# Five Minutes of Blackness

# FIVE MINUTES OF BLACKNESS

## DOUG SMITH

The Mottled Speck

TAMWORTH, NH

*This story is dedicated to Bill W. and Dr. Bob,*
*two men I never met who changed my life.*

"My strength will be measured by how I confront my weakness."

*Sometimes, the obsession is so strong that I would give up everything I have for five minutes of blackness.*

# 1

IT'S BEEN FORTY-ONE HOURS SINCE MY last drink. Who's counting?

My commute through the Gas Lamp Quarter is painful. I stare into every open barroom along the way.

"Can't I have just one?" I ask myself.

"You've never had just one!" I answer myself.

San Diego locals have names for their highways. They refer to "The Five," or "The Fifteen." I drive toward "The Five," but my mind is a thousand miles away. My mind is in Colorado. That's where my wife, Maggie, just moved.

"This time it's for good," she said.

I glance in the rear-view mirror and cringe at the gin blossoms. My hands still shake, and I might be sick again. For the millionth time, I vow to quit.

I am so accustomed to the stop-and-go traffic that I drive by remote control. As I wait for an endless red to turn green, I watch three small kids standing on a street corner. Something seems strange; the kids look scared, and the oldest, a scrawny girl of ten or twelve, is trying to corral the other two. She looks overwhelmed as the little ones look up for guidance. My cop instincts slowly come to life.

The light changes. The traffic slowly moves ten feet forward, and then we stop again. Now I'm right next to the kids. There is new turmoil as the middle one, a boy, tries to break away. The older girl chases him. She shakes him and yells. He cries, and she cries, too. They hug. It seems to be them against the world. An uneasy feeling is tugging at my heart.

I'm convinced that stoplights in San Diego are longer than in any other city. I move a block, sit at another light, and think about the kids. Are they part of a family? Where are the adults? For a brief moment, my mind has stopped thinking about me. I turn right at the next corner. Three more right turns bring me back to the kids. I park across the street. The oldest girl is now on her knees talking to the boy. I walk very slowly in their direction.

"Hi guys," I say, trying not to sound like a creep.

Three adorable little heads jerk up. They are siblings with blond hair and freckled noses. The boy is still crying and looks at me through his tears. The baby of the group, a Shirley Temple look-alike, peeks up with big eyes, curly hair, and a guarded smile. She is looking for a friend. The oldest stares at me defiantly.

"Where's Mom?" I ask.

The oldest steps in front of her younger siblings No one answers.

"Do you live around here?"

Still no answer, and now I know that something is wrong.

"You probably don't like french fries, do you?" I ask.

"Frenth fries?" Shirley Temple says with a little lisp.

"I'm gonna have some fries in that diner, right across the street"

"I like french fries!" The boy nods his head up and down.

"I like french fries, too," says the baby.

The oldest speaks for them all. "We are fine, thank you."

"The problem with french fries," I continue, "is that they always put too many on my plate. I can never finish them."

I have their attention.

"Could you help me finish my fries?"

The three kids all look toward the diner at the same time.

"Some people like ketchup on their fries. Other people like gravy. What do you guys like on your fries?"

"Ketchup," says the baby. "Yeah, ketchup," says the boy.

The oldest crosses her arms and glares.

"So," I pause, "My name is Jesse. I'm a policeman, but I don't have to wear a uniform."

I look at the boy. "What's your name?"

He stands up tall and says, "I'm Andy, and I'm eight."

"Hi, Andy." We shake hands, and he pumps hard.

I look at the baby of the group.

"Can you tell me your name?"

"I'm Abby."

"Her name is Abigail," corrects her brother.

"Mom said it's OK to say Abby!" She hits him.

I look toward the oldest and smile.

"My name is Amy," she says, very quietly.

"How about some fries?" I ask again.

I reach out my hands, and the two smallest kids each grab one.

"No!" The big sister says. She is defiant. "No! We cannot go with you. Thank you anyway."

She gently removes Abby's little hand from mine.

"Let go of his hand, Andy."

The two little kids shriek at the same time. Their scream is so loud that it's almost scary. People who are walking by stop and stare.

"Amy!" They both yell at their older sister at same time. They look at her with disbelief. They have hate in their eyes. They implode and drop to the sidewalk. They have a breakdown right in front of us. Crying! Choking! Yelling! This is not a show. It's a physical, emotional, and nervous collapse.

"Not fair!" Abby shouts, as she kicks her feet and slams her little hands onto the cement.

"Not fair!" she screams, again. I am amazed how loud she gets.

"I am hungry, Amy. I want fries. Please."

Andy stops crying and rolls on his back. He glares up at his big sister. He makes little fists and shouts.

"Why do you hate us so much?"

"I don't hate you," Amy drops to the sidewalk and pulls her brother and sister in for a group hug. Now they are all crying

"OK." She looks up at me.

"Fries. That's it. Just fries."

She stands up and helps her siblings up, too. She takes their hands, and the three of then walk toward the diner ahead of me. I follow.

# 2

THE RED PLASTIC BOOTH IS BIG enough for six adults, but we huddle. Our elbows are touching.

Amy looks at the waitress. "We will have fries, please. Just fries."

I quietly whisper to the waitress.

"Could you please bring chicken nuggets and apple juice for everyone, too?"

When the food is delivered, the kids dig in. I'm amazed at how quickly they eat. As we finish up, I wander back to the forbidden subject.

"So, how's Mom doing?"

"Thees thick," says little Abby.

Amy glares at her little sister. "We can't talk about it!"

"She's sick," repeats Andy.

I change the subject. We talk about TV shows and cartoon characters that I have never heard of.

"What's Mom's name, anyway?"

"Sara," they all answer at the same time.

"How long has she been sick?"

"Thinth thith morning," Abby answers.

"She told us to leave, 'cause Daddy hurt her," says Andy.

"Andy! We are not talking about it!" The big sister seems even taller than before.

We eat more fries, but they are all thinking about Mom.

I'm thinking about Mom, too. I don't want to blow the little bit of progress I've made.

I try a new tactic. I decide to get myself out of the picture and bring in a hero. I talk very, very slowly. All ears are tuned in.

"A friend of mine is a mom. She has a little boy just like you, Andy. I bet my friend would like to go visit your mom. Just to say hi and see if she is OK. I think it's a good idea, don't you?"

Amy is torn between keeping the secret and helping her sick Mother. There is a long, painful pause. She slowly nods, and gives up the address.

I flag the waitress and order the biggest banana split on the menu. "Four spoons, please."

As the kids shovel in the ice cream, I stand up, walk two feet away, and dial my friend from the station.

"Hi Erica. It's Jesse. I need to ask a big favor."

I quickly tell her the story and ask her to take a duty cop to the address.

"I don't know what's going on, but it's bad. I'll take the kids home with me.

# 3

AFTER WE FINISH THE ICE CREAM, the kids seem exhausted from their long day and comatose from the fried food and sweets. They seem comfortable with me.

"Let's go to my house." Since I just fed them, they trust me enough to get into my car. All four of us squeeze into the front seat. As I drive, Abby seems normal. Andy plays with the radio. They giggle and poke each other. Amy sits by the window and stares. When we get to the house, I show them around, and no one seems to mind the mess. I suggest that Abby and Andy climb up on my bed.

"Do me a favor and see if it's comfortable."

They don't answer, but they each fall asleep in a heartbeat. Amy picks up a blanket from the floor and covers her little brother and sister. She is the caretaker.

After Amy and I walk into the kitchen, she starts a one-way conversation.

"My daddy was away for a long time," she says. "When he came home last night, he was so loud. He yelled at my mother, and she cried. He was hurting her. They fought all night. This morning, he hit my mom! Daddy hit my mom! She fell down and couldn't get up."

This brave young girl starts to cry.

"I tried to hit Daddy, but he's so big. He was mean. He said bad things. He swore at me. He pushed me and told me to get out. Mom was crying, and she told me to take the babies.

"I told my mother that I didn't want to leave her.

"'Please, please get the babies out of here,' she said.

"Dad said, 'Don't come back!'

"I dragged my brother and sister out of the house, but we had nowhere to go. We walked and walked. We were all so hungry."

She looks up at me and her eyes start to mist.

"Thank you for feeding my brother and sister," she says.

My phone rings. I walk to the living room and take the call.

"It's terrible," says Erica. "Tenement. A neighbor said there was a fight, but she minds her own business. Sara's door was unlocked, and she was on the floor. Unconscious. Broken forearm. Broken finger, from clawing, probably. She was beaten bad. Blood. Probably raped. The ambulance is taking her away right now."

"Thank you, Erica. Any sign of the man?"

"No, but three uniforms are coming down to talk with the neighbors. Do you want social services to take the kids?"

"Not until tomorrow. They've had enough crap for one night."

I slowly walk back to the kitchen to give Amy an update. Fortunately, her head is on the table. I carry her to the guest room and tuck her in. I grab a pillow and blanket and tip-toe toward the couch.

Early the next morning, I hear Abby and Andy whispering, but before I can get to them their big sister finds them. Amy crawls into bed with them. They all fall back to sleep. I fall back to sleep, too.

At 6am, my phone rings, and I grab it, quickly. Erica has been working on this case all night.

"We found him. OD. There's more. He was in jail for two years. Got out a few days ago and went back to his old tricks. The rest you know about."

"How's the mom?"

"Not good. Why don't you bring the kids to Mercy after lunch? I'll meet you there."

# 4

I KNOCK ON THE BEDROOM DOOR, and Andy says, "Hey, no loud noises!"

"Does anyone like McDonald's?" I whisper.

Three hands go up.

At the local Mickey D's, they eat like animals. We have seconds of hash browns and chocolate milk.

I tell them that Mom is getting better and that we should go see her in a while.

"Will we have to thee Daddy, too?" Abby asks.

"No, Daddy won't be there."

I look at the kids in the morning sun. They are filthy. Hair is matted, faces are dirty, and clothes are hand-me-downs.

"Let's go to Target," I say. They stare at me.

Amy finds new clothes for her little brother and sister and picks out an outfit for herself. We have fun shopping. They laugh at each other as they try on clothes. We buy new sneakers.

We head home, and I put Amy in charge of baths. The kids clean up good. Now they look like middle class yuppies on the first day of school. We spend the morning with cranberry juice, cookies, and cartoons.

When we get to the hospital, we get visitor badges. Suddenly, the kids seem mature. We stand outside their mom's room.

"Your mom will be so happy to see you," a nurse says, as she walks by with a cart full of meds.

We all hold hands for courage and walk in.

I've been in too many hospital rooms, and I've seen too much abuse. Sara looks terrible. She is a shade of gray. One eye closed. Bruises. An IV. A cast. Bandages. She looks at the kids, and a smile slowly starts to form. A bit of color returns to her cheeks. I think she might be a great mom. She looks at me with questions in her eyes but doesn't ask. She looks back at her family and slowly starts to cry. The kids see their mom crying, and they cry, too. They all crowd around the bed and try to hug their mother at the same time.

The kids talk about hash browns, new sneakers, and the banana split.

"Abby ate all the chocolate!" Andy says.

"Did not!" She hits him.

Erica walks in and gives me a hug and some good news. She and her husband will take the three kids until Sara is feeling better.

"My boy would be happy to have some friends to play with."

There is hope.

# 5

As I DRIVE HOME, I REFLECT on my previous twenty-four hours. It was good for me. The kids gave me something to think about besides myself. For a short time, I was happy. For a short time, I was part of someone's life. For a short time, I didn't even think of drinking.

I am proud of myself. This is a turning point in my life. This is the sign that I have been seeking.

I decide to give up drinking for good. I will be the kind of person that little kids look up to. I will get sober!

I take scenic Route 101 up the coast. The sun is starting to set, and the panorama is spectacular. As I reach Del Mar, my stomach growls, and I realize that my last meal was hash browns. As I inch through the traffic, a parking spot opens up in front of my favorite restaurant.

I go to Bully's Pub too often, but I'm a sucker for the big portions and the chaotic atmosphere. The lobby is packed, music is playing, and people are laughing. A girl smiles at me.

"There will be a twenty minute wait," the hostess says, "but there's a seat at the bar,"

Since I have just given up drinking, I pass on her suggestion and stand by the door.

When a table opens up, I order a huge slab of prime rib, a giant wedge of iceberg with blue cheese and extra butter for my potato.

The waitress is good at her job and matches my face with a drink. "The usual?"

It happens so quickly that I am blind-sided. Did I nod? Did I say yes?

In two minutes flat, the waitress flies by and places a drink in front of me. She keeps going. I instantly decide to send it back. If I have this one drink, I will want another. Then one more. Then everything will become a blur. I look for the waitress, but she is gone.

I stare at the low-stemmed cocktail glass with powerful, brown liquid. I touch the glass. It's cold and wet. I quickly pull my hands away and put them under my legs.

I stare intently at the drink. A cherry is perched on top of the glass. It's held in place by a long, red toothpick.

It's only a damn Manhattan. What's the damn fuss? Where's the damn waitress? I look around the room again. My drink is still there, but she is still missing.

I think about putting a twenty-dollar bill on the table and walking out.

I think about running out.

I take a sip.

Thirty minutes later, my prime rib is gone, and three Manhattans are gone, too. On the way out, the bartender greets me.

"Hey Jesse, good to see you, again."

Without asking, he places a drink on the bar.

"This one's on me."

I am helpless. I climb up on the stool and stare into the mirror behind the back bar. Who is that pathetic, weak, miserable loser looking back at me?

"I wasn't going to drink!" I say out loud. "How the hell did this happen?"

"What's that, Jesse?"

"Nothing."

I quietly hang my head and stare into the glass. I promise myself that after tonight, I will never drink again. I will definitely quit. I will go cold turkey tomorrow, but as long as I've started, I will finish the job. I will go out in style. This is my last night. This is my last hurrah.

Another drink is in front of me. Within seconds, the drink is gone. Within minutes, my soul is gone.

# 6

THE PHONE SCREECHES. IT SCREAMS. IT shatters my blackness.
I open one eye. The Jack Daniels bottle is empty, but my bladder
is full. There's a Budweiser can in bed with me. As I reach for the
phone, the can jabs me. My voice is two octaves lower than normal.

"Yeah?"

"Jesse, you won't believe this." It's my friend and partner, Fig.
We've worked together for the two years that I have been a San
Diego detective.

"We have a guy sitting in a brand new Jag without any balls!"

"What the fuck are you talking about?"

"God, do you sound terrible," he says. "Did you celebrate last
night?"

"Yeah. I celebrated because my wife left me! Why are you calling
me so early, and what's the matter with your balls?"

"It's not so early, and there is nothing the matter with my balls."

"Then . . . what?" I shout into the phone.

"Jee-sus Kee-riste!" he says. "Check this out. Underground parking lot in La Jolla. You know the one on Prospect Street? We have
this guy sitting in a brand new Jag. Everything is in place except his
nuts. They've been blasted clean off. Looks like three or four shots,

close range. He bled to death, and man, there is blood everywhere."

"Ouch," I say, as the Budweiser can pokes me again.

Fig reminds me again that this is not my day off and I should get my ass to the underground parking lot pronto.

Someone once described a hangover as a dark-green headache, with a light-brown taste in your mouth. I have both. I feel antiquated and dilapidated. I am broken, busted, and disgusted with myself.

I hate the mirror. Today, I feel old and so weak. I am only thirty-nine, but I look seventy. My five-foot, nine-inch frame is slouching. My handle-bar mustache is sad. My blue eyes are bloodshot red. My face is a sickly shade of gray. The spider veins in my cheeks glow in the fluorescent bathroom bulb. They look like neon lines on a psychedelic black-light poster. My doctor says they will never go away.

A lady friend once said that my body was like an old car. My frame is rusty, and it's hard to start in the morning.

After showering, shaving, and spilling Coke on my only pair of clean Dockers, I climb into my car and drive towards the scene. It's another beautiful, California day, but then, aren't they all. The mid-morning temperature is probably seventy-five, but I don't even notice. I turn the AC as high as it will go and direct the cold air to my face. I guzzle three Cokes on the way.

I park the car and put my San Diego Police sign in the window. I grab my darkest pair of sunglasses and walk towards the underground garage. Long strips of yellow tape are everywhere. They say, "Do Not Cross." Blue bubble-gum machines on top of cars have rotating lights that hurt my eyes. My hangover seems worse in the light of day than it did in the gloom of my room.

The first official who arrives at the crime scene is supposed to seal off the area. I should have been here to do this, but since I wasn't, Fig covered for me. Again. He has covered for me a lot, lately.

As I shuffle down the inclined parking area, I see Fig leaning against a squad car. His arms are crossed, and he has a shit-eatin' grin on his face. His full name is Sam Newton, but he has had the nickname Fig since high school. He has a crooked nose and broad shoulders. His biceps bulge under his threadbare blue blazer. His crew cut is salt and pepper. One of his front teeth is chipped, and he has never bothered to get it fixed. He has been through many battles, and some have left scars. The one on his face is long. At five-foot-six, he reminds me of a bulldog that's been well fed but is still looking for the next scrap. He is a great cop and would defend a partner to the death.

"Jesse," he says as gently as he can. "The chief is bullshit! You were supposed to notify the family hours ago. I told him that you were sick, but he didn't buy it. I hate to say this, old buddy, but I just saw a bumper sticker that describes you. It read: 'Instant asshole, just add alcohol.'" His grin turns into a smile.

Fig knows my story. He knows that I have successfully given up drinking twice before. Two years was the longest. He knows I was on the verge of being terminated by the FBI for drunk and disorderly conduct. He knows that, since I left the FBI, my drinking has gotten worse. He also knows that the reason that my wife left me was because of the booze. That's my story. That's my very boring story.

"Let's go look at the ball-less wonder," I grumble. We walk towards the victim's car, and the pounding of my heels on the downward incline jars my temples. I honestly believe that people shouldn't have to work on hangover days.

We show our badges and finally get to the spot where the brand-new Jaguar is parked. I'm sure that it was a great car before someone covered the inside with a testicle shake.

A gray-haired man is slumped over the steering wheel. To a passerby, it would look like he was sleeping off a drunk. At the time of his death, he was well dressed in a business suit, wing-tip shoes, and a starched, white dress shirt. The tie is still in place, and there is no sign of struggle. All dressed up, and nowhere to go. Ever again.

Fig brings me up to date. "We found several bullets in the driver's seat under his crotch. They all went right through his body, and there might be another one or two still lodged in there someplace. It looks like a 32-caliber hollow point. At least four shots, close range, dead center, right on target." My pecker shrinks just thinking about it.

"There was another shot to the heart, just to be sure, I guess" says Fig.

"Ballistics will do the rifling tests to see if they can come up with a make. At that close range, a small pistol would be enough to do the deed."

My mind flashes past some of the hate crimes I have seen. Whoever did this really despised the victim. My first thought is that some lady got tired of the dead man's shit.

"No witness and no visible clues," says Fig. "The lab guys are checking everything. The perp must have been a woman, because no man would be mean enough to shoot another guy in the nuts."

The name on the deceased man's license is Blake Vanderbeek. He just turned fifty. He lives on the island of Del Coronado, and I think the address is one of the streets near the ocean. Million-dollar joints are all you would see in that part of town. I volunteer to go and talk with the family, and I'm glad to hear that someone else has already broken the news. I hate that part.

# 7

ON THE WAY TO MEET THE widow, I stop for a double Bloody. I rationalize that the vodka will stop the shaking. It doesn't.

I don't feel good enough to deal with the security system mounted by the circular drive, so I park on the street and walk towards the main entrance. I start the long trek up the brick walkway past the designer shrubbery and the manicured lawn. Up ahead, I see the mansion, but mostly there is glass. This house reminds me of a gigantic fish bowl, but it also reeks of money. New money. Flashy money. Showy money. It says, "Look at me. Look at my trappings. I have it made!" The house is right on the edge of the ocean. The deceased Mr. Vanderbeek had a good deal, whatever it was.

The massive front door is made of glass and I can see right through the entranceway, and out to a pool in the back yard. Beyond the pool is the ocean. I also see a couple inside, hugging in a very close embrace. Probably an old friend of the family who is consoling the widow, I think. Their eyes are closed, and they couldn't be any closer. They are oblivious to my arrival. As I knock on the door, the woman jumps. She looks towards me and then looks back to her friend. He just glares.

After what seems like forever, she opens the door, and her friend walks out.

"See ya later, babe," he growls, as he pushes past me. A quick evaluation puts him a few years younger than the woman. He is big, and his tank top is bulging. He climbs into a rusty pickup with oversized tires and roars down the circular drive.

I introduce myself and find out that I am talking to a very young Mrs. Vanderbeek. I remember that the victim in the Jaguar was fifty. Mrs. Vanderbeek is a true California Trophy Wife in every sense of the word. She is probably under twenty-five. She is fresh and wholesome with very little makeup. She is tall and trim. Her shoulder-length blond hair has been professionally streaked with fine wisps of silver, and it hangs straight. Her fingernails and toes are painted fire-engine red. Her see-through white tank top fits perfectly. Her Daisy Dukes are a size too small.

For someone who just found out that her husband had been murdered, she looks remarkably calm.

"I'm sorry about your loss, Mrs. Vanderbeek."

"Oh, well," she says.

My job puts me in front of many people who have had a loss. Sometimes there is screaming, sometimes fainting, but usually tears. This, however, is the first *Oh, well* I have ever heard. For most people, the agony of a loss starts slowly and ramps up over the first hour or maybe even the first day. At some point, grief will overshadow all other emotions, but I don't think Mrs. Vanderbeek has any emotions.

I say I need to ask questions, but before she even responds I write one word in my note pad. The word is "insurance," and it has a big question mark after it.

"Mrs. Vanderbeek, do you have any idea who would have done this?" She looks at me and smiles as if we were just introduced at a cocktail party.

"Please, call me Tippy."

"Yes. That's fine. Tippy, do you have any idea who could have done this?" I ask again.

She shakes her head slowly, frowns, and offers a quizzical stare with her eyes open wide. She seems to be posing for a picture.

After a very long silence, I ask another question.

"Did your husband have any enemies?"

Tippy is far, far away and there is still no comment or response. All I get is a smile that could be perceived as flirtatious. Is she coming on to me, or is this the way she reacts to all men? Her husband was just murdered, and she is standing here with twinkling eyes. Her posture is erect, and she is so still that I wonder if she is breathing. I am so mesmerized by her attitude and engrossed with her physical appearance that I almost forget why I'm here. I have been waiting for a reply, but the silence has not been awkward. Just looking at her is pleasant. As I try to figure this young woman out, I ask one more question.

"If you could think of one person who wanted to hurt your husband, who would it be?"

Finally, I get a reaction. Her eyes change as if she has suddenly woken from a deep sleep. Her head slowly tilts to one side, and her smile fades.

"His first wife," she says, almost as a matter of fact.

"Excuse me?"

"His first wife, Sandra. She hated him. She hated me. She hated the fact that we have the money and she has nothing. She hated the fact that we live here in this place, and she lives in a shitty little condo. She hates the fact that I always call her Sandy instead of Sandra. She did it. She killed him."

"Did he see her? I mean did they get together?" I am thinking of the parked car and the crime scene. No struggle. The person who shot Blake Vanderbeek had to be close. Very close. It was not the kind of crime scene that would have taken place between two people who fought all the time. If she hated him, how could she possibly get so intimate?

"She was always after him," Tippy explains. "And she used their son, Alex, as a reason to see him. She constantly wanted to talk about Alex. That boy was a real pain in the ass. He was always in trouble. He scared the hell out of me. I didn't want anything to do with him. Sandy kept saying that Alex should come down here and live with us. She said her son needed a father figure. What that kid needed was a jail sentence. Oh my god! If that spoiled brat moved in here, I would have moved out in a heartbeat, and Blake knew that."

"So, Blake would see his ex, just to talk?" I ask.

"They talked about Alex's therapy, or the trouble he had just gotten into. He was always in trouble, and she always wanted to talk. Blake didn't want to keep seeing her, but I encouraged him to go, because the last thing I ever wanted was for that overgrown baby to move in with us."

After a long pause, she continues. "But I know what she really wanted. She wanted to get into his pants, but not for the usual reasons. She wanted to get into his pants, 'cause that's where the money was."

Tippy has such a warm, compassionate way of sharing.

"Did your husband have any enemies?" I asked.

"I think he had more enemies than friends," she says, starting to open up. "He was always talking to his lawyer, and there was always someone who wanted to sue him. But I know that Sandy did it. She hated him. She hated me. She wanted our money. You should just go over and arrest her!"

"Just two more questions, Tippy. Could you tell me who the gentleman was who just left?"

"Oh, him? Murphy? He's my personal trainer."

"And where were you last night?"

"Well, actually, er, I was with Murphy. We were, er, training."

# 8

AFTER I LET MYSELF OUT OF the mansion, I drive away and focus on my pain. I have the Taj Mahal of hangovers. As I look for the nearest watering hole, I pass the Del Coronado Hotel. I could go into the pub, but they charge for parking. Further on down the street, I see a hand-carved restaurant sign hanging in front of an old, brick building. The Cock and Bull Tavern happens to be a very upscale café, but I can see through the picture window that they have what I need. I need a drink. Before I even walk through the door, I sense that this place is out of my league, but this is an emergency.

The barmaid on duty is trim and stylish. She has an air of sophistication, and I suspect that she had been striking in her day. She is wearing black slacks and a short, tuxedo jacket with a starched, white blouse. Her black-and-gray hair is pulled straight back, and small flowers have been painstakingly woven into a bun. Her complexion is flawless, but she can't hide the tiny wrinkles that come from years in the California sun. Her blue eyes still sparkle, but they peer out at me over tiny, wire-framed glasses. She smiles warmly.

"Hi, there. What a beautiful day! I'm Georgette. What can I get for you?"

"Cuervo, straight."

After pouring my tequila into a fancy, low, stem glass, Georgette returns the bottle to its rightful place on the back bar. She turns and faces me to start the small talk. Within a second, my glass is empty. I say nothing, but in drinker sign language I tap the glass. She understands the signal. She reaches back and retrieves the tequila. This time, before putting the bottle away, she watches to see if this drink will disappear, too, and it does. She stands in silence. She will not need to ask where I am from, or what I do for work. She knows that I am here for annihilation, not conversation.

Within ten minutes, I spend twenty bucks. Wham, Bam, thank you, ma'am. The five-dollar tip is the quickest this fading beauty will make all night.

I've started the process. I have started drinking. Once I have the first drink, I can't predict how many I'll have, how long I'll drink, or where I'll end up. All bets are off for the rest of the night. I'm on a roll. Most people get drunk a little at a time. They can feel the booze sneaking up on them. The average person has a built-in warning system that tells them when to slow down. I don't have that warning system. I just have a switch. My switch is either off or on. My switch flips on.

My favorite drink is always the next one.

# 9

THE ALARM GOES OFF, AND I pull the pillow over my head. It doesn't help. If the alarm clock had been by my bed, I would have heaved it clear across the room. I've killed too many alarm clocks, lately, so I keep the new one in the bathroom. I jump out of bed to shut it off. Getting up so quickly makes me dizzy, and I hold on to the door frame as I take a leak. I close my eyes and feel wetness splashing all over my feet. When I open my eyes, there are black floaters, rotating in front of the wall. I feel faint. I consider calling in sick. I consider driving my car into a cement bridge abutment. I climb into the shower.

When my wife, Maggie told me she was moving out, I thought that living alone would be a blessing. Instead, it's a curse. When Maggie lived here, she was always up first. She would have the lights on. The radio would be quietly tuned to a news station, and we listened to NPR. She would greet me with a cup of coffee and a smile. While I showered, she would make breakfast. We would talk about our day. Or she would listen to my excuses about the night before.

Now that she is gone, the house is dark, quiet, and depressing. Coffee is too much effort, so I take a Coke out of the fridge. There is no breakfast, and the only news is in my head. It's bad news.

I miss my wife so much!

As I back out of the garage, I gulp a Coke and drive.

"Where the fuck am I going?" I ask myself out loud.

I find the address that was scribbled on the back of an envelope.

The difference between the mansion that the new wife, Tippy, lives in, and the condo that the ex-wife, Sandra, lives in, is like night and day. The mansion was bright and tastefully decorated. The condo is dark, and it's a mess. But the living arrangements aren't the only difference. The years have not been kind to the first Mrs.Vanderbeek. Her clothes are loose to hide her size, and she dresses for convenience, not for style. She wears no makeup, and her hair has not been combed in days. The dark circles around her eyes suggest that sleep is not a regular habit. I wonder if the lines under her eyes are from age or pain.

I'm sure that the murder has taken its toll, but instead of despair, there is contempt. Instead of tears, there is anger. The hate in her eyes is obvious.

I introduce myself, and offer my condolences. "I am sorry for your loss, Mrs. Vanderbeek. Are you OK?" I ask.

"No. I am not OK."

"Can you tell me who would have wanted to do this to your ex-husband?"

"About a thousand people!" It was a quick reply. "He hurt people. He took, and pushed, and controlled. He stole. It serves him right," she says. "He left me, you know, for a disgusting slut who performs unnatural acts. I caught them one night, right in my own driveway," she rants. "I was at a meeting and came home early. There they were, right under the spot light. Her head was down in his lap. His pants were around his ankles. It was disgusting!"

I cut her short.

"Did he have many friends?"

"He had no real friends except money. Money was his God. He wanted to make it and to keep it. And now the bitch will get it all."

"Mrs. Vanderbeek, I'm confused. I thought that, in California, there was a fifty/fifty split in a divorce. Did you get less than fifty percent of the estate?"

"He found a loophole." Her eyes are starting to mist. "Family money is not included. His father made all the money, so alimony is not figured on the family fortune. Our son and I got next to nothing. I've had ten attorneys look at the settlement, but no one can find a way to get around the loophole."

"Where were you last night, Mrs. Vanderbeek?"

"Well, this may not sound good, but I was with him. I was with Blake. I had to talk about our son, Alex. He has been acting up since his father left. Constant trouble. Fighting in school, stealing, and now I think drugs. It's his father's fault, and I thought Alex should go and live with Blake, even if he is with that bimbo. I can't do anything with him. But every time I mentioned this to Blake, he'd find some reason why it wouldn't work."

"Can you please tell me about last night?"

"We met at a coffee shop in La Jolla. I wanted to meet at a restaurant, but I know he was ashamed to be seen with me. I've gained weight since the divorce, and he didn't approve. So, coffee. That's it. A god-damned coffee shop."

"I told him about this week's problems with Alex, and he told me it was my fault. He said I was doing a lousy job with our son, and that I had to spend more time with him. I had to listen to Alex more. I had to go to his school activities. Everything is my fault. Like it's my fault that the boy's father abandoned him. Blake and I started to fight, as usual, and I started to cry, as usual."

"Blake walked out of the coffee shop and left me sitting there.

I couldn't stop crying," she continued. "I cried in the car. I cried when I got home. I cried all night. Now, this morning, two policemen came over to tell me he is dead. For some reason, I've stopped crying."

A boy suddenly bursts into the room. His black hair is unruly and hanging in his eyes. He wears jeans with rips in the knees and flip-flops. His Dead Kennedys t-shirt is filthy. He is probably only fifteen or sixteen but big for his age. His red face leads me to believe that he had been drinking. His fists are clenched, and he is ready for trouble.

"This is Alex," says his mom.

"Hello, Alex," I say.

"I don't want to talk to you!" The boy stares at me.

"Alex!" says his mother.

"I don't want to talk to this jerk! Get him out of here, Mom."

"Alex," I start again. "I'd like to ask a few questions about your dad."

"I don't want to answer your questions!"

"Were you angry with him, Alex?"

"*Angry?* I wanted to kill the motherfucker!"

"Alex!" screams his mother.

"I wanted to kill him for the things he did to you, Mom. I hate him. I'm glad he's dead!"

"Oh, Alex!" Mrs. Vanderbeek starts to cry.

Alex's rage turns to fear, and he slowly starts to cry, too. The crying turns into sobs, and his mother goes to his side. As the two of them embrace, I excuse myself and make my exit.

I leave the condo and think about a drink. For some reason, I'm completely broke. I head straight home. As I unlock the door, the phone is ringing. It's Maggie, calling from her mother's house in Colorado. I am touched that she is calling.

"Hello, Jesse," she says.

"Hi, Maggie."

"I have found an apartment in Boulder. It's about ten minutes from my mother's. Were you going to send me some money?" she asks.

"I was planning on it," I lie.

"Have you started to go to AA meetings, yet?"

"I was planning on that, too," I say, as I untwist the cap on a fresh handle of vodka.

# 10

THE SAN DIEGO POLICE ANNEX IS in a dilapidated old building on the edge of the Gas Lamp Quarter. When I started working here, two years ago, I was told that our offices were temporary. This place is like my body: everything is outdated, and nothing works. The single elevator was declared unsafe, so we walk. The leaky toilets and faucets have been completely shut off, and the rest rooms are now dusty storage areas. The building is way too old for air conditioning, and way too cavernous for an efficient heating system, so we shiver in the winter and roast in the summer. But no matter how bad the building is, employees are expected to show up on time.

I'm late to the station again. Chief Bettes calls me into his office. He is large in every sense of the word, and his huge frame fills the doorway. His face is pockmarked from childhood acne, and, even though he lives in sunny San Diego, I have never seen him with a tan. He is balding, and his remaining hair is very fine. It is never in the same place twice. Today, static electricity has pulled his hair straight up, and it is reaching toward the door jamb. His tie is loose, and one of his button-down collars is undone. There's a stain on his tie. He wears a brown belt with black shoes. I try to find fault with my boss to make myself feel better. It doesn't work.

The Chief has had it. In his office, he reads me the riot act. Drinking again, blah, blah, blah. Undependable again, blah, blah, blah. Rehab again, blah, blah, blah. I've heard it all before. He acts pissed, but for some reason he likes me. He stuck his neck out to get me a job as a San Diego detective after my early retirement from the Agency. I spend half my time getting into trouble, and he spends half his time getting me out of trouble.

I am like a little boy who has been called into the principal's office. I hang my head and stare at my feet. When he is finished, I promise to cut my drinking way back. I try to shake his hand, but it's awkward.

I leave the Chief's office and quietly walk to my desk. Everyone in the office is watching. There are ongoing bets. The girls wager when I will get divorced. The guys bet when I will end up in jail. Neither option is too far-fetched.

I get to my desk and start my to-do list. We need to look at the numbers stored in the dead man's Day Timer or Rolodex. We need to check email on his computer. I also want to know if he owned a Blackberry or hand-held device of some kind. I make a call to the insurance commission; I need to find out about the beneficiary of the Vanderbeek estate.

My gut feeling is that, since there was no struggle in the Jaguar, the killer must have been a friend of the deceased. If my assumption is correct, there will be an address, or a name, or a note, or a message someplace. I think that this will be an open-and-shut case, and we should find the shooter soon.

I look at my watch, and it's lunchtime. From my desk, I see people leaving the building. Some of them head out in small groups to a coffee shop. Others use their lunch break to power-walk through the downtown area. A few folks have a brown bag and a book. They will find a quiet place to sit and read.

I, however, have another plan. On this day, like many other days, I get in my car and head south to the warehouse district. It's only a short ride, but it seems to take forever. I am exhausted, depressed, and disappointed in myself. I have such an incredible hangover that I have trouble keeping my head up. When I get to my destination, I park in an area farthest from civilization. After turning off the car, I put the seat back as far as it will go, close my eyes, and fall sound asleep. I have done this on so many hangover days that it seems natural. I don't sleep long, and I wake up without an alarm. After my nap, I reach in the glove compartment and grab the bottle of mouthwash. I gargle, and then I spit out of the window. After parking my car, I sneak into McDonald's to use the men's room. I take a toothbrush and tooth paste out of my pocket and try to get rid of the bad tastes. Back at my desk, I reach into the top drawer and find the Excedrin, the mints, and a fresh package of gum. My hope is that no one will know just how hungover I am. I theorize that if they can't smell the stale booze on my breath, they won't know that I was drinking all night long. I go through this ritual two or three times a week.

The saddest part of the routine is that I can't stop counting the hours until the end of the work day. That's when I can find the relief I need. At the end of the day, I can have a drink.

# 11

IT'S SATURDAY MORNING, AND I AM lying on a chaise lounge by the pool. I am naked and very, very cold. I have an excruciating headache. My body is quivering.

Susan walks out of the house wearing one of my old sweatshirts and a pout. She is much younger than my wife, who just moved out. She is pissed. We had planned to share the most incredible sex of our lives last night, but I don't remember if that happened.

I reach for my shorts and smile at my houseguest.

"Hi, Susan. Did we have fun last night?"

"We did not have fun! You were an asshole. You were weaving all over and slurring your words. You were talking Chinese! We got undressed, and you insisted that we do it out here. We laid down on the lounge, and then you were out like a light. You were snoring in two seconds. I left you here, and went into the house."

"I know, Sue," I lie. I don't even remember getting undressed. I hate black outs!

"How about I make it up to you today?" I smile again. "Let's celebrate this beautiful California morning by having a mimosa."

"It's not funny." She glares. "If you hadn't gotten so wasted last night, we could have had a nice time. You don't like me as much as you like booze! We should have just had a glass of wine and gone to bed. Instead, you wanted to get drunk and screw out here."

As I try to stand up, I stumble and trip over a small table. I bruise my knee.

"Oops," I say. I try to sound light and cheery, although my headache is excruciating. Even my hair hurts.

"Let's have a mimosa."

"Alcohol doesn't solve any problems," she says. "I'd like a cup of coffee."

"I know that alcohol doesn't solve any problems, Sue, but then, neither does coffee."

"You are such a loser," she says. "I'm gone!" Originally she'd planned to spend the weekend, but now she is punishing me for having a few cocktails. Susan is having a bad day, and she will make me miserable if it takes forever. She goes inside to pack without saying another word.

"Well, if you're going to leave," I shout, "I'll have a real drink instead of a pussy Mimosa!" As I say this, I recall that my wife left me because of the real drinks.

I've lost my companion for the day, but I still have my two best friends, Jack and Bud. Jack Daniels and Budweiser keep me company for the day and long into the night. I drink like my insides are on fire. When I run out of Jack, I switch to Bud and suck on the can until it crinkles.

I spend most of the afternoon getting rid of yesterday's hangover. I spend most of the evening working on a new one for tomorrow.

# 12

ON MONDAY MORNING, I FEEL LIKE death, but I am back in the office. I start working on my to-do list. I add the general category: Forensics. I need help with the technical side of this case. What was the murder weapon? Has this exact weapon been used in other crimes in the country? Can we identify any prints on the carpet or outside of the vehicle? Were there hair samples, and, if so, were they male or female? Were there clothing fibers on the seats? Did the dried blood belong only to the deceased, or did the shooter get shot or cut in the process? Were there samples of saliva or semen left at the crime scene?

Like most detectives, I can handle the overall investigation, but I need help with the details. Fortunately, there is a co-worker in my office that is an ace in forensics, and she can help me. Even though she is the best hope that I have for a quick resolution, I am reluctant to see her. Because of our tangled history, our relationship is strained. Today, I need to put my ego aside and visit the one person who can help me solve this case. After filling a dusty ceramic mug with steaming, black coffee, I start the long walk to Erica Ringline's office.

Erica understands my drinking. She understands my pain. She

understands my relapse. Erica understands my alcoholism, because she, too, admits that she is an alcoholic.

Erica knows that I have relapsed. She will see that my eyes are glassy, my face is blotchy, and my hands are shaking. She will also detect the pungent reek of alcohol. A social drinker wouldn't recognize this odor, but another alcoholic can pick it up from ten paces. She knows that I am hooked again, and that makes each of us uncomfortable.

I am drinking almost every day, and Erica is sober.

I met Erica on my first day as a San Diego detective. I had spent the morning in the HR department filling out forms, and went for a walk at lunchtime. My stroll took me down a quiet side street past a pub called The Squire. I stopped in for a quickie. An attractive, well-dressed woman was staring into her half-empty glass. The lemon twist suggested that she might be drinking a martini. I ordered my drink and asked the bartender to give one to the lady. She smiled and said that she never drank at lunchtime, but she had had a fight with her husband the night before. She thought that one little drink might help calm her down. She said that the only two things that she really liked were her son and her job. Before I could ask what her job was, she glanced at her watch, and her whole demeanor changed.

"Oh my God, I'm late for work!"

Without saying goodbye, she was gone.

Later that day, when the Chief introduced me to his staff, I met the lady who had just shared a drink with me.

"This is Erica," said the Chief.

"Hello, Erica," I said.

Neither of us acknowledged that we had just a drink together at the Squire. This anonymity formed a bond and the beginning of a long, strange friendship.

The next day, Erica stopped into my office and asked if I would like to sneak out for a quick drink at lunch time.

Erica and I have worked together for the past two years. It didn't take us long to realize that we drank alike. Sometimes we would drink our lunch. A few times a week, we would stop on the way home for a quick one that would last for hours. Once in a while, we even walked out to the parking lot during the day for a nip from the glove compartment. We would meet at a lounge before the office Christmas party or at a bar after the company picnic. Sometimes, we would drink to get fired up, and sometimes we would drink to wind down. Regardless of the reasons, we drank a lot.

We had trouble with our spouses. We were both written up at work. We each spent nights passed out in our cars. During this whole time, neither of us considered ourselves alcoholic. We always got up the next day and made it to work. We thought we were doing just fine. Our relationship never became sexual, but we had a bond. Our bond was booze. Our common trait was denial. We shared stories that only an alcoholic could understand. As time went on, our stories grew more desperate.

One night, Erica told me about a low point in her drinking career. She had been out on a binge, and, when she got home, her husband had locked her out of the house. She became violent and tried to break down the front door with a shovel. When her husband called the police, Erica was arrested on a domestic violence charge. She was taken to jail and put in an empty cell. As she crawled up on a bench to sleep it off, she used a roll of toilet paper for a pillow. Later that night, another woman was put in her cell. Her new roommate grabbed the makeshift pillow from under Erica's head to use it for its intended purpose. The next morning, Erica and her cellmate, a black prostitute, were handcuffed together and taken to court.

Erica was given a choice of extended jail time or Alcoholics

Anonymous meetings. She chose the meetings. By the time she got to her first meeting, she had hit bottom. Her husband and son had left, and she had been fired from her job. She had been sleeping in her car. She was beat! Literally! She had black and blue marks from a barroom fight, and she looked like death. Her clothes were filthy, her hair was in knots, and she smelled like vomit.

I had been going to AA meetings for three months when she walked in. She saw me and smiled. It was a very sad smile, but it was a smile just the same.

At Erica's first meeting, she looked so scared. Going to your first AA meeting is like walking into the middle of a movie. You are trying to figure out what's going on. When they asked her to share, she talked slowly. She sobbed, shook her head, and talked in a low whisper. She honestly wanted to stop drinking, but she couldn't imagine living without alcohol. On the other hand, she knew that if she didn't stop drinking, she would die. I knew the predicament.

Erica also wanted to get her son back. She broke down and sobbed some more. I've never seen anyone more deflated than Erica.

After the meeting, a few caring ladies gathered around Erica and gave her love and encouragement. They shared their stories. They told her that things would work out. It was amazing. Regardless of how bad she looked or smelled, the other women didn't even notice. They understood. They had been there, too.

After the meeting, one of the women, a complete stranger, took Erica home and let her shower. The filthy clothes were washed, and she was given a home-cooked meal. Another sober woman came by to say that she had a temporary place for Erica to sleep. Several women took turns driving Erica to AA meetings. One gal got Erica a job as a waitress, even though she had never waited a table in her life. Within two weeks, the black-and-blue marks were gone. In a month, she looked normal. In two months, she looked clean, wholesome, and rested. In three months, she radiated. She got her old job back on probation, and she was granted visitation rights to see her son.

When she returned to work, we were inseparable. We went to AA meetings together. Sometimes we met at morning meetings on the way to work. Many times, we went to a lunch meeting in the Gas Lamp, and sometimes we met at an evening meeting.

When we were drinking, we only had one thing in common, but when we were trying to stay sober, we had everything in common.

As time went on, I got the "terrible toos." The meetings were too far away. They were too long. The chairs were too uncomfortable. I had too much to do. I became too busy for meetings. Eventually, I stopped going all together. One day, in desperation, I picked up a drink and couldn't stop.

Today, Erica is still sober, and I am a drunk, again.

Today, as I walk into Erica's lab, she looks at me and almost starts to cry. She walks to me slowly, and we hug. She holds on tight. As she shakes her head, she whispers, "We all miss you."

She looks at me again and asks, "How are you?"

"Fine. Actually, I'm fine," I lie.

She smiles slowly and spells the word one letter at a time.

"F-I-N-E. Does that stand for Fucked up, Insecure, Neurotic, and Emotional?"

I send a slow, fake punch in her direction, and she ducks.

I change the subject and talk about the murder. Erica gets down to business, too, and shows me three different hair samples from the Jaguar. One sample is straight and blond, one sample is gray, and the third is short, bleached blond, and curly. There is no way to tell for sure if a hair sample is from a male or female, but we can guess. Usually, female hair will have been bleached, colored, straightened, and curled. The new wife, Tippy, has long, blonde hair.

So that leads us to believe that the killer may be a woman who has short, curly, bleached-blonde hair.

Erica continues her recap. She has found several sets of fingerprints in the car. The obvious matches are from Blake, his wife, and a few employees. There is also a set that cannot be identified. We assume that the strange set of prints belong to the killer. Erica has already searched state and national records and checked fingerprints with the feds. The prints came up negative. Since they were not found in any databank, we figure that the killer is a one-hit-wonder.

"We have a preliminary make on the gun," Says Erica. "The 32-caliber bullets seem to have come from a Kel-Tec P-32. I've put a request in to the FBI's Drugfire Database to see if similar casings have been found at other scenes around the country."

Erica doesn't have to tell me that the Kel-Tec is the smallest handgun on the market. It is only ¾ of an inch thick. In the beginning, the Kel-Tec was considered a toy by most serious shooters. It would barely stop a rabbit. But now, when loaded with semi-jacketed, soft-tip, hollow-point bullets, it will rip a person apart. As the bullets enter the body, they explode into fragments that do tremendous damage. Factor the type of handgun used with the assumption that shots were fired from very close range, and this pistol is deadly! There were also gunpowder burns, confirming that Blake was shot at very close range.

The person who did the shooting could easily have hidden this gun in a pocket or purse.

We have little else to go on.

I thank Erica, and as I leave she squeezes my hand.

"I pray for you," she says.

"I'm fine." I say again.

"F-I-N-E," she repeats.

# 13

DURING THE NEXT WEEK, I SPEND a lot of time checking into the dead man's life. I go through his Day-Timer, but I see no meetings scheduled for the night of his demise. I grab his Rolodex and assign the task of following up on every single name and number. A rookie detective gets stuck with the grunt work.

I check his cell phone, and listen to every incoming message. There are no phone messages that relate to a meeting on the night of the Vanderbeek murder. There is no correspondence of a personal nature, no scribbled phone numbers anywhere, no Post-It notes sticking to a calendar, no invitations or announcements, and no crumpled-up letters in the glove compartment of his Jaguar.

I also interview everyone who will talk with me. I meet with neighbors and employees. I interview associates and the office-building superintendent. No one has any idea of where Blake had been on the night that he was murdered.

There are no facts, but there are opinions. Everyone that I spoke with had the same sentiment. The world was better off without Blake Vanderbeek. I suspect that a lot of people would have been interested in helping with that transition.

My partner, Fig, has also done some research. He has gone

through the deceased's checkbook. He has talked with the gardener, the manager of the country club, the service station attendant, and the owner of a restaurant where Blake had a house charge. No one could tell him of Blake's whereabouts on his last night. No one had any dirt to offer or crumbs to sweep up.

Late in the afternoon, I head out to the village of La Jolla, where Blake was murdered. The words *La Jolla* mean "the jewel," and everyone loves this town. There are miles of public lawns along the water's edge. People who live here spend their lives outdoors. The grassy slopes offer warm air and cool ocean breezes. This is where you would have your birthday party, your wedding, your love affair, or your solitude. The La Jolla cove is a swimming haven where folks in skintight wet suits become one with their snorkeling gear. A few miles away, Blacks Beach caters to thousands of nude sunbathers every day.

When the June gloom burns off, and the morning haze dissipates, hordes of people flock to La Jolla. They enjoy the endless water view, the clear blue skies, and the seventy-five degree weather. At the end of the day, watching the sunset is a religious experience.

A block away on Prospect Street, gigantic palm trees tower over upscale restaurants, art galleries, and boutiques. This is a town full of beautiful people who drive Beemers, Benzes, and Hummers. The men are middle-aged retirees in shorts, sandals, and baseball caps. The women are stay-at-home blondes with cell phones and bottled water.

Today, I'm not here to shop, ogle, or drool. I'm here to find a witness. I take a recent photograph of the deceased Mr. Vanderbeek to the bars, restaurants, and clubs. I'm looking for a needle in a haystack. I'm looking for a bartender, parking valet, or waitress who may have seen Blake before he was gunned down.

I interview people for hours, and continuously strike out. Just before dinner, I walk into a fashionable upscale restaurant called Georges-in-the-Cove. Georges is on the second floor of an office building, and has a full glass wall overlooking the water. This restaurant and bar attracts the movers and shakers. I talk with a stylish, thirty-something waitress who looks fabulous in George's uniform. She is wearing a short black skirt, black stockings, low heels, and a freshly starched white blouse. Her own personal touch is a white ribbon tied into her ruby red hair. She is folding white cloth napkins.

"Have you seen this man?" I ask, placing the photo in front of her.

"Sure, He comes in here a lot," she says.

"How about last Friday night?"

"I think that I might have seen him early on, but it was cocktail hour and the place was packed. I can't be sure."

"Would it help you to concentrate if we went down to the station?"

"Actually, I remember now," she says. "He was sitting at the bar for hours."

"Who was he with?"

"He was talking with some blonde bimbo for most of the night, but I don't know if they came in together. Maybe he picked her up. It happens all the time."

"Tell me about the blonde."

"She was short and had curly blonde hair, but I only saw her from the back and frankly, she's not my type. I didn't pay too much attention to her."

"Why do you remember him?"

"He's gorgeous."

The waitress slides into another world, and she slows down. She looks at me with misty eyes.

"I would love to meet someone like him," she says. "He is such a hunk."

*Hunk of dead meat,* I think to myself.

We schedule an appointment for a sketch artist to meet with the waitress.

As I walk away, I wonder if Blake's last hours were with the curly-haired blonde at this restaurant. It would make sense that, after the stressful meeting with his ex-wife, Blake went out for a drink. He met a stranger at the bar and she walked him to his car. She got in for a goodnight kiss, and then popped him. But what was the motive? I doubted that it was a robbery. His wallet and cash were still in his pants.

Maybe a better story might have been that his disgruntled wife waited near his parked car until the strange blonde got out. Then she climbed in and took care of him there.

If I were a betting man, I would put my money on the first wife, Sandra Vanderbeek. She had the biggest motive to get rid of Blake. They had been together that night. He had made her upset, and she had a reason. That reason was hatred. The motive was revenge. Open-and-shut case.

# 14

THE STORM IN ASBURY PARK, NEW Jersey, was titanic. Hailstones, lightning, and sheets of rain came down from the heavens. Two blocks away, staggering ocean waves crashed over the sea wall. Storm drains were full, and parking lots were flooded. The sky was black. Trees were down and streetlights were out. What little traffic there was, moved at a snail's pace.

No one in his or her right mind would go out on a day like this, unless they had an important mission. Kiki Sullivan had an important mission. She went out.

The driving was terrible but she made it to the Federal Express office before they closed. She needed to claim her delivery. She didn't want her parcel sitting at the pick-up counter for a minute longer than necessary.

When she returned to her condo, she locked the door and set the dead bolt. She closed the blinds, and, in the privacy of her condo, she turned on a light.

Her raincoat was dripping on the kitchen floor, but she didn't care. With shaking fingers, she ripped open the white cardboard box and then used a sharp steak knife to cut open the inner carton. She carefully removed the item that FedEx had shipped clear across the United States.

Kiki carefully pulled the shiny metal item out of the container. The second that she had her hand on her prize possession, she felt better. With her finger on the trigger of her tiny Kel-Tec P-32 pistol, she was in control. Her pistol gave her the feeling of security and self-preservation. Her Kel-Tec gave her strength.

A therapist had told her that when things get tough, she had three options. She could accept the situation, leave the situation, or change the situation. She had finally decided to change the situation.

She felt remorse settling in, even though she had thought about this deed for a long time. She battled for the courage to make the right decision. Kiki had been wronged, and she took revenge. It was that simple. In the end, it's easy to kill someone who deserved it.

After getting out of her raincoat and drying her hair, Kiki turned on the national news. There was no mention of the killing in La Jolla, California, two thousand miles away. Nothing! She was quite sure that the attack in the Jaguar had made it into the San Diego papers, but it apparently wasn't a big enough story for the networks. Well, no news is good news

Although she was watching the evening news, there was not a sound coming from her TV. Her apartment was completely silent.

Kiki took a long, hot shower, dried off, and climbed into her most comfortable pair of flannel PJs. She pulled on a pair of oversized sweat socks. This was the outfit that she reserved for long, cold, lonely nights. She took a chair to her hallway closet. While standing on her tip-toes, she reached up to the top shelf and pulled down a delicate, weathered, overstuffed shoebox. In a trance-like state, she moved the box to the bed and gently removed some of the contents. The shoebox contained pictures of her lovers. She enjoyed taking pictures, and had preserved all of them. She had hundreds of pictures. All of the pictures were neatly organized in groups. Some of the pictures were tied together in ribbons. Others were tied in string. Smaller groups were paper-clipped together. A few batches were stuffed into envelopes. But they were all stored in a simple filing system. They were sorted by date.

She thought of the old TV show: "This is your life!" These pictures were her life. Or, realistically, they were the part of her life that never was. Tonight, she spent hours looking at the pictures of guys she had dated, her old boyfriends, and her old lovers. The one-night stands didn't matter because they left no marks. A few relationships left bruises. Some left scars and mutilations.

Each batch had a hand-written note attached. She had taken the time to jot the guy's name, and the years that they dated. There was a brief paragraph about the relationship, and another paragraph about the breakup. Or the heart-break. Or the dump! She focused on the reasons. They all had reasons. The reasons were all different, but in a sick way, they were all the same. And it really didn't matter. She was dumped. Again. And again. And again. She despised every one of these bastards! No love. No like. Only hate!

Tonight, she felt that she could finally start to clean out the shoe box. After taking a positive action, she could remove one batch of pictures. She felt her heart rate increase, and she felt giddy. Tonight she took one group of pictures out of the pile. She no longer needed to look at pictures of her old lover, Blake Vanderbeek.

She took her scissors and cut each picture of Blake into tiny little pieces. She ceremoniously flushed them down the toilet, just like he did with their relationship.

# 15

AFTER WORK, I FINISH SOME ERRANDS and realize that I am hungry, angry, lonely, and tired. I haven't had anything to eat since breakfast. My blood sugar is on a roller coaster.

I could go home, but, since my wife moved out, there are a few problems. First of all, there is no food. Second, even if I could find food, there are no clean dishes.

I call Erica to see if she would like to go to an AA meeting with me, but she is home with her family. Since I no longer have a family, I am alone.

On the way home, I pass a greasy spoon called The Egg and I. The nearest parking place is two blocks away, but I dump the car and walk back.

A cyclone must have hit this place. Every table is covered with dirty dishes, leftover food, and filthy silverware. Crumpled napkins and french fries are on the floor.

There is one waitress in the dining room, and she is sitting at a corner table. She reminds me of an abandoned car at the town dump. I can envision a flat tire, dented sides, and a cracked windshield. Her hair is hanging in her eyes. Her shoes are untied. Her uniform must have been white at one point. It's now multicolored from mustard and chocolate sauce. She has experienced meltdown. Her ashtray is full, and she is lighting another cigarette. Normally, I would just walk out, but I am already here. I am hungry, and tonight I want to eat in a place that doesn't serve alcoholic beverages.

I stare at the waitress. She offers a half-smile, and holds up a cigarette. It's her way of saying, "Don't bother me."

I pick a booth by the window that is relatively clean, and I bus the table myself. I move the dirty plates to a plastic tub, put the silverware on another table, and wipe the crumbs onto the floor.

I walk to a corner cupboard and fill a cup with stale, lukewarm coffee. It tastes great. I slide into my booth and accidentally sit on a newspaper. It's covered with stains and grease spots. The paper is folded open to the horoscope section, and, since no one is watching, I read my sign.

> *LIBRA: What would it be like, Libra, if you could go a whole day without fear? No fear of whether you are good enough. No fear of whether people will like you. No fear of having mayonnaise on your chin. Well you can!*

I read no further. This message was written for me. I've spent most of my life in fear. I am sick of my own drama, but, today, I realize that whatever doesn't kill me will make me stronger. To waste time, I take out my notebook and start to list my fears. It's an exercise that I learned while I was in AA.

I am afraid that I will become financially dependent on others. I am terrified that I will end up alone. I dread that I will become senile. I am frightened that I will hurt people. I have fear of rejection. I suffer from self-pity, procrastination, and resentment. I am overly critical and lazy. I have been selfish, dishonest, self-seeking, inconsiderate, and unrealistic. I am egotistical, oversensitive, immature, self-centered, and delusional. I am an egomaniac with

FIVE MINUTES OF BLACKNESS

a low self-image. I constantly compare my insides to other people's outsides. And I feel like I don't belong.

The waitress is standing behind me, reading over my shoulder. She seems to be OK with my list and she takes my order for a cheese omelet, hash browns, and more coffee. Without a sound, she leaves to place my order. Or perhaps she will go into the kitchen and cook it herself. At any rate, it's better than eating at home, all alone.

When I get back to my big, dark, lonely house, I see the tiny red light blinking on the answering machine. Fig has called.

"Jesse, a friend of mine said that there is a great AA meeting in Carlsbad, tonight."

Fig cares more for me than I care for myself.

The AA meeting would have been a good idea, but I am afraid to leave the house. I don't want to wrestle with the steering wheel every time I pass a cocktail lounge.

# 16

My goal for tonight is to get to bed without having a sixteen-ounce vodka. I want to touch down safely before I lose control. It's not that I am tired; it's just that I don't trust myself.

I don't notice the condition of my bedroom. I step over the clothes, the shoes, and the beer cans. The bedspread has been on the floor for weeks. I think about picking up the Domino's box with stale crusts of pepperoni pizza. Maybe tomorrow. A blanket has been draped over the curtain rod to keep the early morning sun out of my eyes. It keeps the evening stars out too.

I crawl into the big, empty bed and feel sand and dirt against my skin. I remember that, two nights ago, I went to bed with my shoes on.

When I go a day without drinking, I start to think about the important things in life. Tonight, I lie motionless and think about Maggie. I miss my wife so much. Maggie is the only person who understands me. She has been my best friend, and she has always taken care of me. Maggie humors me. Maggie loves me. Because of my drinking, Maggie left me.

As I wait for sleep, I think about better days. Maggie and I met on a blind date, in our late teens. She was in nurse's training and I was in my freshman year of college. I had a car, and my roommate wanted to double date. He and his girlfriend wanted to be in a warm, private car instead of on a cold, public park bench, so he fixed us up. Maggie and I both tried to get out of the blind date, but our friends had too much at stake. They were persistent.

In our little college town there wasn't much to do on a date, so we ended up at the drive-in. Within two minutes of attaching the speaker, our friends were acting like rabbits. The windows were steamy, the car was shaking, and the moans were embarrassing.

"Would you like to go for a walk?" I asked Maggie.

"Absolutely!"

We walked for a full mile in the freezing winter night until we found a coffee shop. We sat and talked for hours. In the bright light of the coffee shop, I got a good look at my blind date. Maggie was about five-six, with short, blond hair. Her smile was genuine, and she was easy to talk with. She wore a plaid, pleated skirt, a wool sweater, knee socks, and penny loafers. She had a great figure, and she was classy.

Maggie was an intelligent nursing student who had a high level of self-confidence, and she acted like a queen. I, on the other hand, was a stupid college kid with low self-esteem, and I acted like a clown. My jokes fell like bricks. I suspected that she would never want to see me again.

After gallons of coffee, we walked back to the drive-in. Our friends were sound asleep.

As we dropped our dates off at their dorm, I politely kissed Maggie on the cheek. I was prepared for a letdown, but I asked the question that had been on my mind all night. "May I see you again?" I quietly whispered.

"How about tomorrow?" she answered with a smile.

We saw each other almost every night after that, and got married within a year. Later, as I started to substitute booze for coffee, our fairy-tale relationship went downhill.

Tonight, the silence in the house and the voices in my head are colliding. I reach over and click on the radio. Rick Price is singing a country song that hits me between the eyes. "I'm sure close to lonely, tonight."

I fall asleep.

# 17

I WAKE UP SLOWLY, NATURALLY, PEACEFULLY. I can see a sliver of daylight sneaking past the quilted cotton bedspread that had been hung over the window. The sound of a bird chirping slows me down and helps me focus on today. This is my day. It's Saturday, and I wake up without a hangover. I have a strange feeling of peace. Today, I feel refreshed and renewed.

I think about my addiction, and, for the first time, I acknowledge that I am powerless over alcohol. I admit that my life has become unmanageable. They say that this is the first step in recovery. I lie awake and stare at the ceiling for a long, long time.

I brew fresh coffee and take my cup to the deck. I watch, almost hypnotized, as steam rises off the pool. This was Maggie's favorite time of day. Many mornings I would find her quietly sitting here staring at the mist. Sometimes I thought that she might have been praying. Other times, after I'd had a bad night, I thought she might have been crying.

I walk back into the house and look around at the pigsty that I call home. In keeping with my new feeling of progress, I spend an hour cleaning the kitchen. I am a man on a mission, and I wash dishes, I organize the bedroom, change the filthy sheets, fill a plastic bag with empty beer cans, and put away my shoes. After I start a load of laundry, I walk into the bathroom.

I spend an hour in the smallest room in the house. I gag as I clean the toilet, wash vomit out of the sink, wipe the floor, and clean the mirror. I admire my work and decide to give myself a treat. "Time for some fun," I say to no one.

I back the car out of the garage so that I can get to my Harley. It feels good to sit on the saddle again, and I hit the start button for the first time in months. The roar of the V-Twin shakes the building. I slowly inch the bike out onto the driveway and park under a tree. I wash, scrub, and polish my classic Road King. When the chrome is sparkling, the tires are factory white, and the spokes are spit shined, I get ready to roll.

California has a helmet law, but there is no firm consensus on what's acceptable. After years of debate, the courts still can't agree on what they mean by DOT approved, so any helmet is OK. The smallest helmet that I own is called a beanie, and it's covered with stickers. One says: "DILLIGAF." Another says: "God made alcohol so that ugly people can get laid."

From my town in Southern California, a biker can only ride north or south. If you go west, you'll be in the ocean, and if you go east, you'll end up in the desert. I decide to head north. I guide my bike onto the 101, and as I head toward Oceanside, I start to accelerate. I feel the fresh, crisp, morning air in my face. I love to ride, but during my worst drinking days, I am afraid to even get on the bike. I instinctively know that if I ride while I am drunk, I will end up in a box.

Today there is no June gloom. The early morning fog that lasts for most of the summer has finally burned off. The air is clear, and the road is as smooth as a baby's ass. My FLHT is running like a dream. As I turn on to The Five, I ride past Camp Pendleton and the road widens. There isn't much traffic at this early hour, so I pull back on the throttle and let my speedometer touch eighty. A quick check in the rearview mirror shows a clean tail, so I roll up to one hundred. After a brief adrenalin rush, I ease back down to a respectable seventy. I am so invigorated with twenty-four hours of sobriety that I wonder why I don't just quit drinking. I contemplate what life would be like if I could feel this good every day.

"Why is it so hard to get sober?" I shout over the roar of the engine.

I pass the San Onofre Nuclear Power Plant and look at the huge identical twin towers. Each tower is five stories high. They look like gigantic Hershey's Kisses, but the locals refer to this landmark as the Dolly Parton memorial.

It's an easy ride to Venice Beach, and, after I exit, I head toward the ocean. I find an empty spot in front of a local's bar and look through the open door. A single customer is trying to hold his glass steady while he knocks back his first hit of the morning. "What a waste," I say, loud enough for him to hear. He turns and gives me the finger.

I slowly walk toward the cement boardwalk. There is no dress code in Venice Beach, but there are many uniforms. A circus couldn't be more colorful. Teenage boys with spiked mohawks wear low-rise baggies that hang below their underwear. They chain-smoke, spit, and swear for effect. Young girls in tiny bathing suits try to look mature and older women, who shouldn't wear tiny bathing suits, try to look young. Two men walk by holding hands. They are wearing identical neon thongs. There are street-vendors selling cheap jewelry and chicken on a stick. Yuppies in pink shirts weave in and out of the crowd on roller blades.

I stop at the outdoor gym called Muscle Beach where body builders sweat to please the tourists.

In Venice Beach, there are basketball players and ex-beauty queens. There are hawkers, stalkers, and gawkers. Musicians and fire-eaters perform for tips. Hare Krishna dancers with shaved heads chant in a cloud of incense.

I grab a slice of ham-and-pineapple pizza and walk to the drum circle where the energy comes as much from the spectators as it does from the performers. The constant pounding vibrates my brain and reminds me of my worst hangovers.

A block away, a scratchy disco beat is blaring from an ancient eight-track. A tall black man on roller skates is leading a routine. He is wearing very tight nylon shorts and an orange cowboy shirt with wide lapels. There are seven white girls roller-dancing in step.

I find my bike and head south to the Mission Beach area of San Diego. I exit on Grand Ave. and inch through the traffic toward the pier. I am enjoying my day immensely. Life is so good when I am straight! I love riding my bike at eighty, but riding slowly near the beach has its own rewards. Today, most of the rewards are wearing skimpy bathing suits.

Up ahead on the right I see at least at least fifty bikes, mostly Harleys, neatly backed into parking slots on one side of the street. They are parked in front of a bar called Plum Crazy. My kidneys are overflowing, and this would be a good place to take a leak. When you are on a bike, you should never pass up a chance to fill your tank or empty your bladder.

The noise in the bar is deafening. Punk rock is blaring and I am in a sea of shouting, yelling animals all dressed in black

I hear my name screamed from behind me, but before I can turn around, I am engulfed in a crushing bear hug. Huge arms fold around me, and I am lifted high into the air. I almost hit my head on the ceiling fan. My assailant starts to spin me around, and, as he does, my legs extend straight out. People jump out of the way,

FIVE MINUTES OF BLACKNESS

and I am clearing a path of about ten feet in circumference. My feet smack an innocent bystander in the shoulder as they go flying by. The laughter in my ear is unmistakable, and I recognize the voice. I am in the grips of the tallest cop on the San Diego police force.

"Tall Paul, you asshole! Put me down."

Tall Paul can't resist swinging me in one more circle. As I spin, I kick the glass out of a biker's hand.

When Paul puts me down, I am dizzy. He gives me a brotherly hug as if we haven't seen each other for years. It was actually Wednesday.

"What are you drinking?" he shouts over the noise.

"Coke," I scream back.

He disappears and comes back with four plastic glasses, two for him, two for me.

"It's two-for-one Saturday," he screams.

I take a big swig of the Coke, but swallow a mouthful of booze. The liquor flips my obsession switch to the "On" position.

"Is this rum and Coke?" I shout.

"No, you asshole, it's *Bacardi* and Coke!" His shout is followed by a huge laugh.

"Drink, drink!" he says. "You have a lot of catching up to do."

I can't be mad at Tall Paul. He doesn't know that I am trying to quit drinking.

The glass is already half gone, so I finish the job. In my mind, I plan to have just this one.

Two rum and Cokes turn into four, and then six. I start ordering doubles, and I insist on paying for the drinks. My low self-esteem has me trying to impress people I don't like by buying them drinks they don't want with money I don't have.

After an hour of non-stop drinking, Paul says, "I've had enough!" He weaves towards the door.

*How does someone know when he has had enough?* I wonder.

I order another double.

After Tall Paul leaves, a biker with an attitude squeezes into a space two inches from my face. His breath stinks.

"You kicked the glass out of my hand, fucker!"

"Fuck you," I say.

His huge fist heads in my direction and I am too drunk to respond. My nose snaps, and blood is everywhere. I fall backwards and land on the floor. I start swinging. The biker jumps as high as he can and lands right on top of me. His weight slams me down, and my soft head crashes against the hard wooden floor. The lights go out.

# 18

ON MONDAY MORNING, I LIMP INTO the office with a huge black eye and a taped broken nose. People in other departments snicker, but the guys in my group laugh out loud. I don't bother telling anyone my side of the story.

Tall Paul walks up and laughs hysterically. "You were so loaded," he shouts. "How many doubles did you have?" The whole office waits for my reply. My boss stands in his office doorway, waiting for my reply, too.

At lunchtime, Fig and I leave the building. I am taking Tylenol with codeine by the fist-full as people stare at my grotesque face. Fig acts as if everything is normal, which, unfortunately, it is.

We go to In and Out Burger, where the only two food groups are burgers and fries. I order a double-double cheese, animal style. In plain English, that would mean a double cheeseburger with extra cheese, topped with fried onions and mustard. And I order the largest Coke on the menu.

To get the topic off my broken nose, Fig starts talking about the dead man in the Jag.

"This is cool," he says. "One newspaper reporter has named our killer the Honey Badger. According to the reporter, the Honey Badger is the meanest animal in the world. In battle, it goes straight for the balls."

The newspapers have started writing about the event, and there's been some TV coverage. Since we have already started to receive crank calls, we have purposely left out some of the details.

Fig tells me that the victim had numbers stored in his cell, but they seemed to be mostly convenience listings, like restaurants, airlines, hotels, and car rental agencies. The tech guys were checking his computer, looking in deleted files for outbound and incoming mail.

"What's happening on your end? What did you find out?" he asks.

It's painful for me to carry on a conversation, but I try. "I talked with three people who were close to the dead man. I have good suspects with bad alibis."

I go into detail about Tippy. I describe her gorgeous body, her Daisy Dukes, and her

see-through tank top. "She had no bra on, old buddy!"

I tell Fig about her blasé attitude and the personal trainer. I tell him about my call to the insurance guys. "Tippy will have about two mil to spend on toys and boys," I say.

Then we discuss the first wife, with her resentment, and I tell Fig about the teenage kid, Alex, with his pent-up rage.

"So, the new wife wanted some money, the old wife wanted some justice, and the kid wanted some blood."

# 19

LATER THAT AFTERNOON, FIG SAUNTERS INTO to my office. His eyes are wide open, he has half a grin, and he looks way too cocky.

"Good news and bad news," he says.

"I hate games," I grumble.

"The tech guys have been looking into Blake's computer, and guess what they found."

"I hate games."

"Lots of email."

"Can you be more specific, detective?"

"They found a bunch of messages from someone named Kiki. Seems that Blake Vanderbeek and this girl named Kiki were old friends. She talked about getting together for a drink on the night that he was murdered. The meeting was to be at a restaurant called George's in La Jolla."

"Oh my God. That's great!" I jump up.

"Where were the messages sent from? Let's go!"

"Slow down, cowboy. That was the good news."

"Don't call me *cowboy*. Why is there always bad news?"

"The emails had been sent from a free Hotmail account.

"What's that got to do with anything?

"Free accounts are untraceable. It gets worse."

"How can it be worse?"

"The ISP is Manhattan."

"The ISP? What the hell is an ISP? Let's go!"

"There are eight million people in New York City, and half of them use the internet. It gets worse."

"Why are you doing this to me? What's worse?"

"Here's the worst part," he says. "They were sent from a cyber café."

"Cyber café?"

"There is no reason to get on a plane. Forget it."

As I drive home, I get caught in "The Merge." This is where two highways try to use the same space. The Five and The Eight-Oh-Five join together, and eight lanes of traffic slowly squeeze into four. This traffic nightmare backs up every single night and commuters sit and fume. Some nights the delay adds an extra hour to the ride home. The Merge causes sober men to think about drinking. It causes alcoholics to think about killing. I get off the highway in Solana Beach. The Belly-Up Tavern is at the bottom of the hill.

Sometimes, just walking into a bar adjusts my attitude. The air conditioning is on high, and the music is on low. The smell of alcohol is in the air. An overstuffed brown leather bar stool sucks the tension from my body. Chatter comes from across the room. Someone laughs. The bartender smiles as if we were best friends. For the first time today, I feel comfortable in my own skin. I let out a sigh of relief. All this happens before I even order a drink.

Tonight, I will try a new trick. I will control my drinking. If I just have one, I can prove to the world, and to myself, that I am not an alcoholic. Since I am only having one, I order something decent. A double martini is a fair compromise. The first sip of cold gin and dry vermouth is as rough as sandpaper. The second is as smooth as silk.

The third freezes my tongue and burns my throat at the same time.

After the fourth sip, I become alert. My mind starts to race from one thought to the next. Not having to focus is a blessing. A pleasant humming sound starts somewhere between my ears, and my head feels remarkably light. I try to sip slowly, but each sip is bigger than the last one. There is a hole in the bottom of my glass. This isn't fair. I hold it up and look at the bottom of the glass. The bartender laughs. I order another. My mood changes, and I fit in. I belong to the human race. I smile in the darkness.

I think about Maggie. Since she moved out, there is no reason to rush home. I should wait until the traffic eases up. And anyway, Maggie won't know how many martinis I have had. Maybe I should order food. I'm not hungry. I order another martini for me, and I buy a drink for the stranger next to me. I want to be liked. My glass is full again. Now it's empty. How did that happen? I hate to have an empty glass. The sound system is clear, now, and Bonnie Raitt's slide guitar vibrates in my brain.

I wonder if I should stop, now, but the stranger buys me a drink. Nice guy. We shake hands. I tell the bartender to give him another drink, too. We all laugh. I was only going to have one. Now I am up to five, or maybe six. Who cares? It doesn't matter. No one will know if I come home early, late, or not at all. Now I have two drinks in front of me and a new best friend sitting next to me. Life is good.

# 20

I DRIFT IN AND OUT OF sleep. It's probably a beautiful morning, but I can't tell; the blinds are drawn, and the blanket on the curtain rod is keeping the sunlight from blinding me. Today, the chirping of the birds is driving me crazy. My head is exploding, and my mouth tastes like a pickle. I get up and take four aspirin with a beer chaser. This is the best hangover cure that I know.

As I lie in bed waiting for the medicine to take effect, I think about the past few years. I wonder if accepting early retirement from the FBI was a wise idea, but the timing of their offer was too good to pass up. The Agency was ordered to cut payroll, and they made it easy for some of us to get out early. I had expected to be fired for drunk and disorderly conduct anyway. An opportunity to get a pension while holding my head up was a blessing.

When the offer came in, my drinking was totally out of control. Mornings were horrendous. My ability to deal with everyday issues had become intolerable. I thought that having no job would be the perfect solution. Maggie didn't agree, but I accepted the deal. Of course, having too much time on my hands was not a blessing. I had only one hobby, and that hobby was drinking.

Luckily, my neighbor, who was the San Diego Chief of Detectives, was in a bind. Because of a rash of Mexican-gang-related robberies, he was ordered to add to his staff. He was having a hard time filling some posts.

"If you had a chance to have a job with the city, would you take it?" he asked.

"That's a different kind of work," I said.

"It doesn't matter. It's all cop work, and that's what you do best."

He understood my boredom and convinced me to go back to work. Instead of working for the Feds, I would work for the city. Most of the projects that I got involved with were "Smash and Dash." In the old days, we called them "Break and Entry." There was a lot of domestic violence, a few bar-room murders, and some gang bangs. Most of it was pretty cut and dry. I fit into the routine, and I liked the job, but being in a cop outfit didn't stop my drinking. I am in the same bad place that I had been with the FBI. I am with myself.

# 21

I AM IN A ROOM WHERE everything is white. The walls are white, the sheets are white, and a nurse is dressed in white. There are white straps tied to my wrists. Wires that are attached to my chest lead to a monitor. A flat white line moves slowly across a screen.

Friends and family are looking at me. Some of them are in white suits, some in white t-shirts. My wife is in a long, white dress. She wears white lipstick.

"Hi guys," I say, but no sound comes out of my mouth.

A feeble old priest in a white cape shuffles to my bedside. He opens an ancient Bible with dog-eared pages and brushes off the dust. He starts to mumble something about a valley and the shadow of death.

I am still trying to get someone's attention.

After the reading, my nurse unfolds a big, white sheet and throws it over my legs. She straightens it out and starts to cover me. She slowly pulls the sheet up over my chest.

The phone next to my bed starts to ring. No one in the room seems to care. No one moves to answer the phone. The nurse unhooks the wires that were attached to me and pulls the sheet up to my neck.

The phone keeps ringing.

"Hey, why are you covering me up?" I scream at the top of my lungs, but nobody hears.

As the sheet is finally pulled over my head, the ringing phone becomes unbearable.

I can't see a thing. The phone rings one more time, and it jars me out of my nightmare.

It's Fig's wife, Libby. "It's a beautiful day for a Padres game," she says. "We have an extra ticket and we want you to join us." As she talks about the Padres line up and the beautiful weather, my tortured mind races as fast as it can. The aspirin and beer haven't kicked in yet, and my hangover has me paralyzed. The last place that I want to be is in the bleachers. Fig and Libby are great baseball fans and go to a few games a week. They each have a hot dog and split a beer. I don't care about the hot dog and I need twenty beers.

"I have a bunch of stuff to do," I lie. Her disappointment is genuine.

Even though I pass on the game, I force myself to get up. I need some fresh air, and the best place for that is Mission Beach. The ten-foot wide cement boardwalk separates the sand from tiny vacation homes that have been squeezed onto postage-stamp-sized lots. Hundreds of young locals are rollerblading and skate boarding. Hundreds more are jogging. A member of the gray-haired, pony-tailed set is slowly peddling by on a fat-tire beach cruiser. A bungee cord holds a portable radio in place. Tourists are amused by the spectacle. I am, too. These sights help change my mood.

I also know that, as I walk along the boardwalk, I will never be far from my two biggest needs. At any given time, I can plant my ass on a bar stool, or my head in a toilet bowl.

# 22

I HAVE ALWAYS LOVED MISSION BEACH. Maggie has always hated it.

I think about a day that Maggie and I had lunch at a Mission Beach restaurant. I had three martins and she had three glasses of iced tea. My tongue was thick, and I started to slur my words. After lunch, I insisted that we walk toward the old wooden roller coaster. The walk would give us quality time, I argued.

As the martinis wore off, I bought a quart of beer to go. It was served in a brown paper bag. Maggie was still upset about the martinis, and she was uncomfortable with the bag. I pointed out that other people were drinking from brown paper bags, too.

"There's a small difference," she said with disgust. "The other people are homeless."

As we started our walk, I was feeling no pain. I pointed out an interesting sight to my wife: A young man was lying on his back with a camera. He was trying to take a picture of the sun, and he would have succeeded, except that his girlfriend was standing over him. Her crotch was in the way. I made the mistake of yelling that I'd like a set of prints. The guy laughed, his girl laughed. Maggie fumed.

A little further along the boardwalk, a young girl who was stoned out of her mind stepped right in front of us. We almost bumped into her. She totally ignored Maggie and grabbed my hand. With a big smile, she said, "Sweetie, could you put some suntan lotion on my back?"

Maggie turned and walked toward the ocean and sat on the beach. I apologized to the girl. By the time I got to my wife, she was in tears. I guess that day was the beginning of the end for us.

That was a lifetime ago. Today, I am looking for any girl who needs help with suntan lotion. Today, the leisurely stroll along the boardwalk is good for me. The fresh ocean breezes and the warm California sun start to nurse me back to health. I can imagine that color is returning to my cheeks.

In a short time, I am dry as a bone and hungry as a dog. The only breakfast I had was a beer and four aspirins. I stop at the Green Flash Restaurant for real food. I find a table in the sun and order an extra, extra rare burger with bacon, double cheese, mayo, and butter.

"Hold the lettuce and tomato, please."

I order a draft and a shot of tequila. The beer and shot are gone within seconds. When the waitress comes back with the silverware, she looks at the empty glasses and then at me. I smile and order another round. I feel good for the first time today.

In the background, a local radio station is playing Cheryl Crow. She sings "If it makes you happy, how can it be so bad?"

I suspect that the two girls sitting across from me are tourists, because they are not wearing bathing suits. The brunette has on slacks and a sweater. The blonde, who is in a skirt and blouse, is taking advantage of the sun in the only way that she can. She has her skirt hiked clear up to her waist. As I look in her direction, she is pouring beer on her legs.

"To get a better tan," she says to me with a big smile. I toast her with my second shot. She asks my name and introduces herself. And she introduces her friend, who just glares.

"We're here for an insurance seminar," she tells me. "I'm from Baltimore, and Trish is from Cleveland. We didn't know each other yesterday, but now we are best friends." Trish stares at her in disbelief.

The tequila is starting to calm my stomach, and my head feels clearer than it did a few minutes ago. I am amazed at how the first drink changes my mood. My attitude improves, and my spirits are lifted. There is actually a smile on my face. The second shot gets my juices going. I order a third, and this is all long before my burger is put on the grill.

The blonde is a party waiting to happen. I can't resist.

"Hey, do you know the difference between a cheeseburger and oral sex?" I ask.

With a big smile she says no.

"Oh good. Why don't you join me for lunch?"

Her face lights up, her smile is brighter than before, and she giggles out loud. Her friend just grunts and shakes her head, but the blonde's body language is loud and clear.

As I order my fourth shot of tequila, the waitress tells me that I had better slow down. I wonder if I may be talking too loudly as I say, "How can I slow down? I haven't gotten started yet!"

A few minutes later, I ask for three shots of Cuervo Gold. I tell the waitress that one shot is for me and I would like to buy one for each of the girls. The waitress looks concerned, but returns with the booze. The blonde knows the drill and immediately rubs a lime on her wrist. Her friend looks at the hiked skirt, the tequila, and me. We all incur her wrath. She wants no part of this scene and gives us both a stern look. The look is wasted as we throw our heads back and devour our shots. I order another shot for each of us, but now the waitress is calling time out. She says that I have to take a break. She is practicing politics as she asks me to wait for my burger.

"I'm not hungry any longer. Could you please cancel the burger? And could you bring a few more shots of tequila," I say, a little more emphatically than before. Restaurant patrons are staring. The manager comes over to my table. "Sir, haven't you had enough?" he asks.

"Enough?" I say, as I jump to a standing position. I open my arms as if I am performing Shakespeare on a stage. I am now loud enough for the whole restaurant to hear. "Enough? I don't know the term enough," I shout. "I know the term more! I know the term some! I know the term none! But I don't know the term enough!"

Some people are smiling. Most are shaking their heads. The blonde is laughing hysterically. Her friend gets up and walks out.

The manager quietly says, "Sir, you will have to leave, or I will call the police."

"Police? I love the Police! Can you get them to play 'Message in a Bottle?' Or what about 'Roxanne?' I love the way Sting does that." I am still standing and I start to sing, "Roxanne ..."

The manager is now serious. "Sir, I am calling the police!" He walks away.

"Hey! Tell your Mom not to drink the next time she is pregnant." I walk out.

The blonde doubles up with laughter. She runs after me and grabs my arm. We walk together for a few seconds as if we are a couple.

"I have to go," I say.

"I want to go with you," she says.

"Sorry," I say, as I pull my arm away. I leave her standing as I continue to walk down the boardwalk alone.

I make it to another bar two blocks away. After I order, I take a few seconds to reflect. I am very proud of myself. I have gotten thrown out of a restaurant in less than twenty minutes flat. It's a record, and I consider writing a letter to Guinness. I think about the blonde. The fact that her skirt was up to her waist amused me.

If I had brought her with me, I would have had fun. Maybe even bed. But I've known for years that it's more fun to drink alone than to be with someone who might put a damper on my fun. Maggie told me many times how sad this was. And here I am, leaving a potential romp, just so I can enjoy my drink. I don't care. I want to escape. I love the end result that all alcoholics secretly crave: the ultimate feeling of numbness just before I pass out.

# 23

"FUCK UP!" THAT'S WHAT THEY HAVE been saying behind my back. My friend Fig has been saying it to my face. The Chief has been yelling it to my face.

My day at the beach yesterday was another lost adventure. I have no idea what time I got home. I don't know if I had anything to eat after I canceled the burger, or what time I passed out. All I know is that I am staggering around trying to get ready for work. Before I climb into the shower, I gulp a handful of Excedrin. I think about the blonde and wonder if she found someone to pour beer on her legs. I shake my head and wonder why I left. The grip that booze has on me gets stronger and stronger.

Chief Bettes shakes his head as I walk in late again. I'm sure he is thinking that the booze will be the end of my career, or of my life.

"Come in here, Jesse," he says.

I'm not in the mood for another lecture, and I walk into his office with my tail between my legs. I am trying to think of an excuse, but this time the Chief ignores my condition.

"Jess, I talked to an old friend of mine last night. I don't know if I ever mentioned Don Henderson." It's a question, and I shake my head. "We went to high school together," the Chief says, "and we both ended up in this racket. He's in Charlotte."

*Charlotte? Charlotte? Where the hell is Charlotte?* I think to myself. My mind is racing. *He is going to transfer me. He is going to send me away to someplace called Charlotte? I don't want to move! I'll give up drinking! I'll go to a rehab again!*

The Chief speaks in a whisper. "Jesse, the Ball Buster was just there."

"What?"

Don is now the Chief of police in Charlotte," my boss continues. "He had seen some of the intelligence about our case on the internet reports but didn't think much about it. But then, guess what? He called me at home, last night. Check this out. Parked car. Five shots, close range, right to the groin. Blood everywhere. Man propped up behind the wheel. There are too many similarities to our crime here in La Jolla to be a coincidence."

The Chief is rambling, and I'm in a total state of shock. I thought that the Blake Vanderbeek murder in La Jolla was a one-shot wonder. I never imagined that the perp would go on a spree, let alone a spree that stretched thousands of miles away.

"Jesse," the Chief is saying. "My friend Don has heard about your reputation as a detective. He said you were terrific. Evidentially they still talk about you at the agency. Dammed if I know why!" He shows a half smile. "Anyway, he asked if you would gather your notes and observations from the La Jolla murder and shoot down to Charlotte for a few days. He'll pick up your per diem."

I am stunned. I was happy to get out of the agency, because I hated the serial crimes. I was going nuts. There were too many killings, too much blood, and too much pain. I joined a local police force to get away from senseless, big-city violence, and here I am getting sucked right back into the madness.

I promise Chief Bettes that I won't embarrass him with any

"drunken episodes." I promise myself that I will not drink until all interviews are completed. I understand enough about drinking to know that if I don't have the first drink, I won't have the second. "Don't pick up the first drink" is what they say at AA. I used to say it all the time. Now it's all I can hang on to. I'm hanging on to my job, too.

# 24

I PACK A BAG AND CATCH the next flight to Charlotte. On the plane, I put my seat back and try to rest. The flight is turbulent, but it's nothing compared to the bedlam in my mind. Being called in as an expert is unsettling. I have never been an expert. I have been lucky! I have been in the right place at the right time. I have found a few leads that other people overlooked, but I've never been an expert. There's no magic to this job. There are only hours of research and days of tiny little details. This job takes perseverance and persistence.

Unfortunately, now that I am drunk half the time and hung-over the other half, I don't have the energy I once had. I am a falling-down drunk, and I am falling down on my job. I can't follow up on cold prospects or track down hot leads. I am a loser. I know it. My friend Fig knows it. My boss knows it. My wife knows it too. This is so evident to everyone, but I can't stop! I can't break the cycle. I can't quit!

When I get to the airport, I grab my bag and head towards the taxi area. As I pass a newsstand, I see a headline screaming from the front page of the Charlotte Observer. Parking Lot Killer Hits Charlotte!" I buy the paper.

In the cab, I unfold the paper and read the feature article. The story goes on to say that a lunatic has been killing victims in many cities and has now chosen Charlotte. It speculates that the killer is a prostitute who is murdering strangers for revenge. It suggests that she is picking men up in bars, taking them to their cars, and then shooting them in their private parts. She then goes to another city and does it again. This is mostly bullshit and conjecture, but it sells newspapers.

I turn to the entertainment section for some reliable news. There are at least a hundred bars and clubs in Charlotte. They all seem to advertise in this newspaper. Most bars have a blurb in their ad about "Beach Music." Almost every bar has a Beach Music Night. I thought that I had the English language down pat, but I've never heard of Beach Music.

When I get to the station, I confront the desk clerk, a broad shouldered thug with a tattered uniform that hasn't fit since graduation. His brass buckles are tarnished, and his teeth are stained. His uniform was slept in, and his eyes could have belonged to a bloodhound.

"I'm looking for Don Henderson."

"So isn't everyone."

"He's expecting me"

"He's expecting a lot of people."

"Is he here?"

"Yup" Then there is a long silence. This desk clerk is on a control trip, and he wants to have his five minutes of recognition. I play the game.

I introduce myself, and he shakes his head.

"So, you're a cop, huh? I thought you were an ex-con."

"May I see him, please?"

"He's in a meeting."

"What do you know about the parking lot killer?"

"Nothing."

"Did you know the victim?"

"Nope."

"Was he originally from Charlotte?"

"Don't know."

My patience is running thin. I ask one more question.

"What's Beach Music?"

The clerk's brow furls up. He is thinking for the first time this week. "What the hell kind of question is that?"

"A damn good question. What's beach music?"

"You know, Beach Music!" he says.

"No, I don't know. What is Beach Music?"

"Beach Music is ... well, just Beach Music!"

This guy isn't too bright. He's spent too many years with one hand on a siren and the other on his dick.

The local Chief, Don Henderson, is a nice guy. He is about six feet tall, and wears a short-sleeve shirt that shows off his bulging muscles. He might be a part-time weight lifter. His hair is parted in the middle and combed back on the sides. He looks more like a movie star than a cop. His wide smile is genuine.

"We're glad y'all came down here to help us. We can't figure this one out, that's for damn sure!"

Don takes me to the crime scene, and on the way he fills me in.

"The victim's name was Woodrow Winters. Everyone called him Woody. He was forty-two and single. He owned a restaurant near Albemarle called The Black Dog Tavern." According to Don, The Black Dog was a real clean business. Woody hosted fundraisers for local charities and sponsored a kids' little league baseball team. He had a lot of friends. He had a live-in girlfriend of eight years.

"A real cutie pie," says the Chief. "They were gonna get hitched in a few months."

The Black Dog is about thirty minutes outside of town on a stretch of highway that the locals call Barbeque Trail. There are about fifty barbeque joints within a stone's throw of each other.

"I hope y'all like Barbeque," Don says, with a big grin.

We find the location of the crime, and although it's not as concealed as the underground garage in La Jolla, there is still plenty of privacy. A crime like this could go unnoticed for hours. There are so many similarities that it scares me. The body has been moved to the morgue by the time that I get there, but the crime scene has been roped off.

After walking the scene and looking at pictures, we head to the lab. Don tells me that the bullets were 32-caliber hollow point, and rifling tests conclude that they came from the same gun that was used in the California crime. Photographs show that the victim had been left in his car in the same slumped-over position as the man in La Jolla. Again, anyone walking by would think that he was sleeping it off. Instead of a Jaguar, Woody had been sitting in a Jeep Cherokee with a roof rack and a Charlotte Pops bumper sticker Instead of a neatly tailored business suit like Blake Vanderbeek's, Woody had been wearing jeans and a sport shirt. On the back seat there was a box of menus, some large, restaurant-sized containers of spices, and a few cooking utensils. I have prints, fibers, and hair samples sent back to Erica in San Diego for comparison.

# 25

WOODY'S FIANCÉE IS DEVASTATED. HER NAME is Kitty, and we meet in her condo. She can't stop crying. Kitty is petite, attractive, and soft-spoken. Her hair is shoulder length and combed straight. She is wearing a huge "Black Dog Tavern" sweatshirt. Her faded jeans have small rips at the knees, and all of the seams are frayed from years of wear. She wears no lipstick, there is no polish on her nails, and no color on her cheeks. The ex-bride-to-be has a red nose and red eyes. She is clutching a Kleenex in her hand. A roll of toilet paper is on the table. A paper bag on the floor is full.

She stops crying long enough to tell me about the night of the murder.

"I was having dinner with a girlfriend," she says.

"Woody usually closes the restaurant on Saturday nights, and while they are cleaning up, he lets the kitchen guys have a few drinks. He has a few, too. I really don't like it," Kitty tells me, "but they are all so wired after a long night that they just want to relax. Sometimes he gets home late, and I never wait up for him. Last Sunday when I woke up, Woody wasn't here. I called the kitchen manager and got him out of bed. He said that Woody didn't stay around after closing but actually left before last call."

After a heart-wrenching pause, she continues her story. "I started making some other calls, and then two policemen came to the door. The minute I saw them, I knew that something bad had happened."

She starts crying again. I let her cry for a long time before I ask a few more questions. We talk about life insurance, and as far as Kitty knows, there is none. "He promised that he would get that taken care of before we got married." She cries again. I rule Kitty out as a suspect.

I interview the restaurant chef and, for some reason, I believe him when he says that his boss left early. "Woody didn't say where he was going," the chef tells me. "I thought that it was strange that he showered and put on some clean clothes before he left. That seemed like a funny thing for him to do, but I didn't question it; he's the boss."

I start to interview the other employees. Everyone says that Woody was a good guy. I also get the universal question. "Who would ever do that to him?"

I do a little research and find out who did the bookkeeping. Her name is Cynthia McBride, and I set up a meeting the next morning at her in-town office. She has a small business with two employees, and has been doing the company books since the restaurant opened. She tells me that she and Woody had been friends for years.

"Woody had some financial trouble when he first opened, but in the last few years he has really pulled it together," Cynthia tells me. I ask if anyone would have wanted him killed, and she just shakes her head. Cynthia is upset, but very professional and pleasant. The interview fails to help, and I say good-bye.

As the days go by and the interviews progress, I talk to a lot of people. I ask about Woody's business ties, his habits, his friends, and enemies. I ask about his biggest competitors. I ask who would want to kill him. I strike out on all counts.

I drive my rented car back to The Black Dog Tavern. There is a "Temporarily Closed" sign in the front door. Around back, I find the kitchen door open, and I let myself. The kitchen is deserted, but I hear voices coming from the bar.

"I can definitely be the manager!" a male voice says, emphatically.

"You can't even manage your girlfriend." a female voice responds. There are laughs from other voices.

"Why do we need a manager?" a girl asks. "We all know our jobs. Let's just do our jobs and keep the restaurant open."

"And who will be the one to call you when you are late?"

"I may be late, but at least I never come in wasted!"

"I may have had a drink before work, but at least I don't come in stoned."

"Stoned? You're the one who comes in fucked up all the time!"

"Excuse me," I say. They all jerk their heads towards me at the same time.

"May I help you?" says one.

"This is a private meeting," says another. "The restaurant is closed."

I look around the bar. It's like a cocktail party without the fun. Empty glasses are all over the tables. The employees are trying to drink their way through the inevitable job loss. They are trying to steer a big ship without a rudder.

I introduce myself and ask to speak with the hostess. She stands up and we shake hands. She takes me to the office. I wait while she rewinds the answering machine. There's a message about functions, another about a lost pair of glasses, and a third message asking about veggie meals. There are no messages that would indicate foul play. And there are no personal appointments on a greasy wall calendar over Woody's desk.

I sit in the office and interview employees, one by one. I believe that Woody's death came as a shock to all of them.

We impound the office computer and have it shipped to the lab in San Diego.

I visit the restaurant supply company, the advertising firm, and the food vendor. I ask questions, but keep getting blank stares. And since the investigation is going nowhere, I also ask everyone that I meet one other question: "What's Beach Music?" No one knows.

During my time in Charlotte, I use all of my magic to stay on the wagon. It's been three days without a drink. It's been tough. I am exhausted all day, and I can't sleep at night. The hotel room is too hot, but the air conditioner is too cold. The people in the next room are screwing, and the bed keeps banging. The ice machine sounds like an explosion every time it drops its load into a plastic bucket. Everyone who gets off the elevator is either way too happy or in the middle of an argument.

At 3:00am, I slip on my jeans and walk to the candy machine. After wolfing down two Milky Ways and a bag of M&Ms, I am wired. I flip channels for hours.

I get back to bed and think about my life. I only have a few issues. I can't relax. I have no hobbies, and very few close friends. I am not happy being sober, but it has been a long time since I have found any escape from booze. At work, I constantly add tasks to my to-do list. One boss told me that I had a severe case of Jewish guilt. I have a problem with self-control, and I'm ruled by others' feelings toward me. I stare at the dark ceiling and wonder why my self-definition comes from someone else's attention? I should stop being so sensitive. I should stop being so needy. I should stop taking everything so personally. I should stop grasping for acceptance. I should stop thinking and go to sleep.

A loud clacking noise scares the hell out of me. The maid is pounding on my door with a piece of metal, or maybe her shoe. She manages to wake me up. It's 11:00am, and I order breakfast. After three cups of coffee, I go back to the station. I review my notes with Don. I tell him I am running out of people to talk with. I admit that I am running out of patience. I reserve a flight back to San Diego for the following morning.

# 26

IT'S MY LAST NIGHT IN TOWN. I break my fast and go out for a little social beverage. "I deserve it," I say to myself. I pick out a bar near my hotel that is having a "Beach Music" night. I walk to the "Beau," and order a very dry martini with a twist.

The gentleman on the stool next to me is working on a martini, too. He is also working on an extra-large cigar. He is a lawyer from Myrtle Beach, and is in town for a little case and a lot of drinks.

"I'm Louie." We shake hands, squeeze as hard as we can, and stare into each other's eyes without showing pain. His handshake is crushing. It's a guy thing.

We share a few Hillary Clinton jokes and I tell him about my new freedom from my wife. He tells me about his divorce. "My wife fucked my neighbor, and I had to give her half of my fortune! Where's the justice?" he asks, still pissed after years. Who says that men don't talk about feelings?

During the next few hours, we tell our worst jokes, share our intimate thoughts, and buy each other many martinis. Our relationship has progressed. I feel a strong bond with my new lawyer friend. I feel that I can tell him anything. I think that I can ask him anything. I get up my courage, look him straight in the eyes, and take a deep breath. I have his attention.

"Louie, I need to ask a question."

"Fire away, buddy." He looks at me seriously.

"What is Beach Music?"

Without missing a puff on his big cigar, he laughs and gives me the news. "That's the music that you heard the first time that you got laid under the boardwalk!"

"Like Motown?" I ask.

"You got it, man. 50s, Motown, The Four Tops, Marvin Gay, The Isley Brothers, dancing, bitching, Beach Music."

I leave the bar without knowing anything about the victim, the killer, or the motive, but I know about Beach Music.

# 27

THE NEXT MORNING I SLEEP UNTIL nine, have a gigantic breakfast, and take a cab to the airport.

I've reserved an aisle seat for this flight, and as I climb into my row, I look at the young lady seated by the window. She is well dressed, stylish, and professional, but she is as white as a ghost. Her head is down and she is staring into the motion sickness bag. Her eyes are wide open and she is taking long, exaggerated breaths of air. She is heaving air, in and out. In and out. She doesn't want to be on a plane, and it is obvious that she is expecting the worst from this flight.

There is an empty seat behind us and I move back one row.

"To give you a little more room," I say.

As the plane takes off, I hear a loud belching noise coming from the row in front of me. The girl's head is still down, but she reaches up and hits the orange flight attendant button. Since the plane is banking during takeoff, the attendant is still strapped into her jump seat. There is another loud retching noise. Thank God for barf bags.

# 28

WHEN I GET BACK TO SAN Diego, I go straight to the office and call a meeting with our new task force. Fig, Erica, and the Chief all listen to my update. It's brief.

"We got us a serial," I say. "And we got us a puzzle! Our two victims had nothing in common, except the way that they died. One guy was wealthy with lots of insurance, and the other was getting by, with no insurance. One victim was disliked by everyone, and the other guy had lots of friends. One was married, and one was single. One widow was glad to see her husband go, and one fiancée was devastated. One killing was in California, and the other was two thousand miles away in North Carolina."

"The prints in the two cars matched," says Erica. "But they have not been found in the national fingerprint database. The person who is doing these killings does not seem to have a record yet."

"What about the hair samples?" Fig asks.

"We have matched hair fibers at each scene. This confirms that the same person was in both cars. We believe that the killer was a blond with bleached curly hair. We believe that the perp is a woman."

"Have reports come back from VICAP?" asks the Chief. The Violent Criminal Apprehension Program would show if a similar crime had been committed somewhere else in the country. There were no similarities.

"This might be the killer's first rodeo," I say. "Anything else of interest?"

"Yes," says Erica. "We found bloody footprints outside of each victim's cars. They matched. The shoes were high heels, and we could determine from the prints that the weight of the woman was very light. The shoes were size six."

It's Fig's turn. "The lab technicians worked on Woody's computer. The inbox and deleted files contained 11 different emails from someone named Kiki. This is the same name that was used by the person who whacked Blake Vanderbeek in his Jag. Here's the interesting part. In the first killing, the messages came from a free Hotmail account in New York. In the second case, they came from a free Yahoo account in New Jersey. Kiki, whoever she is, has a good working knowledge of computers. I think that these killings were planned well in advance. It wasn't a coincidence that the emails came from two different cities. This would make tracing the messages very difficult. She chose two cities with large populations for anonymity.

"Since the messages were sent from free email accounts," Fig concludes, "there will be no record of a name or address. No personal information is required for free accounts. And free email accounts self-destruct after ninety days of inactivity. In that time, this Kiki person could have set up another free account, in another cyber café, in another city. Finding Kiki will not be easy."

"I love it when they play hard to get." I smile, but no one smiles with me.

Erica adds one more detail. "The DNA tests conclusively confirm that saliva on the lips of each victim matched. We assume from this fact that the killer had kissed each of the men before, or after, they were shot."

"OK," says the Chief. "Let's have a quick rundown. What do we know about serial killers?"

Fig starts with the intelligence factor. "Serial Killers are most likely street smart, and could easily get around," he says. "They may also be charming and charismatic."

Erica says, "Serial killers usually prefer hands-on weapons and these two murders were definitely hands-on."

The Chief puts in his two cents. "We've always felt that a serial killer is well organized and since these killings were well planned, they fit into that profile."

And when it's my turn, I add the only other thing that we all feel confident about. "Serial killers have usually had a terrible childhood. They may have been born out of wedlock, or were probably physically, sexually, or emotionally abused as kids."

The Chief starts thinking out loud, and we all tune in to his thoughts. "Most serial killers pick random targets. The victims are usually in the wrong place at the wrong time, but I think that this case is different. Because of the emails, it's obvious that "Kiki" knew the victims before-hand."

"Kiki may have been jilted by these guys, and may be going after her old lovers," says Erica. "Blake was five years older than Woody, but they each could have been involved with her. This would make sense."

"No, it doesn't make sense," I say. "It doesn't make sense that a girl would just go out and kill her old lovers. There must be more to her story. Something is missing.

"This girl has a disturbed personality," I say. "I suspect that she started to slip through the cracks years ago, but no one was there to catch her. Unfortunately, we might not catch her, either."

"Why do you say that?" the Chief asks.

"She might be on a mission, and when the mission is complete, she might just disappear.

"How about this," I add. "If we can't go forward with our investigation, let's go backward. What do we know for sure? Or what do we suspect?" I sum up: "I believe that these murders were planned well in advance. I believe that the killer knew the victims for a long time. I believe that she traveled a long distance to get to the scene of the crime. I believe that she is very organized, savvy, very determined. I believe that although she may be very ordinary looking, something is different about her. Her actions don't define her state of mind. She might be found sane in every measurable way. It's not *what* she does, but why. She might believe that these men are guilty of some crime, and she is punishing them. So we have to find the crime that she is punishing them for, before we can find her."

There is more silence as we all think about crime and punishment.

Fig breaks the silence with another unsettling observation. "The killer has had two successes. She now has a genuine taste for this adventure. She is getting good at this killing thing. She seems to be able to get in and out of a town, and I bet we will see more of her work."

"There are a few possibilities for an early break," I say. "First of all, the killer might feel remorse and confess. Second, someone who knows the killer might turn her or him in. Third, the killer slips up. Fourth, we find an acquaintance that the victims had in common. This last option is our best bet at this point."

I ask Fig to go back and talk with Tippy and the first Mrs. Vanderbeek. We also want to talk with Kitty in Charlotte again. We will ask them for every name and address of every contact that the deceased might have known. It will take time, but that is all we can go on now. We will start a big-mother list of every person that the dead men knew. We need to look for similarities. If we get enough names, hometowns, and occupations, we can have the computer do a search and look for the one name or city that might come up in common.

I also ask Fig to start a task board in my office. A USA map with crime-scene locations pinned. I ask Fig to call the families and get photographs of each victim. I want pictures of them with their friends and acquaintances. I want pictures of them enjoying their favorite hobbies. I want group pictures of them at work and at parties. I want pictures of them in their homes, and older pictures of them in college or high school. I especially want pics of their old girlfriends and lovers. I ask Fig to start a collage of each deceased person.

Our goal is to find out what the dead men have in common. How did Kiki, if that is her real name, know these two men? Why did she kill them? Will she kill again? How many men are on her list?

The killings are a month apart, and I wonder if there will be a pattern. Will there be another incident someplace in the country in four weeks? The clock is ticking.

One other question comes to mind. "Here's the part that really bothers me," I say. "How did she get around? If Kiki traveled by plane, how did she get her pistol past airport security? Did she drive between the two cities that were two thousand miles apart?"

"Where do you guys think that she might live?" Fig asks.

"I think that she lives in the Northeast," I say, "because that's where the emails were sent from."

Fig is the expert on getting information. We brainstorm to build a list of possible links. Did the two deceased men go to grammar school, high school, or college together? They are not the same age, so a school relationship seems unlikely. Did they come from the same small town somewhere in the country? Were they somehow related by a second marriage or were they distant cousins? Did they work together years ago? Did they play for a sports team? Did they belong to a business association, or a club? Were they involved in a business deal?

I ask Fig to cross-match airline reservations and rental car records in and out of San Diego and Charlotte. This won't be easy because the only name that we have to go on is Kiki. It's probably a nickname. But we will look for similarities in any records.

"Let's also check every motel and hotel in each area," I say. "The shooter must have been covered with blood and might have cleaned up someplace. Try to find a maid who has found a pile of bloody clothes."

We start a countdown to the next full moon.

I strongly suspect a borderline personality disorder, and I am beginning to feel that, from all outward appearances, our killer probably looks very normal. To get in and around airports, if that's how she traveled, she would blend in and not cause any undue attention or interest. She is probably neat, well dressed, organized, and thorough. I am thinking that the person who committed these crimes is a professional who knows how to communicate. But, if she is a good communicator, why were there no phone messages on answering machines? Why were there no common call-backs logged on cell phones? Why were there no incoming or outbound phone numbers on the murdered men's phone statements from either New York or New Jersey?

The list of unanswered questions goes on and on. My mind goes on and on.

We all sit quietly and think. The silence is deafening. I am wondering how we will find a perpetrator who has no criminal record and no apparent motive. How will we find someone who has gotten within kissing range of two people who live two thousand miles away from each other? What is the missing link? My mind is overtaxed from playing out possible scenarios.

# 29

KIKI'S RETURN FLIGHT FROM CHARLOTTE LANDED later than scheduled. The baggage carousel was out of order, and the porter had to bring all suitcases up the elevator one at a time. By the time she got to the Federal Express office in Asbury Park, it was closed.

She unlocked her condo door and looked around. *It's good to be home,* she thought, but she knew it was a lie. She took off one of her high heels and threw it clear across the room.

"Why don't I have a man in my life?" she wondered, as she unpacked. "I don't even have a roommate."

With the exception of a fair-weather acquaintance at work, she was in her own world. When her coworker asked about her weekend, she always had a story ready: "A friend and I came into the city, and we climbed up to the top of the Statue of Liberty," she would say; or, "A friend and I went to the Tavern on the Green, and then we took a horse-drawn buggy ride all the way to the Village."

On Sunday mornings, she would read the paper to find out where the flea market was, or she would look for a review of a new art show. She would go alone, just to have the details for Monday morning's story. In every story, there was always a fantasy friend.

The reality was that she got up alone, she had her meals alone, and she slept alone. Sometimes her loneliness felt as if it was closing in on her, drowning her, suffocating her.

She stood on her deck and felt the ocean mist gently brush her face. She wiped a tear from her eye and went back inside. She took the small leather-bound notebook out of her desk and crossed another name off of her to-do list. Blake and Woody were gone.

Kiki reached up to the top shelf of her hall closet and gently took her shoebox down. She found the pictures of Woody and attacked them with a pair of scissors. She let her rage explode through her fingers and cut, stabbed, and shredded the pictures until they were not even recognizable. She put the remains of her life with Woody in the toilet and flushed the bad memories away. Woody was gone from her life. Period.

There was a sense of accomplishment, but there was also a sense of loss. Her world was getting smaller. She wondered if her anguish was being fueled by her actions.

She flopped on the bed and glided in and out of sleep. She was exhausted, but couldn't relax. She should be happy, but all she did was cry.

Kiki woke at daybreak, and turned on the news. News Seven mentioned that there had been another parking lot murder. They talked about a tragedy in Charlotte and said that the killing had a lot in common with a shooting in La Jolla. Pictures of the two parked cars were flashed on the screen and pictures of the victims were also shown. There were no clues.

"Don't panic, folks," said the newsman. "These two crimes are isolated, and although there are similarities, no conclusive evidence can be reached yet. News Channel Seven is conducting its own investigation."

Then the picture changed.

"We interrupt this program for breaking News." A reporter was standing in front of a sign that said Welcome to Charlotte.

"In an exclusive interview with former ex-FBI detective, Jesse Collins, News Seven has learned that the same small handgun was used in both crimes. Someone traveled from California to North Carolina, but we don't know why these two men were targeted. Other than that, there is not much to go on," he said.

Kiki stared at the image of the detective. *What a nice-looking man,* she thought. She would like to meet him. Maybe he would like her. Maybe they would be friends, or even lovers. Or maybe, if he got too close, she might have another plan for him. On a whim, she added his name to her to-do list. Something would have to happen with the detective. In the back of her mind, she knew that she would never meet Jesse, because he would never find her. How could he? No one would ever put the pieces together.

As usual, although the TV was on, her apartment was completely silent.

# 30

As the sky grew light from the morning sun, Kiki walked to the beach. On the way, she stopped at 7-11 for coffee and Zebra cakes. No one cared if she ate healthy or filled up with junk, but she knew that the coffee and sugar would bump her mood up a notch. She walked across the boardwalk and kicked off her flip-flops as she stepped onto the sand. She loved the feeling of the fine, white sand as it sifted through her toes. She didn't care if she stepped on broken shells or cut glass. That would only make her tougher in the long run. The tide was going out, and the waves were low. There was beach tar everywhere. She looked around. It was early, and she was alone. She hiked her dress up to her thighs, and walked into the ocean. The cool, salt water felt good as it crashed against her legs. She pulled her dress up further, and walked in up to her waist.

She was still way ahead of schedule, and she sat on the sand as she had done a thousand times before. The morning sun was warming her entire body, and it felt good. She lay back and wiggled until the sand was the shape of her body. She pulled her dress up again so that she could dry. She moved her heels into the sand, and they set into little indentations. She closed her eyes and dozed off. When she slept, she felt as if she was becoming one with the sand.

When Kiki awoke, she watched a flock of seagulls as they played in the wind. She loved to watch them swoop toward the ocean and glide back up. They were free and didn't have a care in the world.

She went to the FedEx office, and, as soon as they were open, she picked up her package. Then she headed straight for her condo and locked herself in. When the door was secure and bolted, she unpacked her pistol. Just having her Kel-Tec back in her hands made her tingle.

She gently caressed the handle and stroked her cheek with the barrel. She kissed the tip and let her tongue glide back and forth on the tiny opening. She slid the barrel as far into her mouth as she could, as she thought about her blueprint for relief.

Her plan had fallen into place over a long period of time. She remembers how she got the idea of shipping her pistol by FedEx. When Kiki was young, the FedEx deliveryman who called on her office always paid special attention to her.

"What kinds of things do people ship?" she asked one day.

"People can ship anything they want," he had said slowly. "I suspect they ship drugs, counterfeit money, and even guns, but I don't care what's in the package. FedEx will ship any package as long as it's not ticking, dripping, or glowing."

Kiki tried this out, and sent a pair of socks to herself. She sent t-shirts. She sent underwear. She found out that she could send any package to any FedEx office with a customer pick-up counter. All she had to do was specify the zip code, prepay for the service, and add a note that said "Hold for customer."

Shipping her pistol to La Jolla and Charlotte had worked like a charm. Kiki was getting good at being a world-class traveler. On each trip, she rented a cheap motel room near the airport. After each encounter, she went back to the room to shower and change. She took extra time cleaning up the room and put all of the bloody clothes into a plastic bag. After she left the room, she went out in search of a dumpster. In La Jolla, there had been a construction container right next to the hotel. In Charlotte, she had found an unlocked dumpster behind a supermarket.

Kiki felt better today than she had the night before. Two painful thorns had been removed from her side. She slipped on her bathing suit and went back to the beach, which was now crowded with people.

She had planned to spend the day catching up on her rest, but the couple on the next blanket gained her undivided attention. The girl was young and very thin. She probably only weighed ninety pounds. Kiki felt sorry for the girl who had absolutely no curves in the front, and was flat as a board. When Kiki saw the back of the girl's bathing suit, she stopped feeling sorry. The girl was exploiting her major asset. The back of her one-piece suit was cut so low that her tiny little fanny was hanging out. The boyfriend was probably ten years older, and he was well taken care of. She was bent over him and licking his nipples in plain sight right on the beach. Of course, there was nothing wrong with this. They were not having sex, but her attention was so subtle and suggestive that Kiki couldn't stop staring. The boy was lying on his back and his hard-on was bulging through his Speedo. The girl's hand was resting on his thigh, and her fingers were doing the walking.

This public display of affection had Kiki's juices flowing. She knew that she should stop staring, but she couldn't look away. Kiki let her mind slip into fantasy mode. She imagined that she was in a fashion show. She could picture herself standing in the wings and waiting for her name to be called. Finally, the announcer read her name from his schedule and said: "Up next in our show tonight is Kiki. She will be wearing a long flowing black and red..." He glanced up and stopped.

"Oh my God," he muttered into the microphone. "She's naked. She is only wearing heels!" The announcer shot a glance at the fashion coordinator but couldn't get her attention. She, too, was staring in shock. The announcer looked back at the runway in disbelief. He was trying to continue the dialog, but the best he could do was stutter. Flash bulbs were popping everywhere. Video cameras were rolling from every corner of the room. Reporters in the front row stopped writing. They were just staring. Two men in the back row were doing high fives. Women were nodding approvingly. There were smiles and applause. Kiki walked to the end of the runway and struck a very elegant pose. Then slowly, very slowly, she untied the scarf that had been draped around her neck and let it hang from her extended arm. She turned and faced in another direction. She did a half curtsey and slowly started to sashay back down the catwalk. Her long legs were stepping out, one in front of the other, and her balance was perfect. She glanced over her shoulder to see that the announcer was still staring. Before leaving the runway, she turned one more time to the audience. Everyone in the room was on their feet, cheering and yelling. People in the back of the room were standing on chairs. She bowed slightly and then threw her scarf into the crowd. Every person in the audience was applauding. Every eye in the room was on Kiki. She envisioned the headlines that would appear the next day in Woman's Wear Daily. "Beautiful fashion model steals the show!"

She woke up from her fantasy dream. The couple was gone. She ran into the water to cover up her own dampness and then she went home alone.

# 31

Erica calls. "Hey Jesse, I have a great idea!"

"Awesome. What is it?"

"Why don't we grab a meeting? If we hurry, we can make the 8pm group in Carlsbad"

"Oh Erica. Thanks a lot, but I have some other plans."

"Jesse. You seem to have a lot of other plans lately. I hope that your plans don't include drinking."

"I'm fine." I say.

"I've heard that before."

I hang up and pour a healthy handle of Bacardi into a chilled tumbler. Erica and I are such good friends, and I know that I am letting her down. She checks on me regularly, and constantly tells me about mutual friends that she sees at meetings. She invites me to join her for cookouts or get-togethers. I respectfully decline. I want to get back to AA. I want to get sober. But more than that, I want a drink.

# 32

"HELLO?"

"Hi Maggie, it's me"

"Who?"

"It's me. Your husband, Jesse."

"Oh, Jesse. I didn't recognize your voice. You sound so hoarse. Are you sick or something? Have you been drinking a lot?"

"I haven't been drinking too much. How's the weather?"

"It's a beautiful day in Boulder. The sun is shining, there's a light breeze, and the flowers are just starting to bloom. It's such a refreshing change from California where the weather never changed."

"Great. Are you in your new apartment yet?"

"Mother is helping me unpack as we speak."

"So, you're really going to stay in Colorado?"

"Yes."

"I was hoping that you would move back here to California with me."

"Jesse, I can't live with you. Your drinking was making me sick."

"It's making me sick, too."

"So why don't you stop?"

"That's what I want to do!"

# 33

KIKI REACHED UP TO THE TOP shelf of her closet, and brought out her shoebox. She thumbed through the informal time line, and went back to the early days. She found a collection of pictures of Tommy Button. Some of the pictures were of him alone, but most were of the two of them. Tommy was such a gentle man. He was a very caring man. Tommy was a man who gave himself to her as well as he could. He took care of her, and they were interested in the same things. But he loved her. She knew this. He brought her trinkets. He gave her attention. They talked about things that most men didn't even notice. He was interested in fashion, and he commented on the latest trend in hair styles. He even felt comfortable discussing her feminine issues. She had never known a man who understood her menstrual cycles, or mood swings, or hot flashes. She had a bond with Tommy that she could have never had with another man. The only strange part of the relationship was that he was very timid when it came to sex. It was as if the intimate part of their relationship was painful. One day, he just walked out. Just up and left. She was devastated. She kept trying to contact him, be he avoided her. She went over the things that she did, and the things that she said. Why would he just leave? The heartache lasted for a long, long time.

# 34

IT'S THE FOURTH OF JULY, AND I have a bang-up of a hangover. Since it's a holiday, Fig and his wife, Libby, are babysitting me. Instead of letting me drink by myself, they take me to a party where I can drink with other people. They even offer to drive. Libby will be the designated driver. I feel like such a loser!

Fig, Libby, Maggie, and I have been friends for years. It's my fault that our foursome has become a threesome.

On this holiday, we go to a very exclusive gated community in Rancho Santa Fe. This gala event is hosted by a young CEO of a software firm. The property is spectacular, and no expense has been spared for this party. A bandstand has been built for the occasion and a portable dance floor set up near the pool. Long tables with red tablecloths are full of shrimp cocktail, crab legs, and smoked salmon. Caterers are everywhere, and they are preparing a buffet table with a carving station at one end. There are three open bars all stocked with top shelf liquor. I am in heaven.

The red, white, and blue candles floating on top of the kidney-shaped pool are impressive, but the focal point of the party is a gigantic American flag that has been hung on one complete side of the house. Spotlights are shining from six eucalyptus trees.

Fig and Libby are my token socialite friends, and they know everyone at the party.

"You have to get out and meet people," Libby is saying.

"I'm not good at being social, Libby. I just don't want to go out and get laid."

Libby is my wife's best friend, and we are not sure if my wife is coming back. We are trying to prepare for the worst.

The five-piece band is blasting an old Chubby Checker tune, and I walk to the bar. It's my third Bacardi. I'm trying to pace myself. I feel a tap on my shoulder and hear a female voice shout into my ear over the music.

"Can you grab me a gin and tonic?" A blonde in a low-cut, white dress with spaghetti straps is asking the question. The girl is taller than I am, and as thin as a fashion model. Her hair has been braided with red, white, and blue ribbons that hold short pigtails in place. She has freckles, crooked teeth, and a warm smile. As she leans toward me to take the drink, her dress falls open. Her strapless bra is red and I'm impressed with her patriotism.

I offer a toast. "Here's to Independence Day!" I say

"And to the fireworks!" she replies, with a wide-open smile and crooked pearly whites.

"Did you know that all guys are like parking spaces?" she asks.

I smile and just shake my head.

"The good ones are taken, and the ones that are left are either handicap or way too small!"

After I stop laughing, she tells me that she is here on a blind date.

"Is he handicap or way too small?" I ask.

We laugh again.

"My boss fixed me up," she says, "so I have to be polite. My date is out on the dance floor doing the twist with my boss's wife."

The conversation flows easily, even though the music is loud. We talk about dating, dancing, and drinking.

"I hate all of these southern California yuppies," she says. "They all stand at cocktail parties drinking lite beer and white wine. Their breath stinks, and nobody has fun. If you are going to drink, just get to it." With that she empties her glass. I down mine, and get refills.

She tells me another joke, and, with the punch line, she puts her arm around my neck and hugs very tight.

"Do you know the difference between hard and dark?" I ask. She shakes her head no.

"It stays dark all night."

She laughs, and I share a few more of my favorite one-liners. The band starts to play the first slow song of the evening. Without any discussion, we start to dance. With one hand on each other's shoulders and the other hand on our drinks, we do very well. The girl holds on as tight as she can with her free arm. She is an excellent dancer, and she follows me perfectly. I can feel her body pushing into mine. She smells good, and I can feel her breathing in my ear.

After the song ends, the band takes a break, but we are still standing in an embrace. Out of nowhere, her date shows up and takes her hand from my shoulder. He leads her away to a table on the other side of the dance floor. As she is being kidnapped, she looks back at me and mouths the words, "Call me!"

Hours later, when Fig and Libby are ready to leave, I am trashed. As we walk to the car, I tell Libby how much I liked the blonde with the crooked teeth. I tell her that we had so much in common. Before we drive away, I say that she wanted me to call her, but I don't even know her name. My mouth is like a motorboat. Putt-putt-putt.

Two days later, Libby calls. "OK, Jesse," she says. "You owe me! It took some time and it took some digging. I had to call twenty people, and I hope that you appreciate it."

*What the hell is she talking about,* I wonder?

Libby goes on. "Mandy, that tall blonde that you met at the party. She lives near the beach in Lucadia. She would love to see you. Here's her number," she says. "Call her!"

I think about my wife, Maggie. She left me, and I am going through all the stages of withdrawal including anger, denial, over-eating, and over-drinking.

A man has to move on. I call Mandy.

# 35

MANDY AND I HAVE DRINKS. WE have snacks. We tell our worst jokes.

We laugh and hug.

I use my best line.

"You probably don't like hot tubs, do you?"

It works every time.

When she comes out of the bathroom, she is wearing one of my Harley Davidson t-shirts, and a pair of white panties.

"Damn it" She looks concerned. She pulls up the tee shirt and yanks a tag off of the undies. "They're new," she says.

It's about 10pm when we finally climb in the hot tub.

"So, Mandy, I have one question," I say.

"Uh oh, what's the question?"

"Well, the problem with the first date is the goodnight kiss at the end of the night. Just thinking about it causes anxiety. It's such an awkward situation that it puts a man under tremendous stress. Just think of all the questions that go through a guy's mind. 'Should I kiss her? Will she say OK? Will she say no? Will she slap me? Will she laugh at me?'"

"So what's the question?" she smiles.

"Can I have the good night kiss now, in the middle of the night, and get it over with?"

"Good idea."

The goodnight kiss in the middle of the night is wonderful. Her tongue is on fire, and it pierces my mouth. Her long arms tighten around my neck, and we get very, very close. We are half-standing and half-leaning against the edge of the hot tub as her legs start to slide open. As if by magic, her panties start to slide out of the way, and I start to slide in.

I think I might be squeezed to death.

"Where's the protection?" she asks.

"Excuse me?"

"Protection!"

"What?"

"Protection! You know, the condom, the contraceptive, the rubber, the party hat!"

I just look at her, as her arms drop away from my shoulders.

"The what?" I bang the side of my head twice, to signify that I can't hear.

She gently pushes me back.

"What about protection," she persists.

"I have protection!"

"Good. Where is it?"

I am slowly moving in and out, just trying to make the moment last. I flash my biggest smile and kiss her on the cheek.

"Where is your protection," she asks again.

I ignore her and continue to glide in and out.

"Where is your protection?" she demands. Now she is getting forceful. "Do you have protection?"

"Yes"

"Where is it?"

"In Hartford" I say, moving faster, hoping to finish my mission before it's too late.

"Why would your protection be in Hartford?"

I start to move faster.

She asks again. "Why is your protection in Hartford?"

"I have New England Life!"

Splash! I am pushed completely out and she leans on my head. I almost drown. It's over before it's over.

"I don't believe this," she says, as she lets me up to breathe. "The world is full of AIDS, and you don't have any rubbers?"

"Mandy, I have never used a rubber in my life. I wouldn't even know how to put one on."

"Well I'll be! Damn it! That's it! We can kiss, and touch, but no fucking."

I love it when they talk dirty!

Ten minutes later, I walk to the kitchen to get more drinks. Water is dripping off my naked body. Puddles are everywhere. Barry White is crooning so loudly from the CD player, that I can barely hear the phone ringing.

"Hi there!" I shout into the mouthpiece.

It's the Chief calling me on a Sunday night. This is the first time that he has ever called me at home. I'm sure that he can hear Barry, and I'm also sure that he knows that I am hammered.

"Jesse, the Ball Buster just struck again. This time she has hit three thousand miles away in Provincetown, Massachusetts."

Before he hangs up, he says, "Be in here early tomorrow morning. That's a fucking order!" The phone slams down.

# 36

ON THE WAY TO THE OFFICE, the morning sun is attacking my eyelids, but squinting magnifies my headache. My temples throb, but worse than the physical pain is the emotional downheartedness. I feel miserable. I am on an elevator going down, but I can't seem to get off.

"Why can't I get sober?" I shout.

I concentrate on getting to work on time, but I need caffeine and grease. I stop at McDonald's to get my heart going. I take my McMuffin, McCoffee, and McHangover to a corner table and sit quietly.

As I burn my tongue on the first sip of coffee, a school bus unloads the summer camp field trip from hell. In two minutes, I hear kids screaming, babies crying, doors slamming. I see lips bleeding, fingers stepped on, brothers pushing, and sisters pulling. There are teachers yelling and aides shouting. My headache is magnified by 1000%. I grab my java and escape to the privacy of my car.

When I get to the office, the Chief grabs me. Physically. He squeezes my arm and railroads me into his office. He slams the door.

"Sit the fuck down." He shouts, more than talks.

"Jesse. God Damn it! You have become my worst nightmare! Your drinking is a joke with everyone in the office. Your barroom brawls, and your bathroom belching is all that I hear people talking about. What a lot of fun you are! But you are not fun for me. Your drinking is going to be the reason that I have to fire you. I don't want to fire you, but, believe me, I will do it! I cannot have a detective of mine behaving like a show-off, childish, pain-in-the-ass, king baby. If you fuck up one more time, I will have your ass and your badge. Is this clear?"

Without waiting for a reply, he walks to the door of his office, opens it, and shouts at the rest of the team.

"Let's have this meeting! Now!" I stare at my feet.

"It's only been three weeks since the last massacre. Here we are again," he says. "The pace is picking up! Now she's in Provincetown, Mass. This killer is now a coast to coast celebrity. She just nailed a guy named Tommy Button."

Fig is thinking out loud, "I wonder if the time lapse between the murders is getting shorter by design, or if this is happening by chance? Sometimes, serial killers get better at their sport and speed up the pace. After a few successes, they might feel more confident."

"We need to continue looking for clues," says Erica. "Maybe she has left a personal item, or maybe there is a motel that will recognize her."

"I wonder if she flew in to that town, or if she rented a car from the Hyannis airport." I add.

"Jesse, I want you to get to Provincetown at once."

As the meeting ends and people start shuffling out, the Chief grabs my by the arm again. He turns me around. He is two inches from my face.

"Stop embarrassing yourself. Stop embarrassing me! Stop drinking!"

# 37

I LEAVE THE OFFICE, GO HOME, and pack. While sitting on the long flight, I have time to think about my destination. Provincetown. New Englanders call it P-Town. At the tip of Cape Cod, it's a destination for people who practice alternative life styles. Gay bars are everywhere. Closet queens come out to play and drag-queen balls are commonplace. In Provincetown, it's like Halloween every day. It's not unusual to see a six-foot man walking through town wearing a pink-ruffled tutu. I've seen a man with a beard wearing a mini dress and another man in a nurse's outfit, carrying an enema bag.

Although some sections of P-Town will raise eyebrows, other areas attract the straight people of the world. There are bars, restaurants, and gift shops. There are beaches, sand dunes, and hiking trails.

Maggie and I went there years ago for a long weekend. It was bizarre. Wherever we went, we saw women holding hands, women hugging, women openly kissing. There was too much PDA.

"Public Display of Affection," I explained. On our second day in town, we noticed a sign that explained everything. The sign said, Welcome to Women's Weekend. Once a year, lesbian lovers descend on P-Town and let it all hang out.

The long flight from San Diego to Boston has a two-hour layover in Chicago's O'Hare.

I think about a beer. Instead, I have coffee and walk from one end of the airport to the other. I know that if I have just one beer, I will be flying without a plane. I can't afford to lose my job. I can't afford to let my boss down. I can't afford to have another hangover like the one I have today.

I start to feel sorry for myself and my condition. I experience immense self-pity until I see a man in a wheel chair. He has a suitcase on his lap and is moving rapidly to catch his plane.

When I get to Boston's Logan, I have a short layover, and then take a small puddle jumper to Hyannis. Sitting on a plane all day makes me jumpy.

As I deplane, I see reporters everywhere. "There's Jesse," someone shouts. A dozen people come to life. A microphone is shoved in my face. Questions are being yelled, and reporters with notebooks stand in my way.

"Where is the Ball Buster going to strike next?" someone shouts.

Flash bulbs are exploding in my eyes. I wonder how they knew that I would be on this flight? Did someone from the office tip them off?

*"Is it true that she has killed twenty people, and the police are hushing it up?"*

*"What's her blood type?"*

*"Where did she get the gun? Was it registered?"*

*"How did she get the gun past airport security?"*

I quickly push past the reporters and give my standard, "No comment."

A thirty-something, prim-and-proper female reporter pushes her way to the front of the pack. Her business suit is conservative, her hair is short, and her teeth are sparkling. Her smile is genuine, and

I am impressed with her poise. She looks more professional than the rest of them. A back-up photographer is right behind her. She might be with a national syndicate.

She stands right in my way. When I step to the left, she moves to the left. When I step to the right, she moves in that direction too. I cannot get past her. She flashes a winning smile and stares me right in the eyes.

"Does she fuck them first?"

I shake my head in amazement. I physically push her out of the way, and walk to the car rental area.

When I get to the Avis counter, I sign the forms and decline the extra insurance.

"You have to take the insurance," the salesgirl says. "Your own insurance may not cover you." The salesgirl is on commission.

"That's bullshit!" I say, loudly enough for everyone to hear.

I feel badly for taking my frustrations out on the sales girl, but I pick up the keys and storm off to the shuttle bus.

Two men appear out of nowhere and quietly follow me on to the bus. One man is obese, and the other one is sickly and meek. In this small bus, all seats face inward, and I take a seat halfway down the aisle. As I settle into my seat, the rotund man sits directly across from me. He has a dark complexion, very little hair, and he is sweating profusely. He moves uneasily in the small, shuttle-bus seat, and his weight is a burden. He has enjoyed a lifetime of gluttony and is now paying the price. He smiles, and I ignore him.

The other man, who is much smaller, walks past us and takes a seat in the back of the bus. He is five feet away. Neither of these men have a suitcase, but the small man puts a leather bag on his lap. I didn't see either of them in the airport, and I wonder where they came from. I am still fuming from the onslaught of reporters, but I try to relax.

As the bus starts to move, the fat man speaks.

"Hello Jesse,"

"Who are you?"

"I'm Sonny Crackly, from *The Daily Informer,*" he says, as he tries to give me a business card.

"Please leave me alone," I reply. "I have nothing to say." I turn in my seat to face the front of the bus.

"We will offer you a handsome retainer to work with us on the story."

"What story? There is no story." I twist my body completely around and look out the window behind me.

He continues. "We have pictures of the deceased from each morgue, and we have pictures of the three death cars," he says, "but what we really want is your perspective. We want you to bring us up to date and then take us through all of the upcoming killings as they happen. Sort of like a reality show host. We would like to publish your profile of the killer and then, after each new killing, update your evaluation. Our readers will love it. They will buy papers just to see how your mind works. Doesn't that sound rewarding?"

I stare at this predator. I am repulsed. I try to ignore him, but there is no way for me to escape.

"Is it true that she is taking body parts as a souvenir?" he asks. "We plan to run that idea as a headline soon, but it would be much more exciting if you can comment on what parts she is taking, and what she does with them."

I gawk at him in disbelief.

"Our readers would be interested to know if she eats the parts, or just uses them, if you know what I mean." He smiles.

I feel like I am going to be sick.

Sonny continues talking as if this were a two-way conversation. "I have another great idea. You could predict the city that she will hit next. If you guess that the next murder will be in New York, just imagine the amount of papers we could sell in that city. You could predict a different city each week, and we can run special editions for each city.

"Get away from me. I hate your sleazy newspaper; I hate the stories that you fabricate. Now I hate you."

He sits quietly for a second, and then slowly starts talking again, but this is a brand new conversation. "Here's something you might be interested in, Jesse. We've been working on a story about you."

Slowly, I turn back to look at him. "What the fuck are you talking about?"

"The story is finished and ready to go to press. This would be a good time to publish it. Now that you are famous, our readers would like to know about your life. They have a lot of questions."

"What questions?" I fall into his trap.

"Well, they would like to know why you were dismissed from the FBI."

I stare as his words sink in.

"We have all of the details about that episode in your office: the bar room fight and the dates of your DWI convictions. We have a very interesting mug shot of you that was taken during your last incarceration. Not too flattering! But if you work with us on this Ball Buster thing, we wouldn't need to run the story about you."

He looks at me and smiles.

I am in shock. I am being blackmailed by a sleazy, overweight, bottom-sucking scumbag. I can feel my temples pound as my pulse races into overdrive.

Sonny speaks again. "How is your wife, Maggie, doing in Colorado? She moved to Boulder, right?

"What?" I snap.

"Did she leave you because of your drinking?"

I explode. "Fuck you," I scream, as I fly across the little bus. I hit him broadside and grab him by the neck. I start pounding his head against the seat. We both fall to the floor. I keep swinging.

Instantly, brilliant bursts of light start bouncing off the ceiling. The small man in the back of the bus is taking endless pictures with rapid-fire flash bulbs. "I've got him, Sonny!"

In a heartbeat, they have fifty pictures of me assaulting a fat man on a bus.

The driver calls his dispatcher. "One customer is attacking another customer on the bus!" In seconds, I hear a siren. This is a perfect ending to a less-than-perfect day.

I spend the next hour in a police station in Hyannis, Massachusetts. I explain my rash behavior, and the officer understands. He takes me back to the rental center, and I get my car.

The two-hour drive to Provincetown is excruciating. I keep replaying the scene on the bus; I can't believe how that slimy bastard lured me into a scuffle. Now, my life history will hit his front page. Pictures of me in a brawl will sell more papers than anything that he could dream up. Fact always sells better than fiction. Maggie will be disappointed. My boss will be pissed. I will be drunk.

# 38

WHEN I GET TO PROVINCETOWN, IT'S 2am, and I am emotionally charged and physically drained. I toss and turn until daybreak.

Before breakfast, I walk around the hotel property. The humidity is high, and the heat is oppressive. Even though it is only 8am, my armpits are wet and sweat is running down my chest. My shirt needs wringing.

When I get to the station, I ask for Nicholas Davis, the Chief of Police.

"Don't call him Nicholas," says the desk clerk.

"Do I have his name wrong?

"No, you got the name right, but only his mother calls him Nicholas."

"And what do you call him?"

"We all call him Nickel."

The Chief is in his mid-fifties. His lean, weathered face is tan. His light brown hair is showing strands of gray, and he wears a neatly trimmed goatee, a short-sleeve Hawaiian shirt, tan chinos, and a pair of very dark sunglasses. Is Jimmy Buffet in town?

Nickel spends a few minutes on small talk and then gets down to business. He has been following our killer's spree, and makes some comparisons. "This murder was not committed in a garage or parking lot, like the others," he says. "The shooter did the deed on the backside of a gigantic sand dune. I think it will be better to take you out to the scene, rather than try and describe it." He picks up his car keys, and walks toward the door. I follow.

On the way, Nickel confirms that the victim was Tommy Button, a year-round resident of Provincetown, Mass.

"Folks said he was gay," he says.

When we get to the sand dune, I am amazed by the size. It's at least thirty feet high. This is the kind of scene that could have been in an action movie with an ATV flying overhead. The location of the dead man's parked car is roped off with uniformed men standing at the perimeter. We are relatively close to town, but not visible from the road. It would have been a thirty-minute walk for the killer to get back to civilization, and there are motels, restaurants, and a gas station on a bike path along the route.

Back at the municipal garage, we get to see the victim's car. It is a meticulously restored 1930 Model A Ford. It's a five-window coupe, with semi inflated all-terrain tires. Someone poured a lot of time and money into this antique. The outside of the car is lime green. The inside has been tricked out with white-leather upholstery, but it's now covered in blotches of black, dried blood and unidentifiable body scraps. There are small, neat, holes in the seat where bullets entered the crotch of the victim. Another hole in the seat back shows that a bullet went through Tommy's chest.

We view the body at the morgue. Tommy had been thin and pale even before the murder.

I ask more questions about the victim. The Chief tells me that Tommy and his life partner, Farron, operated a jewelry store on Commercial Street.

"They made a bundle from the tourists."

My first stop is the jewelry store. It's right across the street from Mayflower Family Dining. "Established 1929," reads the big sign.

Tommy's partner, Farron, is tall, thin, and effeminate. He is bald by choice. He flaunts the tell-tale stereotypes of a gay man. He talks with a slight lisp. His wrists seem to be attached by strings instead of bones, and they are as limp as a noodle. And he keeps saying, "Oh, my dear." He is genuinely overcome with grief.

"Tommy lived in P-Town for about five years," says Farron. "We had been in a committed relationship for most of that time. Tommy lived in Key West before he moved here, and he had no family, or at least no family that he ever wanted to talk about."

Farron tells me that Tommy was quiet, law-abiding, and respectful. "He couldn't possibly have any enemies. The only excitement that Tommy ever had was driving his dune buggy out on the sand. He never drove fast and just liked being able to get away from the tourists."

We talk about Tommy's last night. His partner remembers that something was wrong.

"He insisted on going out by himself. He said that he just wanted to go for a ride. Usually we went together. I was so hurt."

"Did Tommy have his own computer?"

"He had a laptop at home. He was always on it. Drove me crazy," Farron says. "He was involved with raising money for AIDS research, and who knows what else."

"I'd like to borrow his computer," I say.

"Whatever."

It's hotter than it was earlier, and the sweat is rolling off my brow. I am tired and cranky. After leaving the jewelry store, I grab coffee and walk along Commercial Street. I pass tiny gift shops and restaurants. Tourists in tank tops and shorts shuffle through town. The women are enjoying the shops, and the men look bored. Most out-of-towners never leave this street, so the traffic moves at a snail's pace. It is much faster to walk than to drive, but most visitors drive anyway. I wonder if Kiki flew into Hyannis and drove here, like I did. Maybe she drove all the way here from her hometown, wherever that is? Or maybe she took the ferry from Boston? However she got there, our killer really gets around.

I go back to the Provincetown station and talk to the lab techs. I ask the Chief to ship Tommy Button's laptop to San Diego overnight.

I call the office and have a conference call with Fig, Erica, and the Chief. A few strands of blond hair had been found in the dune buggy. There were fingerprints that matched the two other killings. If there were footprints, they were now gone. They had been covered by sand.

Something else was missing, too. There was no matching DNA on the lips of the victim. The killer did not kiss this last guy. All along I thought that the killer was a woman who had a grudge toward her old lovers. Although I didn't meet Tommy, I was convinced that he was gay. My idea of a scorned woman was out the window.

I have asked Farron to send photographs of the deceased to San Diego. I ask Fig to post the new location on our task board in my office. The USA map now has a triangle. Rifling tests conclude that the same gun was used in each crime. I ask Fig to continue working on his list of the victim's activities. We are looking for something that they might have in common. The list now includes general categories like home town, schooling, family ties, religion, hobbies, and business interests. We are still striking out on all fronts.

I go back and talk with Nickel. The air conditioning in his office is working overtime, but it just can't seem to catch up. We recap our time together, and I share my feelings about this case. I am convinced that the killer does not live in this town.

"She had some kind of previous relationship with each of the victims," I say. "She's a seasoned traveler, a computer whiz, and a great communicator. Somehow, she is convincing people to meet with her and then turning the screws on them at the last minute."

"Why would they meet with her?"

"They all seem to be old friends. Email messages show that she is calling on them to talk about getting married. But the same scenario has happened at least three times, now. I believe it's just a ploy to get these guys to see her.

"Here's the confusing part," I say. "So far, there have been no phone calls that we can trace, or phone messages on any of the victims' answering machines. All communication has been by email. All mail has come from untraceable accounts."

"So, if I get an email from an old girlfriend, I should walk away, right?" says Nickel.

"No. Run! At any rate, I've done as much as I can in this town," I say.

"Have a safe drive back to Hyannis, and a great flight back to California. Come back and see us on vacation sometime."

I reserve an early flight out of Hyannis the next morning and check out of my Provincetown hotel.

I load up on coffee and start the two-hour drive back from P-Town to Hyannis. My eyes are falling back into my head, and staying awake is a challenge. The Cape Cod scenery is beautiful, but for most of the trip my eyes are crossed. My plan is to get a room near the airport and sleep for twenty hours straight.

# 39

I CHECK INTO THE AIRPORT HOTEL near the Hyannis circle. I notice the humidity again when I lug my suitcase up the stairs. When I step into the room, I feel relief. The air conditioner has been on for hours. I kick my shoes off and climb under the covers. Not only is the air conditioner doing a great job of cooling the room, but it is also producing a low drone that is blocking out all noise. I zone for hours.

When I finally wake up, I realize that I have slept through lunch and dinner. It's 8pm. I was originally going to sleep right through the night until tomorrow morning's flight, but I'm hungry.

I take a long shower and put on some clean clothes. The night is young, and Hyannis is so beautiful. My only responsibility tomorrow is to sit on a plane back to San Diego. I think that I can handle that task without screwing it up. I plan to have dinner and a drink. Or maybe a drink and dinner. *What's the worst that could happen?*

I head out to route twenty-eight in Yarmouth, where there are only four types of businesses. The tourists spend their money on t-shirts, miniature golf, restaurants, and bars. I pick the fourth option.

The Schooner Pub sign says steak, lobster, and seafood, but it looks like a bar to me. The lighted sign also says that it's Nuts and

Bolts night, and the parking lot is packed. This is the place for me.

I find a spot at the far end of the lot and walk to the entrance. The doorman has a jarhead crew, a baby face, and gigantic muscles.

"What's the Nuts and Bolts thing?" I ask.

He flashes a smile. "The first fifty guys get a bolt. There are big bolts and little bolts, fat bolts and skinny bolts. Some are metric, and some are sheet metal. The first fifty ladies get a nut. Again, all different sizes and shapes. Each bolt only fits into one nut. The trick is to find the nut that your bolt fits into."

"So, although there is no guarantee that you'll get laid, you might get screwed, huh?" I ask.

He laughs. "Unfortunately, you're too late to get a bolt, but you might get screwed anyway. Five dollars cover, please."

As I walk towards the bar, I hear the dialogue. Everyone is talking about their nuts and their bolts. The conversations are interesting. The innuendos are endless.

"Can we get our things together?"

"Do you think that we would be a good fit?"

"Can I put my bolt into your nut?"

"Wanna screw?"

So here are fifty guys walking around trying to get their bolt into some poor girl's nut. There is plenty of potential screwing going on.

There had been a buffet set up on the dance floor, and waiters are in the process of cleaning up. As I look around, there are still lots of tiny cocktail franks and cold meatballs on little red plastic plates. I haven't eaten all day, so why start now?

There is one long bar against the wall that runs the entire length of the room. The bar is packed with people who are exchanging mindless chatter and playing with their nuts and bolts.

I gently push my way through the crowd and make it to the bar. I try to make eye contact with a tall, thin bartender, but he is busy.

He is a professional, and I watch him pour two drinks at a time, pull three beers out of the cooler with one hand, and bang keys on the cash register in seconds. Every once in a while, he flips a bottle and catches it in mid-air while filling a glass with ice at the same time. He is also singing to the music. His long, blond hair is combed back into a neatly trimmed ponytail. His black, button-down dress shirt and black vest are classy. While I am waiting, I hear someone call him by the name Tyson. As he looks in my direction, I point at him and call him by name, too. "Hey Tyson," I shout over the music. "How have you been?"

Tyson comes over and shakes my hand as if we are long lost cousins. He tells me that it's so good to see me again. I don't bother to mention that we have never met. He asks what I'm drinking, and I order a Black Jack on the rocks. He grabs a large glass and pours a healthy double shot of Jack Daniels, Black Label. He pushes it to me and tells me that it's on him. As he leaves to wait on another customer, I pound the double Jack. Within minutes, he is back with a refill. I put a ten spot on the bar and he pushes it back. He says that it is so great to see me.

"How is work going? Are you still dating the blonde?" he asks, but he really doesn't expect a reply. He races off again.

Thanks to my new best friend, Tyson, I am on my third double in a heartbeat. I remember that I haven't eaten all day, but that doesn't stop me from enjoying the mistaken identity and the free drinks.

When Tyson comes back, I try to give him money again, but the drinks are still free.

"Sorry we can't talk, man," he says, "but this place is a zoo."

He walks away and stops three stools down. He makes a drink for a red-head, and I watch him fill another glass with Jack Daniels. He slides the drink to me from six feet away. It stops directly in front of me. Tyson winks.

I wonder how many drinks I have had. Was it eight drinks in thirty minutes or thirty drinks in eight minutes?

All of a sudden the alcohol shifts into full gear. It permeates every pore of my body. The drinks that flooded my empty stomach have backed up into my blood stream. They have formed a tidal wave that goes straight to my brain. My head starts spinning. No warning. No advance notice. No coming attractions. I go from sober to drunk in five seconds flat. I have trouble standing. The room is at a forty-five degree angle. At once, the lights seem darker. My eyes start to water and my peripheral vision is shot. I can't tell what song is playing, but the ringing in my ears is deafening. The smoke in the room creates a haze that hovers over everything. I can't see my feet. My legs feel like rubber. I start weaving, and hold on for the ride of my life. Tyson is yelling to me, but I can't see his face. It's moving in circles. I feel my head tilt slowly forward and then it jerks back. I'm afraid to take a step, but I have to leave this place.

As I transfer my weight from one foot to another, the room tilts again. Am I on an ocean liner? Are we in the middle of a storm? One knee buckles and I lose balance. I fall towards the bar, but the railing saves me. I look towards the exit and plan my trip so that I won't fall to the floor. My plan doesn't work. I fall flat, and my soft head hits hard wood. I touch my temple and it's wet. To avoid looking drunk I quickly get up, but crumble again. I manage to crawl to a support post near the dance floor. I don't care that people are staring. I stumble past the bouncer, and smash into the cigarette machine as if I am a pinball in an arcade game.

"I hope you can drive better than you can walk!" he shouts. I fumble with the key and open the door. Sticking the big key into the small lock takes forever.

Food! I have to eat! Eating will save me. I need a big, greasy burger. I start driving in the direction of my hotel. Driving while intoxicated is not a new experience for me. I have done this for most of my adult life. Driving while absolutely blind drunk, however, is always a challenge. The white line in the middle of the road is wavy. Is it a single or a double? My eyes are glassy, and the oncoming headlights blind me. Why does every car have their high beams on? Every time a car passes, I have to close my eyes to refocus.

There is an all-night diner near my hotel and I look for a parking space. My rental car seems way too big, and most spaces seem way too small. As I back into a parking space, my foot slips off of the brake and slams on the accelerator. My car shoots backward, and I hear metal smashing against metal. The crash is loud, and as I look in the rear view mirror, I see white. A white car. A big white car. It's as big as a boat. Out of nowhere, there are three huge black men pounding on my doors. Without thinking, I jam my rental car into drive and lunge forward. Tires are spinning and gravel is being shot up behind me. I am racing out of the parking lot onto the highway. Suddenly, the big white car is right behind me. I am in no shape to drive under normal conditions, but being the point person in a chase is totally absurd.

I pull on the wheel and turn sharply onto a side street. This is so stupid. I have no idea where I am, and I am trying to elude men who have probably grown up in this town. I pray for my adrenalin to kick in.

The sound of a siren is a blessing. I weave to the side of the road, but for some reason, the Caddie flies right past me. Why didn't they stop too? My door is yanked open, and I am pulled out. I fall. Guns are pointed at me. I am picked up and pushed face first against the door. My hands are pulled behind my back. The cuffs are out and the officer is getting ready to click them shut. *Did he read me my rights? Did we even talk?*

Then a miracle takes place. A call comes in over the police radio that changes everything. A female voice is shouting. "Attention all units! Proceed at once to Damien's Lounge on Main. A riot is in progress. All units proceed to Damien's lounge at once!"

The cuffs are off my wrist, and the cop stands two inches from my face. He shouts. "This is your lucky night, asshole! Get this fucking car off of the road. If I see you again tonight, you will be in jail in a heartbeat!" And with that, they both run to their cruiser and roar off with their siren blaring and red lights flashing.

I stand there motionless. There is no noise except for the pounding of blood as it races through my temples and the involuntary jerking of my body as it rattles against the car. It takes me a few seconds to realize that I am free. The men in the Caddie are gone, and the police are gone. I am alone. I get in to the car and slowly head back to my hotel. My hands are firmly anchored to the steering wheel in the classic ten and two position. Adrenalin has finally taken over, and I am wide-awake drunk.

The morning wake-up call comes too early. I am on top of the bed fully dressed. Even though there is vomit on the bedspread and urine in my pants, I realize how lucky I am. I lie there and relive the night before. If a riot call had not come in, I would be in jail right now.

I stand up too quickly, and the room gyrates. I am nauseous. When the wave of dizziness subsides, I stagger to the bathroom. I fall on my knees in front of the toilet and puke blood. When there is nothing left, I slowly lift my head. My eyes are too glassy to see.

The whole room spins again, and my head jerks forward. I reach out to catch myself, and hit the toilet seat. As the seat slams down, it smashes against my upper lip. There is fresh blood everywhere. I stay on my knees and let my head drop directly into the bowl as I cry.

"Dear God, please help me."

I don't think God is listening.

# 40

"Hi Kiki. Your package has arrived from Provincetown."

"Thank you, Fred," she flirted.

The Federal Express agent was always so pleasant. When he saw Kiki coming in, he ran over to wait on her first. He offered a genuine smile and put out his hand. She let him hold it, just a little too long.

He talked slowly and made sure that she could read his lips. Somewhere in his past, there must have been a deaf person.

On one of her first visits, he told her how to remember his name.

"Just take the letter *R* out of Fred and you end up with Fed. That's me. Fred the FedEx Man." He laughed. She laughed, too.

"Did you have a nice trip?"

"I had a very nice trip, thank you." She smiled as she signed the release.

"I've never been to P-Town," he said, "but I hear that it's fun. Did you go alone?"

"I went to see a friend, but I won't be seeing him anymore." She laughed, took her package, and said good-bye.

As she drove back to her condo, she thought about Fred the Fed. He sure was cute. He must work out, because of those bulges in his shirt, and what about that bulge in his pants? She smiled. She wondered if they could have a relationship.

She sat at a stoplight and let her mind wander.

All of a sudden it hit her.

"Oh my god!" she yelled out loud. "Fred knows my name! Fred knows where I've been! Fred knows the dates of my trips! Fred knows *everything!*"

Kiki began to hyperventilate. She pulled her car over to the side of the road. She screamed at the top of her lungs, "Oh shit!" She pounded her fist on the steering wheel. "Why did I send my packages from the same FedEx office every time?"

Kiki had planned every single detail of every trip so that there would be no slip up. She had made sure that no one could trace her. She sent messages from anonymous accounts. She bought her airline tickets at an airport counter, and paid in cash. She used her full name for tickets, but her nickname in all email messages. She cleaned up after herself and left no traces at any of the crime scenes. No one was supposed to connect the dots. No one was supposed to put her at any of the crime scenes.

Now, that had all changed. The one person who could identify her knew everything! What would happen if Fred the Fed watched the news and put two and two together? What if he matched the shipping dates to the dates of the killings?

"Oh shit!"

Kiki ran from her parked car into her condo with her package tucked tightly under her arm. She locked the condo door, secured the deadbolt, and closed the blinds. After checking her pistol, she spent twenty minutes working with a pair of scissors. She cut her airline tickets into tiny little pieces. They all ended up in the toilet. She did the same thing with her rental car invoice and the motel receipt. They, too, were flushed. All details of her Provincetown trip were now shredded into confetti and on their way to the town sewer.

Finally, she grabbed the shoebox of pictures, and without even a second thought, cut the pictures of Tommy Button into little pieces. They, too, were flushed, and on the way to their final resting place, with all of the other shit in the cesspool.

# 41

BACK IN THE SAN DIEGO OFFICE, I meet with our computer technician.

"Did you get Tommy Button's laptop from Provincetown?" No answer.

"What did you find?" Still no response. He stares at the huge bloody scab on my upper lip. For some reason he seems more interested in my appearance than he does in my question.

"Same deal," he finally says. "The Sent Files and the Deleted Files have lots of messages to and from Kiki. The account was a free Hotmail account, but it had a different email address than the other two versions. And the messages were sent from a different ISP. This time the messages came from the Atlantic City area in New Jersey. There were lots of messages about getting together. The time and place was set up long before the meeting. This gal really planned ahead."

"When did the messages to Tommy Button start?"

"She sent her first message two days after the murder in Charlotte."

# 42

Kiki thought about Provincetown. She was sorry she couldn't spend more time on the Cape. She remembered a t-shirt she had seen there. It said: "All of my problems have been caused by men: Menopause, Menstrual Cramps, Menial Chores, and Mental Illness."

Men had caused every single one of her problems, and, now, three of her problems had been solved. Three men had gotten what they deserved. They had been such cruel bastards. Leading her on like that and then dumping her just because of her little difference. She was sick and tired of people rubbing her nose in her disability.

Why couldn't men be as loving as her mother?

What a shock it had been when mother passed away. The money in her estate did not replace her. God rest her soul. She had left an unexpected insurance policy payable to her disabled daughter. Kiki had not known about the nest egg that would pay her one hundred thousand dollars. After the sale of her mother's house, Kiki received another huge gift. Her total net worth was now almost two hundred thousand dollars. This was more money than Kiki had ever seen.

Relatives had tried to help her invest. "Put the money in bonds," one cousin said. "Put it in the stock market," said another. "Let me invest it for you," said an uncle. "I could take care of your money, and you wouldn't have to worry."

They had pushed her and pulled her. They all wanted to manage her life. It seemed to her that everyone wanted to take control of her money.

"My friend gave me a tip about a company that you can invest in. It's the best thing for you," one of her in-laws told her. Some relatives had been so pushy that visiting them became uncomfortable. Kiki stopped going to family gatherings.

Kiki didn't trust anyone. She had never had to deal with money, and she didn't understand stocks, bonds, or investments. While she pondered her newly acquired fortune, she left her money in the bank. When she bought a car, she took out cash. Her banker tried to give her a cashier's check but she wanted the real money. When she bought her condo, she insisted on paying in cash.

Kiki didn't like going to the bank and she didn't like having to explain her actions to a pushy old man in a baggy suit. How could she communicate with a man who mumbled all the time? She couldn't understand what he was saying. He couldn't grasp the concept of looking at her and speaking slowly. He was so stupid. Her reason to withdraw her money was none of his business.

"I would like to take out all of my money," she announced, one day.

"In cash?" He looked shocked.

"Yes, please," The next day, he handed over more than one hundred thousand dollars in cash.

Now she had money whenever she needed it. She didn't ever have to deal with that stupid banker again.

Cash gave her control. It's all about control.

# 43

IT'S A BALMY SUMMER DAY, AND there's a light breeze coming off the San Diego bay. I wish I could be at the beach, or the mountains, or anyplace but here.

I'm standing on the top step of the San Diego police building surrounded by a mob of news dogs. The news dogs are hungry. They want some scraps. I wish I had something tasty to give them, but today there will be no treats.

A news conference is bad enough when there are meaty morsels and juicy tidbits, but today there's an empty dish of questions with no answers.

Local stations have sent cars with magnetized call letters pasted on the side; regional stations have sent fancy vans with loudspeakers, and spotlights. The national networks have sent bucket trucks with high-tech sound equipment. They've been waiting five hours for a five-minute press conference.

"Don't they have something more important to do?" I ask Fig, who is standing between me and the Chief.

The Chief had agreed to an interview with one local station, but the word got out. He makes a quick announcement, and then, to my utter amazement and shock, he turns the meeting over to me.

I glare at my boss.

He walks over to me, smiles.

"Just give some smart answers to their stupid questions," he mumbles. "Have fun."

*"Detective Collins, are you sure that the same person is involved in all of the crimes?"*

"We have identical fingerprints and hair samples from each scene. We are confident that one person has committed all crimes."

*"Has the killer been involved in other murders besides the recent three?"*

"To our knowledge, the killer has not been involved in any murders before the current crimes in La Jolla, Charlotte, and Provincetown."

*"Detective, what kind of profile do you have on the killer?"*

"We think that the killer is a white female between twenty-five and forty. We believe that she is attractive, savvy, and well-educated. She is street smart, and knows how to get around."

*"Why has she picked these particular men?"*

"We think that she is targeting men that she knew from a previous relationship. We think that this is some kind of punishment that she is doling out. This is probably a control issue."

"Do you have any leads?"

"Unfortunately, ladies and gentlemen, we cannot discuss any of our leads."

The questions are endless, and my answers are repetitive. The Chief fidgets for awhile before whispering that we should get this wrapped up.

*"How did the killer pick these three cities?"*

"I guess that she likes warm climates." There are a few chuckles.

*"Where will she go next?"*

"You could check with her travel agent." Reporters laugh nervously.

*"Do you have any advice for the public?"*

"If an old girlfriend calls you, run like hell."

*"Was she having sex with the victims before she killed them?"*

"No one died with a smile on their face." Reporters start to laugh. The Chief steps in front of me and takes over the mike.

"Thank you, Detective Collins," he says formally. The interview is over, but reporters keeping yelling questions as we turn and walk into the building.

The next morning, when I arrive, the Chief meets me at the front door, grabs my elbow, and steers me to his office. His grip is too hard. He is walking too fast. He has a concerned look on his face. I wonder if he has hemorrhoids. He picks up a newspaper unfolds it and turns it so that I can read. It's the Daily Informer, hot off the press. I look at the headline.

## SAN DIEGO POLICE DETECTIVE ASSAULTS REPORT-ER!

The Chief's face is taut, and the veins in his neck are bulging. His eyes are dilated, and he is white as a ghost. I'm staring at a man who is livid.

"The newspapers are having a field day, Mr. Collins. You are a celebrity. You have the distinction of having your life story publicized. Everyone now knows about your bar-room fights, your arrests, your jail time, and why your wife left you . . . again. The picture of you attacking the Daily Informer reporter on a bus was a nice touch, don't you think? Next time, don't forget to smile."

He continues, "I know that you were set up. This could have happened to anyone, but it's bad publicity, and it will take focus off of our mission. I don't know how we became the national focal point for this series of crimes, but we are. Police Chiefs from around the country are having a field day, laughing at our little dog-and-pony show.

I have never seen the Chief like this. His eyes are red. Steam is escaping from his ears. He moves so that he is one inch in front of my face.

He hisses three words at me: "Find this killer!"

Then he gets up and walks out of his own office. I guess the meeting is over.

# 44

I GET TO MY DESK, BUT I am afraid to sit. My ass is still red from the spanking I just got. The Daily Informer article didn't say much, but it was embarrassing.

I try to find my computer. It's here someplace, but it's buried under a thousand leads. We have received suggestions written on lined, yellow, notebook paper, theories typed on legal paper, and handwritten comments on lacy, pink stationary. Every make-believe detective in the country has a hunch. There are legitimate leads and thoughtful suggestions, but there are also wild-ass wacko schemes.

People are talking about the Parking Lot Killer in barbershops and bedrooms. They are telling jokes about the Ball Buster in bar rooms and boardrooms. This might be the most talked-about story of the decade.

I used to be able to handle a case like this in my sleep. My mind was sharp and nothing fazed me. Now, my mind is like a piece of gum that's been chewed so long, it's breaking apart into little pieces. I fail to ask the questions that used to be second nature. I miss obvious clues and overlook details. I have lost my touch. Am I getting old? Am I burned out? I know that answer, but it's painful to admit: I am a drunk!

In the middle of this confusion, the Chief calls an urgent meeting in his office.

"My friend in Charlotte, Dan Henderson, just called. One of his uniforms pulled a homeless drunk out of a dumpster. He was holding on to a bag full of women's clothing. The clothes were covered in dried blood. When his men started dumpster diving, they also found a pair of high heels, size six. Their lab guys found that the blood matched that of deceased restaurant owner Woodrow Winters. Hair fibers matched our suspect, too."

"And I suppose there was no identification," I mumble.

"Nada," says the Chief, "but there was an interesting find. In the pockets and hem of the skirt, there were small amounts of sand. We're matching the granules to known samples. It will take some time, but we can use a technique called neutron activational analysis to determine what part of the country the sand is most likely to be found."

"Activational what?"

"Never mind."

I look at Fig and ask, "Have you been able to find anything on the dead guys? Anything in common?"

"I thought that an easy match might have been college," he says, "But no luck. Blake was five years older than the other two, and he graduated from San Diego State. Woody never graduated from college, and Tommy Button spent four years at a small Catholic school in New Hampshire. They didn't grow up in the same town. They had no common relatives. They didn't work in the same industry. They didn't belong to clubs or groups that would have brought them together."

It's hard to hide my feelings. I am disappointed in our progress. I am saddened that Fig hasn't found a link that ties the dead men together. But most of all, I am frustrated with myself. As I sit in this meeting, I rub the scar on my lip. I know what my problem is. It's clear to me. It's obvious to my boss. It's apparent to my co-workers. I am letting everyone down.

After the meeting, I go back to my desk and continue staring at the pile of leads. I assign a few to rookie detectives. Maybe one of them will get lucky and find a needle in the haystack.

I log on to the network to check email.

As mail starts to download, I absentmindedly scan the names in the "From" column, but my focus is a thousand miles away. All of a sudden, I jerk to attention. A familiar name jumps out at me. My heart pounds. My temples throb. I can't believe my eyes.

I jump up quickly and then back away one step at a time. I stare at my computer from five feet away as if the name might bite me. Then I slowly inch closer. I lean forward, and click on the message with one finger. I am afraid to get too close.

Date: July 21
From: kiki4@yahoo.com
To: jcollins@SDPD.com
Subject: Hi Jesse

Hi Jesse,

We haven't met, but I feel like we are already friends. I see your picture in the newspaper all the time, and you are on TV almost every night. You seem like a very nice man.

You and I have so much in common. We are both successful in business, but we are unsuccessful in relationships. We have been lonely, and we are now alone. We are both looking for acceptance, and we are looking for peace. I never feel like I fit in. How about you?

I just read the article about you in the Daily Informer. I didn't like it. That reporter, Sonny Crackly, is an asshole. In his article, he said that your wife moved away, and that makes me so sad. I have never had a real, long-term relationship, but when I do, I wouldn't leave my man. Oh, sure, I have had brief affairs, but I am always the one who is hurt in the end.

I was also sorry to hear about your battle with alcohol. I think that my father had a drinking problem, because he disappeared. I know that my uncle had a problem with the bottle. He was always drunk. I hated my uncle more than any other person that I have ever met, and I will never forgive God for letting my uncle do those things to me.

I wish you well, and someday, it would be fun to meet you. I think we have a lot of mutual interests. Who knows? We might become friends.

I look forward to meeting you very, very soon.

Sincerely,
Your admirer,
Kiki


I take a deep breath, open my mouth, and scream at the top of my lungs.

"Fig, Erica, Chief—get over here, quick!"

They all come running.

My vocal chords are shot. I back away from the computer and point. They all crowd around my side of the desk and start reading out loud.

"Trace this message *now*," yells the Chief. The technicians all scramble.

Shaken, I leave my desk and sit in the coffee room. It seems that people are taking turns babysitting me.

Within an hour, Fig gives us a recap.

"The email is from an ISP in Connecticut. We now have one

stream from New York City, two from New Jersey, and one from Connecticut. We can't trace any of them but the good news is that all ISPs are all within two hours of each other."

"OK," I say, gaining my composure. I stand up. "It's time to make some assumptions. Let's place our killer in the Atlantic States. Let's assume that her father abandoned her. Let's start to look for a girl who might have been taken away from her family because of sexual abuse. Maybe her uncle is in jail someplace."

"Put out a bulletin to all law-enforcement agencies in New York, New Jersey, and Connecticut for starters. Tell them that we have reason to believe that the parking lot killer lives in their state. Ask them to report any strange behavior. But don't leak this to the press. We might be making progress."

"Should I send a message back to Kiki?" I ask the Chief. "Can we bait her to meet me?"

"Let's wait on that. Maybe we can get close in another way."

"Erica. Please go back and look at those grains of sand from the bloody clothes. See if there is a match to the Jersey shore, or Long Island Sound. Let's put the killer near the ocean."

Before the meeting breaks up, Fig gives me a worried look. "Jesse, I'm scared shitless. Every other email from Kiki has resulted in a death. Are you in her sights?"

There is silence. Erica's eyes start to mist. She reaches out to me and squeezes my hand. Everyone else just stares.

# 45

KIKI WAS ENJOYING HER FREEDOM. THREE tormentors were gone. She was as happy as she had been in years. It was Saturday morning, and she slept soundly until eight. When she woke up, she took a leisurely shower. She poached eggs, toasted English muffins, and found a recipe for Hollandaise sauce that her mother had given her. The sizzling Canadian bacon smelled wonderful and the Eggs Benedict would be a real treat. She pan-fried leftover potatoes with lots of butter until they became crispy hash browns. She added hot coffee and a piece of cantaloupe. She sat on her patio and enjoyed the meal and the ocean view. After doing the dishes and cleaning up her kitchen, it was almost eleven.

"What a beautiful beach day," she said to no one. The Jersey shore was fabulous at any time of year, but summer was the best. The ocean waves were eight feet high, the sand was white and clean, and, when the breeze came from the East, it provided a cool, salty mist that could only be found in this part of the country.

Her new two-piece black bathing suit fit great and showed off all her charms. The bottom was two inches lower than last year's suit, and a line of white skin stood out between the suit and her tan. She added an extra dose of sun-tan lotion. She combed her curly hair into a very short ponytail and added a black ribbon. She checked herself in the twin mirrors and decided that she looked absolutely stunning.

Kiki got her big beach umbrella out of the storage area, packed a small cooler with bottled water and a veggie sandwich. She grabbed her notebook and pen. Today, she wanted to avoid the tourists, so she headed to a secluded spot. She parked her car a mile north of the boardwalk rides and the pizza stands. She was away from the area that her mother had called the Honky-Tonk. She set up the umbrella, wiggled into the sand, and got comfortable. She loved the feeling of the warm sand as it caressed her legs and her fanny.

*This is what paradise must be like,* she thought. Kiki started to daydream about the changes that had taken place over the past few years. She thought about all the pieces and how they fit so beautifully together. It would be nice to journal about the positive experiences in her life journey.

She would like to write about three things: How it was, what happened, and what it was like now. She opened her notebook and dated her entry.

### Date: July 31

*For most of my life, I have been confined to a damp, dark, torture-chamber existence. There was one punishment after another. Over time, I became emotionally broken, beaten, and battered. I was in constant, sensitive agony. Was it self-imposed? It didn't matter, because the pain was real.*

*I had been used and abused by men. They have had their fun and then tossed me to the wind. I was floundering in a storm of turmoil, and sinking below the water level. I had just about given up and was ready to drown, but one night a solution appeared. Sometimes, a locked door doesn't open until we stop knocking.*

*When I saw that old Clint Eastwood movie, my life changed. I watched the heroine settle a score with many men. In every instance, she got up close and personal before pulling the trigger.*

*I don't remember how many times I watched that movie, but I do remember renting it from different video stores to avoid suspicion. The movie gave me hope. I slowly began to formulate a plan. I knew that this would take a very long time, but it gave me a positive project. I have been planning my revenge ever since. Retribution is the only thing that has kept me going.*

*I took a deliberate step and made a list of my objectives. In my mind, I knew it would be a long-term project. It would take years. But the project gave me hope.*

*First, I would investigate handguns and, somehow, learn how to shoot. Second, I would purchase my own pistol. And lastly, I would set sights on my targets.*

*The first part of the project was to learn about guns. I Googled gun clubs, firearms, and indoor shooting ranges. From there, I looked up the website for the National Rifle Association. That led me to the Association of New Jersey Rifle & Pistol Clubs. Then I discovered a general heading called Places to Shoot.*

*I found a site that had some interesting topics. One was called: Refuse to be a Victim, and another was called Stop Violence against Women. The amount of information was gratifying.*

*During the next few months, I started to visit many of the firing ranges in southern New Jersey. My goal was to find someone* who would spend time with me. I needed a coach. I wanted a mentor who would lead me on this journey. I was interviewing people, but in the beginning the process was disappointing. Every single man that I met treated me like a bimbo.

One night after work, I went to a firing range in Neptune called The Doctor's Rifle and Pistol Club.

"I would like to learn how to shoot a gun, or a pistol, or something."

"And why would you want to do that, little lady?"

"I want to protect myself," I lied.

"Well, maybe I can help. My name is Doc, and I own this place."

I instantly liked Doc. He was gentle, and he talked slowly. He treated me like a lady. Doc was short, with a huge, barrel-shaped chest. He had a three-day growth of stubble, and a long, gray ponytail that hung out from under a red bandana. His arms were covered with black-and-purple tattoos. The word "love" was tattooed on the fingers of his right hand, and the word "hate" was tattooed on his left hand. A black stud was in each ear.

Doc tried to look tough, but under his hard shell he was gentle and understanding. When we were together, he smiled a lot. He instinctively spoke slowly, so that I could read his lips. It was easy for me to understand everything he said.

"There many types of hand guns," Doc said. "The decision of which one to buy is very personal, but I have an idea. You come around here once a week, and we'll let you try a different firearm each week. You can tell me what you like and what you don't like. We will find a pistol that will work for you. How about Wednesday nights?"

Doc went out of his way to be helpful. He let me use handguns from his own collection, and he borrowed guns from his friends. Some handguns were too heavy. Some had too much of a kick. But most were just too big. I wanted to be able to conceal a pistol in my purse, but I couldn't tell Doc about my plan.

"This one is not for me," was all I could say.

Doc didn't mind the trial and error. He acted like he was genuinely interested in me. At a time in my life when I was so alone, Doc replaced the brother I never had, a father who had disappeared, and my lecherous uncle who fucked me over and over.

Despite Doc's rough exterior, he was a teddy bear.

"Give us a hug," Doc would say when I walked in each week. Sometimes he would say, "Give us some sugar." Then, as we got to know each other better, he didn't even have to ask. We became good friends.

Doc told me about his past. He spent time in 'Nam, and took shrapnel in the leg. He spent time in prison and was beaten up. He had been married and divorced. He had been homeless, and now he owned a business. His jailhouse tattoos were a living symbol of the bad times. His attitude was a tribute to how much he appreciated the life that he had now.

Doc served coffee and donuts before Saturday morning sessions. He had pizzas and beer after Wednesday night's practice. There was time to talk about weapons, technique, and safety.

*As we spent time together, Doc started to narrow down my choice of a firearm. One night, he met me at the door.*

*"Man, do I have a surprise for you."*

*"I love surprises."*

*I followed him into his office, and he held up a tiny package.*

*I opened the box. My laugh was nervous. "You've got to be kidding me," I said. "Is this a gun or a toy?"*

*"Neither! This is a pistol. This is the smallest handgun on the market. It's a Kel-Tec P-32 semi-automatic. It weighs less than seven ounces, and comes with a seven-round, single-column magazine."*

*My mind was racing. This little pistol was small enough for me to keep in my purse, or even in my bra. It would be perfect to help me accomplish my goal.*

*"Does it really shoot?"*

*After spending ten minutes with the Kel-Tec, I was hooked. "I'll take it!"*

*Purchasing that gun was the best investment I have ever made. Three hundred dollars was a fair price for something that gave me so much peace. I paid him in cash.*

*Doc helped me fill out the paperwork, and soon it was mine. I started going to his range three or four or five times a week. After practice, I would head home and stash the pistol in my backpack with the cash.*

*My plan began to take shape. I decided to confront each of my old lovers one more time. Maybe one of them would realize how well I have aged. Someone would surely fall in love with me again. Maybe one of them would want me back. In my heart, I was convinced that, after we got together, they would each beg to have me back. If not, I was prepared to take action.*

*I have been alone for so long. My pain has been unbearable for years. When I made the decision to see each of my old boyfriends, I began to feel better. Since I have started making my little trips, I feel terrific.*

*I still can't believe how eager each of my old lovers had been to get together with me. They all agreed to see me again, but for different reasons. Blake wanted to fuck me, Woody felt sorry for me, and Tommy Button wanted to explain to someone, to anyone, why he had switched from girls to boys. I met each of them for a cocktail, and then insisted on getting into their car after the drinks. I gave each of them, except Tommy, one last kiss for old time's sake. And then, POW! Guys are such suckers!*

*These guys lived in three different corners of the country. No one will ever know that the murders were related. And for me? When this project is complete, I will find tranquility. For the first time in my life, I will be able to stand tall and smile.*

*Two years have gone by since I started working on this project. Two years between the time that I hatched my plan and confronted my first ex-lover. Now I have completed three successful missions. My list is narrowing down, and I am going to find peace.*

# 46

MY NEIGHBOR IS GETTING READY FOR a party and has just cranked up the music. Later today, his outdoor speakers will be blaring.

I'm no longer invited to his parties. Could it have something to do with my little mishap during the last party? So I fell into his bar. So I knocked over a few bottles. So a few people stepped on broken glass. So what? That's what emergency rooms are for.

"I don't care," I say out loud.

The bougainvillea bushes are shimmering in the breeze. It's exactly seventy-five degrees, and there's not a cloud in the sky. It's another beautiful day in paradise.

I'm sitting by my own pool with coffee, a bagel, and a notebook. I am spending my free time thinking about a killer who is tormenting me. My insides are all torn up and this case is driving me to drink. Or is that just today's excuse?

A monster is on a rampage, and the violence is escalating.

I start to make random notes, as I have done a hundred times before. Three men are dead. They are from three different corners of the country. A woman is traveling thousands of miles between murder locations. She is sneaking into a city, killing someone, and then sneaking out. Is she driving or flying? If she is flying, how does she get a gun past airport security? Is she staying in hotels before or after? How does she lure victims into a car? How many more men will die?

There has not been a new clue in a month. There is no common denominator among the deceased. The killer seems to have an agenda and an appointment for each rendezvous. But we always find out too late.

People are looking to me for answers but I question my ability to do this job. My boss questions it, too. Should I resign and let them bring in a new young gun? The harder I try to find an answer, the more elusive the solution gets. I am slowly going nuts.

The party at my neighbor's house is ramping up. The guests have arrived, and there is laughter. All of a sudden I feel alone.

I had planned to stay home today, but now I need to escape from my own yard. I need to escape from myself. The third drink of the day stays down. It calms my insides and slowly lifts my spirits. My mind starts to race, and I turn my own music up loud. The fourth drink has me flying high. I feel good. I run through the house, trying to find a bathing suit and flip-flops, and head for the beach.

I like the sun and the sights at Mission Beach, but the best part of my day is a stop at my favorite "FLBB." This "Funky Little Beach Bar" is called The Lahina.

The Lahina Beach Club is mostly outside on a massive, wooden deck. It overlooks a six-foot-wide boardwalk that's packed with roller-bladers, joggers, and bikini moms with baby strollers. Along the wall, exhibitionists and voyeurs sit side by side. Beyond the boardwalk is the Pacific Ocean.

The Lahina consists of old picnic tables, a few stools, and lots of people. This bar is small, crowded, and noisy. The beer is warm, the prices are high, and the service sucks. I love this place!

The dress code is skin. People are wearing suntan oil and not much more. Gigantic twin speakers at each corner of the main deck are blasting out oldies, classics, and favorites. Most people know every word of every tune.

A beautiful, tall, tan blonde with a daring buzz cut has climbed up on top of a picnic table and is swaying to the music. She's in her own world, and no one really pays any attention to her. She is a part of the scenery. Her skin-tight t-shirt says "more of me, less of you." The shirt has been cut short, and it hangs about an inch below her breasts. Instead of a bathing suit bottom, she is wearing a tight pair of low cut, faded, jeans. Rips and tears are all in the right places.

The Lahina is full of class and trash. I am in the second category. There is endless noise from the surf, the crowd, and the twin speakers. The conversation and chatter is endless. Girls are talking about their current loves. Guys are talking about their latest conquests.

The drink of the day is pitchers and shots. A bubbly cocktail waitress appears out of nowhere, and stands three inches in front of me. I can smell her sweet perfume. She smiles. Thin spaghetti straps work hard to hold her bathing suit top in place. She takes my order.

"A pitcher of Bud and two shots of tequila, please. You look busy, so I better plan ahead."

"You better have a plan, big guy," she kids, as she pokes me in the gut.

After I place my order, I feel a sudden wave of loneliness. I feel deserted and out-of-place. What am I doing here? Why am I in this bar by myself? I wonder where my friends are. Do I still have any? I know people at work, and I have drinking buddies, but what about friends? I am alone in a crowd, and I am alone in my mind. I start to feel sorry for myself.

Fortunately, my drinks appear, and alcohol comes to the rescue.

I can always depend on booze. Alcohol does what it's advertised to do. The first shot of tequila is like magic. Instead of a rabbit popping out of a hat, my head pops out of my ass. I am instantly part of the crowd, I fit in, I am not lonely. I am ten feet tall and bullet proof. If only I could stay this way. If only I didn't need booze to prop me up. If only . . . If only.

I realize that everyone is staring at the couple at a nearby table and discussing the activity that is going on under the table. The guy and girl are wasted, and they are oblivious to the crowd. Since this girl can't see her boyfriend's lap, she assumes that no one else can see his lap either. I am reminded that a person's peripheral vision decreases as their intake of alcohol increases. The guy is wearing boxer shorts, and his joint is at attention. The girl is having a field day with his pecker. This gal is so creative with his member that people are clapping and nodding in approval.

This is the kind of scene that brings total strangers together.

I feel soft breasts slowly push into my back as a smooth hand gently touches my waist. A stranger leans into me, and we are as close as melted cheese. She rises up and shouts over the music. "She's been touching him for an hour," she says. I slowly turn to see an adorable brunette in a hot pink bikini. She has an athletic body and a golden tan. She has white Zinka on her lips, and huge black sunglasses resting on top of her head. Her short hair might be spiked, or it might be reacting to the oil and the wind. The petite diamond stud in her nose matches her earrings.

"Do they think that no one can see them?" I smile.

"In the beginning, she was just touching him on the outside of his boxers, but after a while it flopped out, and they both smiled at each other. It was their big secret, but everyone in the bar started to applaud and cheer. They didn't even notice. When he put it away, everyone protested, but the couple was in their own little world."

"And you've been watching for an hour?" I ask.

"Yeah, except when I had to dip in the ocean to cool off. I'm burning up," she laughs. She touches her crotch and then quickly pulls it away as if she had put it on a hot stove. She blows twice on her hand.

She stands up on her tiptoes, puts her hand behind my neck and shouts into my ear. "I don't know who is going to come first. Him or me!"

I suddenly realize that all men are pigs. My inner pig is calling, but I try to resist the urge. Instead of talking about sex, I change the subject and talk about something completely different. I talk about parking lots.

"My car is in the parking lot behind the liquor store," I say.

"Let me walk you to your car," she offers. She would make a great Boy Scout.

In the car, it's sweaty, salty, sticky, and sandy. It's sweet. It's special. It is not only good for us, but also for the family that gets into the station wagon next to us. The wife is yelling to David to hurry up. I can't tell if David is the freckle-faced boy who is staring at us with his nose pushed against the car window, or the hen-pecked husband who's trying to find his keys. The pink bikini bottom is draped over the rear view mirror, and the brunette never misses a beat. I guess she thinks that no one could see us because the convertible top is up. It's that old peripheral vision thing all over again.

After she leaves, I go back to the bar for more tequila.

Five minutes before sunset, a serene calm comes over the entire beach area. Music is turned off, conversation stops, and everyone faces west. The gigantic sun starts its nightly descent into the ocean. People stand on tables. Girls climb on their boyfriend's shoulders, and couples hold hands.

Everyone watches the spectacle as if for the first time. The whole process only takes a few minutes, but the crowd is solemn. You can hear a pin drop. As the sun fades into the horizon, it gets smaller and smaller until it finally disappears. When it is out of sight, everyone applauds and cheers.

The music comes back on, and I order another shot.

# 47

THE FOLLOWING DAY IS SUNDAY, AND I drive to a coffee shop. I take a table by the window and relax. This is a good place to think about how I am going to get my wife back, but I can't do that. My mind keeps going back to Kiki.

Kiki is subconsciously chipping away at me. I think I am afraid to dig deep. For some reason, I am afraid to really look at her. I don't know anything about this killer!

In my past, when problems have been insurmountable, I was encouraged to turn my facts into assumptions. I need to break my thoughts into tiny little pieces. I open my notebook and ask the waitress for a pencil. I want to know who Kiki really is. I need to know what makes her tick. I want to figure out what she wants. What are her goals? What does she plan to accomplish with this very complicated, highly structured mission?

Before my drinking had fogged my mind, I would have known everything about her. I would have done a character analysis. I used to be the best profiler in the business, but now, I haven't even started the process. I go back to basics and create a check list. #1: What can I learn from her body language? #2: How does she react to others' activities? #3: What are her positive and negative habits?

#4: How does she talk? What are her mannerisms? Does she use regional slang? #5: How does she dress?

What do I know about her? I start to write. She is smart, because she can move in and out of airports. She is most-likely attractive, because a lot of men are interested in seeing her. She is very computer savvy, because she knows how to set up self-destructing accounts and leave messages without a trace. She is resourceful, because she has figured out how to convince men see her. She has significant financial resources, because she can pay cash for plane tickets. She is classy, or at least well-dressed, because she wears high heels. She must be loving, confident, encouraging. Men like to be around her, and they feel comfortable enough to invite her into their car. She is small. She wears size six shoes.

Now for the assumptions: Her father probably abandoned her. Her uncle probably abused her sexually. Her mother is probably out of the picture. She probably lives alone. She probably lives in the Northeastern states.

How do I personally feel about her? Am I challenged, flattered, intrigued, fascinated, or charmed? Am I interested or amused? Am I scared, nervous, or frightened?

First of all, I must admit that I am flattered. Not many people reach out to me. She speculated that we might be friends. Is she lonely? Is she picking me out of a crowd, or is she genuinely concerned with my feelings? Can I use this attraction to my advantage? Should I write back to her and suggest a meeting? Would she see through that and run like hell?

I take a copy of her email out of my pocket and look at her musings. She said that we have so much in common. If that is right, what do we have in common? She said that we were both successful. What was she successful at? She said that we were both looking for peace. What kind of peace does she want? Does she want to get caught? Does she want this chase to be over with? She said that she has never had a long-term relationship. Was that because of her abuse at the hands of her uncle, her father, or the men that she has killed?

And lastly, what clue are we missing? What did the victims have in common? We need to go back to the drawing board.

# 48

AT 3AM, KIKI PULLED HERSELF UP into the fetal position. Ten minutes later, she rolled over onto her stomach. Her sheets were tangled up and damp from night sweats. Her mattress was as comfortable as a washboard, and her pillow felt like a bag of kitty litter. She made a fist and punched the pillow before turning it over to the cool side.

She poured herself a glass of water and took it out to the patio. She looked east toward the boardwalk, but the lights from the amusement arcade were dark. Most normal people were sleeping.

Kiki was second-guessing her decision to eliminate the men who had crossed her. She sat on the patio floor and gazed up toward the sky. She let her mind drift back to her dating days. She knew that, in the beginning, each one of her men had been attracted to her because of her looks.

"You are so beautiful!" they would say. "You are gorgeous!' She was the magnet and they were the steel.

Men were also overwhelmed by how well she performed after the lights went out. When it was dark, she didn't have to read lips, or follow the conversation. Late at night, she shined. She could devote all of her energy to the job at hand. When her man was still, she knew how to communicate.

Her relationships with men were all short lived. Each one of her lovers had stayed for a while, but it was only a matter of time before they disappeared.

They said that she cried too much. Or that she was too demanding. They said that they couldn't give her enough attention, or that she was too good for them. They said that they needed time to think it over. What assholes!

Some guys never made a dent. Other men left scars that would never disappear.

As Kiki thought about her old lovers, she became more and more depressed. Sometimes she could shake it off, like you could shake off the cold. Other times, she started gasping for air. She didn't like being suffocated, but it was too late. It would be a long, lonely night. A white hot ember started to smolder in her temples. A migraine was about to explode. Every time she let herself think about her old lovers, she became drained.

Kiki knew, after years of therapy, that there was only one way to achieve some peace of mind. Her analysts all encouraged her to journal. They told her to keep track of her progress with cathartic healing.

As far as she was concerned, it was like chicken soup; it may not help, but it couldn't hurt.

Years ago, a doctor had asked Kiki to write down the definition of catharsis. It was written on an old, tattered piece of lined notebook paper. She had read it a thousand times.

> *"When you write, you will experience a therapeutic release of pent-up feelings and emotions. You will bring repressed pain into the consciousness. When you let your thoughts flow, you will find release. You may even find closure."*

Cathartic healing helped sometimes. Other times she just wanted to tie her lovers to a tree with barbed wire and shoot out their kneecaps.

Tonight, she was so overcome with heartache that she didn't know where to begin. The trick with journaling was to start someplace. Anyplace. Start with some fact, and keep going until she was drained. The real truth usually didn't come out until she had written many, many pages.

Writing was like having a spider on a blank page. It would weave a web until loose ends were tied together. She needed to focus on her fears.

"Start with something," they said. "Let the pen do the talking. You will be amazed at what comes out. Be brave, and heal yourself!"

Kiki stood up and walked inside to her desk. She grabbed her journal and flipped through previous entries. It was easy to see how things had changed. Sometimes she could look back and laugh. Sometimes she cried.

Tonight Kiki prayed for release. She turned on a tiny light over the desk and found a blank page.

### Date: August 14

*Where do I begin tonight? I am trying to justify my actions. I am trying to rationalize. I have to release the pain, or I will explode.*

*After years of being dumped, I became suicidal. People at work asked about the cuts on my wrists. They asked why I had become so thin. They asked why I was crying all the time.*

*"I don't know," I would say.*

*I've tried to run away from myself, but no matter where I went, there I was.*

*I knew that if I didn't get professional help, I would die. Therapists have all had the same diagnosis. They used words like self-absorbed, controlling, egotistical, and clinging. They said that I was too needy.*

*I don't understand. When I look in the mirror, all I can see is beauty. I see love, I see compassion. What's the problem?*

*I became obsessed. I wasn't sleeping. I wasn't eating. I was losing my ability to focus. I had no friends, no love life, and no outside interests. My pain was a cancer that was spreading too fast. I was deserted in my dreams and isolated in my relationships. I was terminally alone.*

*There has been a hole inside of me that I have tried to fill with booze, pills, shopping, self-mutilation, religion, drinking, eating, starving, and sex. I have blamed my handicap. I have blamed my father. I have blamed my uncle. But mostly I blamed the lovers who left me. I decided to bring those relationships to closure. I wanted to start my life over again. My decisions were justified.*

*No one else can fix my problems. No one else can make me happy. If there is to be change, it is up to me. I am now in control. It's all about control.*

After writing, Kiki felt better. She started to relax. To forget about the past, she escaped to a different time, a different place. She was good at taking on a whole new personality. She did some role-playing in front of her twin mirrors. She went to the closet and took out her new heels. When she was on the Cape, she treated herself to the sexiest pair of red spikes that she had ever seen. They had tiny little ankle straps with dainty brass buckles. She loved them, and, man, did they show off her legs. She also bought a new red silk scarf. It didn't take long to get dressed with an outfit like that. She admired herself in the mirror. Even at forty-two, she had a better body than anyone she knew.

Kiki pretended she was walking down Fifth Ave. in NYC. It was a beautiful, clear, spring day, and the traffic was at a standstill. When she got to Forty-Second Street, she jaywalked to the south side of the street. She headed toward the New York City Library and cut in front of a yellow cab. Out of the corner of her eyes she could see the cabbie waving his arms and shouting. He jumped out of his taxi, and she could read his lips.

"Oh my God. That broad is naked!"

# 49

THERE'S A BAR IN OCEANSIDE, CALIFORNIA, with the best name of any bar in the world. The name of the bar is "One more, that's it!" A big neon sign on the side of an old brick building says it all for me. I can relate. I just want one more, that's it! I want one more of everything. One more drink, or one more drug, or one more dish of ice cream. I want one more potato chip, or one more handful of M&Ms. I have always been obsessed with more. More control, more money, more love, more attention. For the last week I have tried to stay sober. My intentions are good, but my days are divided into predictable stages. In the morning, when I am reeling from the night before, I decide to quit. By noon, when I feel better, I wonder if I overreacted. By 5pm, I think that one drink would be OK, so I have one. Then I have another one. Then I have one more, that's it.

And then, I stop counting.

# 50

MONDAYS!

I am late to work again. It's the fucking job. It's the fucking case. It's the fucking booze.

We have had no progress in this case. The Ball Buster is showing up in different parts of the country and leaving her little mark. Her mark is a gunshot to the crotch. We have hair samples. It's a girl with curly blonde hair. We have prints, but we have no idea who might have left them. We have bullets and know the kind of gun that was used. There is bloody clothing that was left near a killing. In every case, we have talked with family and friends.

I hear a commotion, and, as I look up from my desk, Fig is running in my direction. He is waving his arms and looks like he is totally out of breath. He is so excited that I wonder if he just got laid.

"I found the thread," he shouts from three desks away. "I found the link. I know where they all met their killer!" Everyone in the office stares at him.

"Great! What is it?" I shout.

Fig is puffing and panting. "Let me catch my breath," he says.

# 51

WHEN KIKI WAS 14, HER MOTHER begged a neighbor to give the young girl a part-time job. As a favor the friend obliged, and Kiki went to work in a small office on Saturday mornings. The teenager started her career dusting desks, sharpening pencils, and putting stamps on envelopes.

The work was basic, and the tasks were routine, but Kiki did a good job. She was always early and wanted to stay late. She was friendly and courteous. Her boss was surprised at how eager the young girl was to please. Without being asked, she vacuumed the office, emptied trash baskets, and cleaned the windows. She replaced toilet paper in the rest room, cleaned the toilets, and swept under the desks. She found things to do before she was asked. She was the busiest person in the office, and the boss liked her.

As time went on, Kiki was given new chores. She caught on to each new assignment quickly, and her energy level was inspiring. During high school, her schedule increased. Saturday mornings stretched out to two afternoons a week. After high school, she was brought on as a full-time employee. Her list of tasks included working with the postage machine, the adding machine, and filing. She addressed envelopes and helped with mailings.

In the early eighties, her life changed. When the owner of the company invested in a Radio Shack TRS-80, every employee rolled their eyes. Everyone, that is, except Kiki. She was fascinated with the black box. She took to the computer like a duck takes to water. She started to read everything that she could about the hardware and software. She signed up for an adult education class on computers. As time went by, she did more and more on the "Trash 80." She showed others in the office how to create simple letters with word processing, and she figured out how to print labels for a mailing.

Since Kiki couldn't hear, the computer became her fifth sense. As the technology improved, Kiki improved too.

When email was introduced, Kiki started to shine.

Kiki loved the Internet. Communicating was finally easy for her and she thrived on email. As she became more proficient, she realized that she could communicate without fear of identification. She learned how to set up free accounts with phony names and addresses. She realized that after she stopped using a free account, it would self-destruct. She discovered that sending messages from cyber cafés was untraceable. In the beginning, it was a game. Later on, it was an obsession.

Kiki got in touch with each of her old flames by email. When she sent the first message, she just talked about old times and kept the posts brief. After a few notes went back and forth, she announced that she was going to be in their town for a meeting. A few days later, she sent a note asking if they might get together for a quick drink. She told each of them that she only had an hour between appointments.

Then she sent one last message. After reading it, they were all willing to meet with her.

The plan had worked fine, so far. Three up! Three down!

Now it was time for the biggest challenge of all. Now she focused on the man who had stayed with her the longest, and hurt her the most.

She went to her closet and pulled down her shoe box of pictures. She removed a group of photographs that were tied together with twenty-seven pink ribbons. Why was it that every time she found a pink ribbon, she would attach it to this special collection of photographs? Why was it that every time she looked at these pictures, she would break down and cry? Tonight, she asked herself the question again. What ever happened to Rusty?

Rusty was the most interesting man she had ever met. He was sensitive. He challenged her to excel in her job and in her life. He asked her to marry him. One day, out of the blue, he disappeared.

She spread the pictures out on her bed. Seeing these pictures again brought up so many emotions. The pictures brought up love, hate, and rage. Tonight they brought up revenge.

It was time to find Rusty.

# 52

RUSTY WAS LATE FOR WORK ON this Monday morning. His new twenty-two foot I/O was his favorite toy. He loved it. His wife, Trudy, hated it.

Every time he invited his wife to join him on the boat, there was always a problem. It was too hot, or too sunny, or too breezy. He was going too fast, or he was spending too much time tied up next to his friend's boats.

Over the weekend, he invited his buddy's sister to go water-skiing, and that was the last straw.

"You were paying too much attention to her." His wife said. "You were talking to her too much. You were too nice to her! And when her bathing suit top slipped down, you couldn't take your eyes off her." Blah, Blah, Blah.

He finally took his wife home, and, without even saying good bye, he stormed out of the driveway and went back to the marina. At 10pm, he ran out of gas. He had to wait for another boater to tow him in. He didn't get home till 3am.

Rusty didn't mind being out late, because his relationship with his wife was at a standstill. Trudy was on the warpath. According to her, Rusty only had two problems: everything he said; and everything he did. And she let him know it. She complained about him spending too much time at work, or too much time with his guys. In the winter, it was too much time on his snowmobile. Now, it was too much time on the boat. Ever since she caught him drinking with a customer, it got worse. So what if the customer was the foxy owner of a new hair salon? So what if they were drinking at 10pm? So what if they were sitting together on the couch in her office? So what?

Fortunately, his business almost ran by itself. After Rusty's father had passed away, Rusty took over the family electrical contracting business. The company was very successful, and most of his employees had been with him for years.

When Rusty finally got to his office, he logged on and was blown away by a surprise message.

> Date: August 22
> From: Kiki222@hotmail.com
> To: Rusty@yankeeelectricservice.com
> Subject: Hello stranger
>
> Hi Rusty,
>
> Long time no see.
>
> Well, I was so happy to find you through your company website. It's been so long since we've talked. Communicating is so much easier for me now that everyone has email. How have you been?
>
> I am having fun, and life is good. I have been working with computers a lot and have even learned some programming. During the last year, I designed a new website for my boss. I am single, and there are no kids in the picture. I like it this way.
>
> I have changed so much since the days that we dated. Lots

of counseling! Lots of journaling! I am an entirely different person than the one you knew so many years ago.

How is your business? Are you married? Are there any kids? Boys? Girls?

How old are they?

Drop me a line and tell me what's going on in your life.

Love,
Kiki

What a shock! What a surprise! What a treat! He had a message from an old lover! He left the office and went for a ride, just to collect his thoughts.

Rusty and Kiki had dated for a long time, and, at one point, they had been very happy together. What a great lover she had been. One night, in a weak moment, he'd asked her to marry him. That's when things got bad. She became so possessive that he couldn't come up for air. She was in his face twenty-four hours a day. He couldn't spend time with his friends, he couldn't visit his parents, and he couldn't even go to work without her smothering him. She wanted to know where he had been. She wanted to know who he was with. She wanted to know what he was thinking. He tried to back off, but that made matters worse. He couldn't stand it, so he fled. He took a job in Boston, and told his parents to say that they didn't know where he was. She drove his parents crazy, and it was a cruel thing to do, but he had no choice. He was being buried alive, and he had to find daylight.

Now, however, after all of this time, it was great to hear from Kiki. She sounded like she might have grown, and he really wanted to see her.

When he returned to his office, he spent an hour composing

a positive and upbeat reply. He answered her questions and they became pen pals. Every few days, there was a new message. After each message, there was a witty, creative, and positive response. He felt uneasy about what he was doing. After all, he was married. On the other hand, his wife was going through a change of life, or a change of attitude. He brushed his concerns aside, reasoning that he was just having fun, and that no one was being hurt.

After a month of light and meaningless communication, a message with a different twist showed up.

Date: August 30
From: Kiki222@hotmail.com
To: Rusty@yankeeelectricservice.com
Subject: Guess what!

Hi Rusty,

You won't believe this. Actually, I don't believe it either. I have been proposed to.

I am so full of fear. I just don't know what to do. His name is Bill, and he is really a nice guy. The scary part is that, as you might remember, I get a little possessive during long-term relationships. I need to talk to someone about marriage. I need to find out if it is a good step for me. What are the biggest obstacles?

I have friends who are married, and I could talk with them, but they didn't know me way back when. They have all met Bill, and they all think he is perfect for me. I would love to talk with someone who is objective. I would love to talk with someone who knew me before. Would you give me some advice?

It's kind of a coincidence that my boss wants me to do a little project in Manchester, NH. I remember all the fun that we had in that town. Do you ever go there anymore? Do you think we could get together for a quick drink?

I know you are married, and I don't want to jeopardize your relationship. Also, I know you don't want to be seen in public with a strange woman.

I was wondering if there is a nice restaurant in Manchester that might be near a private parking garage. Maybe you know of a place that I could sneak in and out of, without being seen? If you could send me directions, I could park in the garage, and just meet you at the bar for an hour or two. Just for old time's sake. It will be fun to see you, and I really would appreciate your advice.

What do you think?

Love,
Kiki.

Rusty's hormones started to slam dance. What would be the harm in seeing her just once? After all, she said that she just wanted his advice. And she knew he was married. And it would only be for an hour. And on, and on, and on.

Rusty crafted a reply and sent directions to a parking garage near a brand new Mexican restaurant in Manchester, New Hampshire.

# 53

As the meeting with Kiki approached, Rusty started to feel awkward. It was hard for him to lie to his wife, but he rationalized that he wasn't really lying; he was just guilty of omission.

On the day of the rendezvous, Rusty jumped in his company pickup and raced out of the driveway before Trudy even knew he was gone. During the ride to Manchester, he was overcome with remorse.

"It is only for an hour, and I'm just trying to help a friend who had asked for advice," he told himself.

When Rusty got to Manchester, he found a remote spot in the parking garage and walked down a back alley to Dos Pedro's Restaurant. He was sure no one had seen him. He was a few minutes early and ordered a beer. While he waited for Kiki, his mind flashed back to memories of their time together.

When Kiki walked in, his heart almost stopped. What a knockout! She was as beautiful now as she had been way back then.

Kiki was oozing with sex appeal. More than that, her smile was warm and genuine. Her teeth were sparkling. Her blonde hair was short and curly. She was dressed in a very short blue jeans skirt and a low-cut, starched white blouse. Red high heels made her tan legs look perfect. The red scarf draped around her neck created a picture. And, man, what a picture! He was hooked.

Every other man in the bar was hooked, too. Heads turned as she walked in.

Rusty started to walk over to her. His heart was pounding. They smiled at each other from across the room.

"Hi Rusty."

He heard his name being called, but something was wrong. His name was being called from a different direction. It wasn't Kiki talking. He turned around.

"Rusty, over here. What are you doing? Is Trudy with you?"

He looked towards the voice, and stopped dead in his tracks. He stared straight at his mother-in-law. She was sitting at a table ten feet away. His jaw dropped open, and his head thrust forward in disbelief. He stood there staring at her for a full minute.

"Are you OK?" she asked.

As he shuffled toward her table, he fumbled for something to say, but he could barely talk. He slowly made up a story about work and said he had to pick up material for a job. "I was just going to have a beer before I started home," he said.

Trudy's mother and her friend had been shopping. They had stopped at this new restaurant for lunch, and they insisted that he join them. As he pulled up a chair, he saw Kiki walking away. Before she left the bar, she turned, smiled, and shrugged. Rusty couldn't even wave.

An hour later, as Rusty drove home, he wondered why he had picked that particular restaurant. Why did he go on that day? Why did he go at all?

But now, the hook was set. He was already thinking about the email that he would send her as soon as he got home.

Rusty felt like a young man again. He had seen part of Kiki, but couldn't wait to see all of her.

# 54

I'M STANDING AT MY DESK, WAITING for Fig to stop panting. Everyone in the office is waiting for him to stop panting, too. And we are all waiting for his reply. He is out of breath from running across the room.

"You have to get into shape, man!"

"I found the thread. I found out how the guys from San Diego, Charlotte, and Provincetown all met their killer."

"OK, Fig. Lay it on me."

"After months of searching," he said, "I found a link, but it hasn't been easy."

"You're really gonna drag this out, aren't you?" I said.

He ignores my remark. "I started with birth towns, grammar schools, occupations, business associations, family ties, and college graduation details." He looks at a list. "I ended up with different towns, schools, careers, and families. Two of the dead guys graduated from college, but they went to different schools, and one didn't graduate at all."

"OK, Fig, I ain't got all day. What's the link?"

He is still ignoring me, and there is a smile on his face. He is enjoying this way too much.

"I wasn't making any progress, so I dug deeper. I opened the files one more time, and went back to college records. I ordered a complete transcript of their educations. Blake graduated from San Diego State. Woody's last school affiliation was at a restaurant school in Rhode Island called Johnson and Wales, but he didn't graduate. And Tommy graduated from a small catholic school in New Hampshire called Saint Anselm. Nothing matched. But, as the transcripts started to come in, I saw a pattern."

"Hold that pattern. I'm going out for a beer," I say.

He gives me the finger and continues. "Blake Vanderbeek was kicked out of BU in his freshman year. His family enrolled him in a small school in New Hampshire called Saint Anselm College. He lasted three months but was expelled from Saint Anselm's, too. That's why he didn't show up in the original records. Then his family sent him to San Diego State, where he finally graduated. Woody spent the first semester of his freshman year at Saint Anselm's and then switched to Johnson and Wales, where he met his wife, Kitty. They moved to Charlotte, and opened The Black Dog Tavern. Tommy spent four full years at Saint Anselm's."

"So all three victims went to the same college, at some point?" I ask, paying attention for the first time.

"Bingo!"

"Why the hell didn't you say so?"

We barge into the Chief's office, and I ask Fig to tell his story in one sentence.

"The three dead guys all went to the same college in Manchester, New Hampshire."

"Jesse, I want you to get to that school and start digging. Go ASAP! Go and find Kiki before she kills again."

I book a flight to Manchester, New Hampshire, for Monday morning.

# 55

HELL IS A PLACE OF TOTAL separation from God. Hell is full of eternal misery and suffering. Hell can be any condition of extreme evil and pain. This definition from Webster's dictionary is, of course, pure speculation. Hell is a myth that has been created by the religious community. Preachers talk of fire and damnation. They shout about endless torment and agony.

No living person has any idea what Hell is like.

Except for Kiki. Tonight, Kiki was in Hell. She was living in endless torment and agony. This could have been a nightmare, but she was wide-awake. Her past had crept up on her again, and it was like being caught in a suffocating, revolving door. She kept going round and round and round. She couldn't breathe.

Her past revolved around her uncle.

When other little girls were playing with dolls, she was playing with Uncle Emmett. Or, rather, Uncle Emmett was playing with her.

Sometimes she went for months without thinking about him, but then, for no reason, he came back into her mind. Tonight was one of those nights. She could hear him, and she could smell him. She could taste him! Tonight he had a bone-crushing grip on her. Tonight, his memory was cutting off her air supply. She was gasping.

Kiki couldn't escape from her thoughts. For the past two hours she had been curled up on the floor in the fetal position. She was sobbing uncontrollably. She was quivering and shaking involuntarily. Even though her room was warm on this balmy, summer night, she was freezing. She pulled a blanket off the bed and covered her body.

She held a razor blade between her thumb and forefinger, and started a faint red line. Kiki could not ignore her childhood trauma. It may fade away someday, but for now, Uncle Emmett was alive in her mind. He was right there, touching her, probing her, using her.

Tonight, her thoughts slid back . . . back in time . . . back to that place . . . back to that person. As she relived the horror of her childhood, she started trembling. She expected that if she didn't do something therapeutic, she would end up in a convulsion.

Even though it was 3am, she considered getting in touch with her therapist. God knows she paid him enough! But he would just tell her to get out of bed and journal. He would tell her to write it out. He would gently suggest that she seek cathartic healing.

Tonight, it would be best to get up and write her childhood saga, again. She had performed this exercise a thousand times. Catharsis had worked for her in the past, and she prayed that it would help tonight. She wiped away the tears and bundled herself in the blanket. She opened her journal to a clean page and thought about writing. Where should she start this time?

## Date: October 1

> I hated that private boarding school for the deaf. It was strict and rigorous. For as far back as I can remember, I was away from home from Monday until Friday. I was at a prison for little people.

*When I was home on weekends, mother had to work, and I didn't see her often. She worked constantly to pay for my school and tutoring. And she had to pay for weekend babysitters. Back then, I couldn't understand why I had to stay at that school all week, or why I couldn't be with my mother on weekends. I was always alone. I was always confused. I was sad. I was so hungry for attention that it hurt. I remember I just wanted someone to talk to me. I wanted someone to play with me. I wanted someone to pay attention to me.*

*I liked the days that Uncle Emmett came to visit. He was chubby and soft. He always had a red face, and he smelled funny. He was always drinking, and sometimes he had me fill his glass for him from the big bottle.*

*"Get your old uncle a little nip," he would say, slowly, so I could understand.*

*After Uncle Emmett's wife moved out, he was at our house often.*

*One day, Mom asked him to become my Saturday babysitter, and he jumped at the chance. He said that it was good for him to have a purpose. It was good for me to have some stability. I knew that every Saturday I would be with my favorite person.*

*My uncle paid attention to me. He would hug me and have me sit on his lap. He was the only adult who had time. He would read to me and tickle me. He would lift me up and have me straddle him so that we could sit face-to-face. I liked that, because I could read his lips. We would play patty cake. He loved me. Sometimes he would make believe that I had been a bad girl, and he would spank me. He would put me across his knee, pull up my skirt, and pat my fanny for a long, long time. We would both laugh. My Uncle Emmett was my knight in shining armor.*

*When I was at Uncle Emmett's house, we had fun, and we had secrets. He would give me ice cream for breakfast and tell me that it was our secret. He would give me candy for lunch and tell me that it was our secret. No one would ever know our secrets.*

*And when we started playing his games, he said, "This will be our biggest secret."*

*How old was I when we started playing games? Was I four, or was I five?*

*As I look back, I realize that in the beginning he was testing the water. He wanted to see how I would respond. And I must have responded beautifully. He was spending time with me, and I would have done anything to please him. I loved his devotion. I loved being in his spotlight.*

*I remember the first secret game that Uncle Emmett made up. "Just for friends," he told me. He taught me the underwear game. It was fun. We would show each other our underwear. I would pull my skirt up a little at a time and show him my underpants. Then he would pull his slacks down a little at a time and show me his shorts. It was exciting, and it was a big secret.*

*One Saturday, he taught me a new game. We played doctor. He would examine me, but, as I think back, he was still testing. He was taking it slowly. I was in my underwear, and he poked and prodded me while I lay on the bed. Then he encouraged me to examine him. I was too young to know about right and wrong, but, even at my young age, this felt very grown up. I was on an equal level with an adult.*

*The following week, he suggested we have a real doctor's examination. He smiled. "No one will ever know about our secret game."*

*We took turns going into the bathroom and covering up with a towel. He examined me first, and, when I lay on the bed, I was stiff. I was scared, but he tickled me until I laughed. As I wiggled, kicked and squirmed, my towel slipped off. He made a production of covering me, but then there was more tickling. The laughing made me relax, and after a while I felt OK with being undressed in front of my uncle.*

*When it was my turn to be the doctor, I had him climb on the bed.*

*"It's your turn!" I said.*

*In the process, his towel dropped. We both laughed, but I had finally seen his thing. It was big and shiny and purple. There was lots of hair.*

*We spent the next few Saturday's examining each other. I loved the attention, and I thought I was the luckiest little girl in the world. During the week, I counted the days until I could be with Uncle Emmett again.*

*One Saturday, he had me examine his thing even more. Instead of just looking, we started touching.*

*"It's my lollypop," he said. I touched his lollypop and pushed it up and down.*

*"Just like the doctors do," he said.*

*And he examined me. For the first time, he really touched me.*

*That day, we touched each other for hours. It felt so good when my uncle touched me. When I went home, I was sore. But I was happy.*

*After that, as soon as Mom dropped me off, we would take our clothes off. Sometimes we would have a contest to see who could get undressed first. I always won.*

*One Saturday, after hours of touching, he asked me to kiss his lollypop. I didn't understand the thrill that it gave him. The moment that my lips touched him, something shot all over my face.*

Kiki had to stop writing. She suddenly became dizzy, and she started to sweat. She felt the sickness coming up from the bottom of her stomach. It burned like a combination of cut glass and hot chili peppers. It tasted like urine.

The projectile vomit happened so fast and so forcefully that it shot three feet across the room, covering everything in its wake. Kiki fell into the mess and started to wail. She pounded her fist on the floor.

"I can't write about this," she cried out loud. "I can't even write!"

# 56

IT'S SUNDAY AFTERNOON, AND I AM packing for my morning flight to Manchester, New Hampshire. I am excited. I will finally get to know Kiki. What is her history? Who hurt her? What drives her? What does she want? How many men does she need to kill? After my suitcase is packed, I run out of things to do. Without a list of tasks, I feel lonely.

I am alone, and I feel sorry for myself. I am under-loved, under-nourished, and under stress. Since Maggie moved out, I feel abandoned. I am desperate for companionship.

I call my partner.

"What a great day," I say to Fig.

"How's your weekend going?"

"Oh, I have lots to do," I lie, "but I was thinking of taking a break. Wanna grab a beer?"

We agree to meet at a seedy little dive called the Boiler Maker's Union. The Union, as it's affectionately called, is right across from the beach and there is an endless parade of tan bodies and tiny thongs. We plan to meet at three. Since I don't have a life, I show up at one.

The Union is dark and dreary. The air smells like a used bar rag.

As I wait for my friend, I order my fourth margarita with an extra shot of tequila. I pour the little shot into the big glass and take a slug.

I turn my back to the bar and scan the big, dark room. As my eyes become accustomed to the gloom, I focus on a young couple in a corner booth. They seem to be so much in love. They are quietly talking, and, every few minutes, they share a kiss. They are oblivious to anyone else in the club. He is bigger than she is, and they are holding hands under the table. They use their free hand to sip their drinks. He pulls his arm out from under the table and puts it around her small shoulder. She snuggles into him with her head on his chest and just stares up at her boyfriend. They look like the happiest couple on earth.

I remember my early days with my wife, Maggie. We were so much in love, too. We talked endlessly about our hopes and dreams. We shared our plans and planned our lives. As the song goes, I didn't want to leave her, I couldn't wait to love her. Now, we live a thousand miles apart.

As I watch the young couple, I feel like crying for the second time today. I miss Maggie immensely. Today, I feel differently about our separation. Instead of just thinking about me, I think about us. I am usually too self-centered to accept responsibility, but I start to consider my part in our broken relationship.

The young couple gets up from their corner booth and saunter slowly across the empty dance floor towards the jukebox. They are barefoot, and he has his hand inside of the back of her shorts. It looks like he is massaging her tiny butt. Suddenly, she shrieks and jumps up. She playfully slaps him and looks at him with her eyes open wide in shock. Then she rises up on her tiptoes and gives him a big, long kiss.

They stand in front of the jukebox and discuss selections. As they search the song list together, he bends over and whispers in her ear. She giggles.

Their happiness increases my sadness.

The young man slides a dollar bill into the machine and punches a few numbers. When the selection starts, he bows, takes his young lady by the hand, and leads her to the middle of the empty dance floor. They listen to Billy Joel, and the guy sings along. "You're always a woman to me," he sings loudly. They start a very slow dance.

The song reminds me of Maggie. She was definitely a woman. She had class, and she had style. She loved me and cared for me. She was totally devoted to me. She worked hard to make my life easy. I took her for granted, I emotionally abused her, I regularly abandoned her, and I finally lost her.

Tears start to run down my cheek.

"Jesse, are you crying?" Fig says from behind me.

"Oh shit!" I grab a dirty bar napkin and wipe my eyes.

Fig laughs at me, and I push him away. Then we both laugh. My laugh is nervous. To take the focus off my tears, I order drinks. A beer for my friend and tequila for me.

Fig just shakes his head. "What the hell is going on with you?"

With my back to the couple on the dance floor, I open up.

"I've got to make some changes," I say.

"Like?"

"I need to give up the booze," I say, as I take a big swig of tequila. "I need to find a killer, and I need to get back with my wife."

"Getting tired of the single life?"

"This is not easy. I am terrible company for myself. I miss Maggie so much." I start to cry again, and Fig looks embarrassed.

We sit quietly for a while, and Fig invites me to follow him home for dinner.

"I'd rather be alone," I say.

He buys me another shot, pats me on the back, and heads toward the door.

After he goes home to his wife, I start to watch the couple in the booth again. I am more depressed than ever. I have to leave this place. I get out of the Boiler Maker's Union and go to another bar for one more drink.

One more; that's it!

# 57

I COME TO. I AM PROPPED against a wall, half sitting and half lying on a cold, hard floor. I am shaking. My mouth is full of cotton. My throat is sandpaper. Even before I open my eyes, I know that there are bright lights. I sense panic and confusion. I hear swearing and yelling.

Did I just wake up, or am I dead? Why am I so cold? Why am I sweating? Every part of my body is quivering. My head is splitting. I am dizzy. I think I am going to puke. I smell like I already have. I seem to have lost a huge chunk of my life. Where am I?

I slowly open my eyes. I am in a large room with a cement floor, cinder block walls, and steel bars. I am in jail.

My mind is racing. How did I get here? I vaguely remember red lights, and I remember trying to walk a straight line. I remember falling down, but the rest is a blank.

Bright lights covered in wire frames glare from the ceiling, and I squint to look at my new surroundings. My eyes are glassy, my vision is blurry, and I am dizzy.

This place looks familiar, and I realize that I am in the Vista jail. This is the first time, however, that I have seen the Vista jail from the inside.

My hands are rough and bloody. I feel my face, and there are scabs. My forehead is pounding.

I think that passing out would be a blessing! I fight to stay awake.

I try to relive the previous night. I remember driving. But where? Did I have an accident? Was I in a barroom fight? I check my pockets. My wallet, watch, and money are gone. My belt is missing, too. My mind races to fill in the blanks.

I am in a crowded cell with twenty losers, and I make no eye contact. Slowly, I pull myself to a standing position and cling to the cell door. I start to take stock of my environment, but moving too quickly makes me dizzy.

There is a pay phone for collect calls, and I desperately want to use it, but who would I call at this hour? What hour is it? There is long, cement bench, but I can't sit on it. A giant black man is taking up the entire space. He has a full, scraggly beard, long, filthy hair, a ripped jacket, and work boots. His shoelaces are untied. He is snoring so loudly that I'm sure he can be heard from a mile away. There is a stainless-steel toilet, but I can't take a leak in it. A very thin, sickly man has passed out with his face resting on the rim. If he drowns, no one will care.

In the center of the cold, cement floor, a man is crunched up in a ball. He is motionless. He is dressed in tan slacks, but there is no shirt. His shoes and socks are also missing. I wonder how a man could lose his clothing on a chilly, California night. What's his story?

I am locked up in a jail cell with the scum of the earth. I have nothing but contempt and disgust for each of them. They scare the hell out of me. Some are sick, some are hurt, and most are hopeless. There have been many losses tonight. The men with fresh cuts and bruises have lost a battle. Others have lost time and money. Most have lost their self-respect. All have lost their freedom.

It hits me like a ton of bricks. Why should I think so lowly of my cell mates? I am in jail, too! I have always had a fear of ending up in prison. I couldn't imagine being locked up like an animal, but here I am!

This is the lowest point in my life. I have fallen from grace. I am locked up with the people I usually arrest. I feel lower than dog shit and as slimy as puke. How did this happen to me?

A flashback makes me lightheaded. I have had a great career. I have a wonderful wife. I have a boss who takes care of me. I have friends like Fig and Erica. I have my health and a decent income. Why am I in jail?

I get up the courage to call Fig collect. His wife answers, and she wakes him. She asks him what the fuck I could possibly want at this hour. He gets out of his warm bed and drives through the chilly, California night to throw my bail. As I hug the locked cell door, I see him come in and talk to the desk sergeant. He is showing his badge. They both look at me and just shake their heads. Then, all of a sudden, the sergeant starts to laugh. It becomes a loud, hysterical, belly-shaking laugh. The thought of a San Diego detective in his Vista jail just cracks him up. Fig is not laughing.

The Sergeant can't resist having fun at my expense. He walks to the locked cell door and yells to the inmates.

"Hey assholes. There is a cop in this cell with you!" Prisoners hate cops, and if they find one in a jail cell, his last few minutes are numbered. It gets very quiet, and everyone sits up. Many eyes are glued on me. Two overgrown bears stand up and start to shuffle in my direction. As they get dangerously close, the Sergeant opens the cell door and pulls me out. Now the entire cell population is yelling and swearing.

I am released. They return my watch, my wallet, my belt, and some cash.

The sergeant laughs again. He pounds his desk.

Fig drives me to my house, and neither of us have a word to say. As I fall out of the car, Fig reminds me of my obligations.

"Remember," he says. "You have a flight to New Hampshire tomorrow morning."

I stumble to my feet, and Fig jams his foot on the gas pedal. The car door slams shut as he drives away. I stagger into the house and grab a full bottle of tequila. I unscrew the top and crush it in my fist. The broken pieces of plastic cut my hand. I throw the broken top as far across the room as it will go. Why would I need the top for a bottle that I am going to empty? As I take a long, hard swig, the liquor runs from my mouth onto my filthy shirt and then onto the floor. I swallow some more as if my life depends on it. I stop for a breath and then take another gulp. I tip the bottle straight up and almost drown in the flood. All of a sudden, the bottle is empty!

# 58

THE ALARM GOES OFF AT 4AM. I'm lying on the kitchen floor in a pool of tequila, urine, and vomit. My flight from California to New Hampshire is scheduled to leave in three hours. I get up and limp to the bathroom. I spend the next five minutes with my head in the toilet. When I run out of vomit, I gag.

What happened last night? I walk unsteadily to the front door and look out to the street. The driveway is empty. I remember Fig bringing me home from jail. Where is my car?

Back in the bathroom, I look in the mirror, and there are black scabs with fresh blood on my face. There is an abrasion on my chin. Did I fall down? My left eye is black and blue. Was I in a fight? My hands are red and bloody. My knuckles are all scraped. My head is spinning. I fall to my knees and heave into the toilet again. I am dizzy and sweating. My eyes are glassy, and I have trouble seeing the toilet.

I pick up the phone and call United Airlines. "I'm sick," I say. No lie there! We reschedule for half past ten, and I pass out. At eight, the alarm goes off for the second time this morning, and I force myself to get out of bed. I have painful dry heaves over and over. My stomach aches from the retching. I try to look in the mirror, but I am seeing double. I feel hot and sweaty, but I am freezing. I have uncontrollable chills.

I call United Airlines to reschedule my flight one more time. We are now shooting for the 2pm flight. I call a cab company and schedule a pick up at noon.

I set the alarm clock for eleven and drag myself back to the bed.

I am on the edge of a cliff. The ground under my feet is slowly slipping away. In the ravine below, there is a fire that is roaring out of control. People are being burned to death. There is screaming and terror. People try to claw their way up the sides of the wall. The few who do climb up slide back to certain death. Even from way up here, I can smell charred flesh. As I look in horror at the crowd below, the sand continues to slip out from under my feet. I am unsteady and shifting from foot to foot. I can feel the heat that is rising up from the pit. I am sweating profusely. I feel myself moving slowly toward the edge, but, for some reason, I don't fall in. I am counting the seconds until I tumble into the pit below and a predictable, horrific death. I wake up. The sheets are soaking wet. My head seem to be on fire.

This nightmare on the edge of a cliff comes to me when I am in turmoil. Sometimes the details are different. In other versions, there have been slithering snakes or giant rats with long, sharp teeth in the pit below. And, as always, people are trying to claw their way up from their deaths. In every nightmare, I stand petrified as the sand slowly slips beneath my feet.

I get up, take a handful of Excedrin, and climb into the shower. After I dry off, I realize that I am still sweating. My shirt becomes soaking wet within seconds. I have trouble getting dressed. Pushing big buttons through tiny buttonholes is impossible.

I vomit yellow, slimy bile into the sink. I have diarrhea. I am shaking and dizzy.

The cab driver leans on the horn to let the whole neighborhood know he has arrived. I climb into the back seat and immediately start to fade. The driver turns around and flashes a gold tooth and a three-day growth of stubble. His body odor would drive a freight train off the track. He is wearing a black cowboy hat with sweat marks and a sleeveless shirt to match. The country station is blaring. He looks at me in the mirror and shouts with enthusiasm, "Man, I hope you like Jerry Jeff Walker as much as I do!" Before I can ask who the fuck Jerry Jeff Walker is, he turns the volume up as loud as it will go. The taxi driver and Jerry Jeff Walker sing together about insane rodeo cowboys, and I am introduced to a new kind of hell.

When I finally make it to the ticket counter, I stand at the end of the world's longest line. There are at least one hundred people in front of me, but I'm probably the only one reeling back and forth.

I have lots of time to think. I think that puking would be good. I think that dying would be good. I think that a beer would be good. I think about a cold, frosty beverage in a chilled glass with beads of moisture slowly running down the side. I think about the white foamy head, and I can see the fizz floating up from the bottom. I can feel the tiny bubbles breaking against my face as I hold the glass to my cheek. I can almost taste the cold brew. I think that this is going to be tough. I think that I am going nuts.

I get checked in and have an hour to wait. I am as nervous as a long-tailed cat in a room full of rockers. With all of the seats in the airport, I sit right outside the bar. I stare through the door and watch the patrons. Other men successfully navigate through life without puking their guts out in the morning. Other men's wives don't move a thousand miles away. Other men don't end up in jail.

I want to have just one beer, but I realize that I can't have just one beer. I have a rude awakening. I am in trouble with my boss. I am in trouble with my best friend. I am in trouble with the law. I am in trouble with my wife. I am in trouble with my health. I am in trouble financially, and I am going crazy!

I grab my cell phone and call Maggie.

It's early afternoon in Colorado, and I catch my wife at home. "Hello."

"Hi Maggie," I say meekly. "I have just decided to give up drinking, and I would like to see you."

"I'd like to see you too, Jesse. Please call me after you have ninety days of sobriety." Then she quietly says, "Gotta go now." The phone is dead. Maggie is the only woman who can pull my chain.

Saying "Fuck it" and going to the bar would be the logical thing to do. Drinking is what I do best!

But, today, I put off the decision to have a drink for fifteen minutes. Instead of a beer, I get away from the bar and grab a coffee. This time I go and sit at the gate. As soon as the plane takes off, I go back to sleep. As we change planes in Chicago, I drink more coffee and order something to eat.

On the next leg of the journey, the plane is almost empty. I realize how exhausted I am. I fall into a deep, hypnotic sleep, and a gorgeous flight attendant who seems bored wakes me to take my drink order. Her hand is on my shoulder. In my haze I order a Jack Daniels, and then, just as quickly, cancel the order. She just looks at me and smiles. She bends over and moves her arm around my neck. I can smell her perfume, and I can feel her warm breath. Her breast is touching my arm. She whispers in my ear. "If you are a little short of cash, this one is on me."

I am a people pleaser; I don't want to disappoint her.

"No thanks," I say and fall back to sleep.

When I get to Manchester, I go straight to the hotel and crash. The physical withdrawals haven't started yet, but the emotional seesaw is in full swing. The best place for me to be is locked in my room without a bottle.

Sleep is non-existent. This will be just like other times that I have given up booze. I will go through days of being exhausted followed by sleepless nights. My body will go through the classic *delirium tremens* just like before. The definition of insanity is doing the same thing over and over, expecting different results. Am I expecting a different outcome this time, without making changes? I know that if nothing changes, nothing changes. What can I change? I can change this moment. They say that it's one day at a time, but for me, it's one decision at a time.

When I get my wake up call, I am in shock. I know that I slept a bit, but mostly I remember the clock flashing big, fluorescent numbers. I saw one-something, two-something, three-something. I am burned out and confused. I am shaky, but I remind myself that this is much better than coughing up blood.

It's been thirty hours without a drink. Today is one of the few times in over a year that I wake up without a hangover. Even without the booze, I am exhausted. Getting out of bed is an exercise in sheer determination.

Today, I have to do my job. I need to get some information on the three murder victims. Before I leave my hotel room, I call the AA hotline number that's listed in the phone book. I need to get a meeting schedule. Many alcoholics who have given up the drink volunteer to answer the calls. They are prepared to talk with someone who is at the end of his rope. I am that person. I am given directions to a meeting at noon. The guy on the hotline ends our conversation by saying, "Keep coming back!"

# 59

MY FIRST STOP AT SAINT ANSELM College is the Alumni office. The lovable lady in attendance reminds me of everyone's favorite grandma. She has all the comforts of home. She has an extra wide lap to sit on, a large bosom to rest your head on, and a smile as big as all outdoors. Her name is Marina and she volunteers her life story. I am not the least bit interested, but I know that she can help me, so I listen. She tells me that she graduated from Saint Anselm twenty-one years ago. She goes on to say that she fell madly in love with her sociology professor. He was fifteen years older than she, but they got married. Her parents objected, but now her parents have moved in with them. They have three kids. She has given up her dream of being a journalist, and instead helps find missing friends and classmates.

She finally smiles and says, "How may I help you?"

I start by asking for information about the three ex-students. I give her the names and show her some pictures. I purposely did not tell this story when I made the appointment. I didn't want reporters camping out at the college. Marina says they cannot give information to strangers, and asks what my interest is in these three men.

I show Marina my identification and tell her that these three ex-students have all been murdered. Her eyes open wide and I think she may have gone into shock. Her complexion becomes pasty, and her forehead becomes glossy. There is no conversation, and she just she stares at me.

Slowly, she comes out of it and adopts my sense of urgency. We start with the only one of the three victims who graduated from the college. She works the yearbooks and the files and finds Tommy Button, who spent his last minutes alive in a Model A Ford in Provincetown, Mass.

Marina thinks that she remembers Tommy, but something is eating at her. Some memory is just out of reach. Her eyes are darting back and forth. She is far, far away. She stares at the wall behind me, and I finally turn around to see if there is a picture.

She bites her lower lip, and something clicks. Her eyes snap open as if she just woke up from a bad dream. She picks up her phone and mumbles something inaudible. Then, without saying a word, she leaves the office. I think she is going to cry. She is obviously becoming caught up in my crisis. Good.

The coffee pot in her outer office is full, and I help myself. I know that in the weeks and months to come, I will substitute a lot of coffee for my alcoholic drug of choice. I finish the first cup and start on a second.

Marina returns to the office with another woman of about the same age. I am introduced to Margaret Lansdowne, one of the teachers at the college. Margaret is a large woman with a receding hairline and a fine, gray mustache that should be trimmed. She has that northern comfort look. She has given up on Revlon, Clairol, and Jenny.

Fortunately, Margaret wants to talk about Tommy Button.

"I heard that Tommy was murdered," she says, clutching a tissue. "It was on the news. Tommy would never hurt anyone. Why would someone want to hurt him?" She stared straight ahead and tried to hold back the tears.

"Tommy and I were friends, and we graduated together. We were very close," she says.

She and Tommy met in the glee club. When she looks at the picture in the yearbook, she becomes pale. There are tears in her eyes, and her voice starts to quiver.

She slowly shakes her head and starts to reminisce. She is talking half to me and half to herself.

"Tommy was my best friend," she mumbles. "We had many of the same classes, and we worked on assignments together. I had a lot of free time, and Tommy did, too. We started to share our stories. We opened up to each other. We talked about life, and school, and our goals. We would sit in the cafeteria and talk for hours."

"Did he have a girlfriend?" I ask.

"Yes. For about a year," she said. "She was a blonde bimbo. Very attractive, but she was no good for Tommy. She wouldn't leave him alone, but Tommy and I still had coffee every day. I remember when he broke up with her, too. It was a very hard time for him, and he needed a friend. I think I was the only one in the whole school who knew the reason they separated. I was the only one who knew what he was going through. I was the only one who knew how much he was hurting. That girl... oh, what was her name? She was devastated. She didn't go to school here. I think she worked in town. I don't know. But she was very immature. Attractive, but she acted like a spoiled crybaby, if you ask me.

"Poor Tommy was becoming so unstable," she continues. "He was unsure of his identity, and having an awful time. He kept to himself more and more, and he was going through so many changes. He dropped out of the glee club and even gave up working on the school paper. And he certainly didn't do sports. I think that after he broke up with … what's-her-name, the other guys started to pick on him. He was kind of effeminate. I shared every ounce of his pain."

"Margaret," I finally said. "What were the changes that Tommy was going through?"

"Oh, I don't think that I can tell you, that. It was so personal."

I look at her, head on. "Margaret, Tommy is dead! Two other Saint Anselm students are dead. Maybe you can help me understand a little about him. It might help us find out who did this terrible thing to your friend."

A long silence followed. Then Margaret started to sob.

"If you put it that way," she choked, "I'll tell you. At the end of Tommy's sophomore year, he decided that he didn't want to date girls anymore. Tommy stopped fighting with himself and accepted the fact that he was gay."

Margaret gave me this piece of news very slowly, as if it would shock me, but I already know the story.

"Can you please try to remember his girlfriend's name?"

"I'm trying, but it's not coming to me," Margaret says. "I do remember that there was something very different about her. She had some unusual mannerism or was a little out of the ordinary. Also, I remember thinking, way back then, how possessive she was. Tommy said that she was obsessive and compulsive. I thought that she was nuts!"

The clock on the wall says it's eleven-thirty. I need to get to the AA meeting, so I say goodbye to the ladies. I ask Margaret to try to remember the girlfriend's name. Also, I ask Marina to start looking up some information on Woody Winters and Blake Vanderbeek.

"I'll be back," I say, as I quickly walk out of the door.

# 60

THE AA MEETING IN THIS STARK, church basement starts promptly at noon. The metal folding chairs are cold and uncomfortable. Some have been stenciled with the name of the church, but most of the lettering has worn off. A few of them still say Saint something-or-other. The overhead fluorescent lights are too bright, making me squint. Styrofoam cups are stacked up next to an ancient coffee maker. The paper sign says, "Hot Water Only." I have my choice of Folgers, Sanka, or Lipton. The store-bought cookies are already gone.

I look around the room at the fifteen or twenty people sitting here, and try to find someone like me. I am trying to identify, not compare. This is hard for me to do.

Some of the people here are eating lunch. They are talking with their hands and laughing. A woman in her fifties is knitting. Most are drinking coffee. They look well-dressed, clean, and happy. They seem to have peace.

The speaker at this meeting starts talking to the group, but he is looking directly at me.

"Hi, My name is Billy, and I am an alcoholic."

"Hi Billy!"

"When I got to Alcoholics Anonymous, I didn't want to give up drinking. I wanted to control my drinking. I wanted to have a cold beer on a hot summer afternoon, I wanted to have a glass of wine with dinner. I wanted to go to a club and have a drink. I tried to do these things thousands of times. But most of the time, I failed. When I have one of something, I need to have another. That's the way it is for me. If I have the first drink, I cannot predict how many drinks I will have, how long I will drink, or where I will end up. Many times, the place that I ended up was in jail.

"One day, I made a decision. I decided to give up drinking. Since I have gotten sober, a lot of changes have taken place.

"My wife doesn't throw ashtrays at me anymore. My kids don't cringe when I come home from work. And I know where my car is.

"I am happy to be sober, today."

Then without any warning, he looks at me and says, "We have a new member here, today. Would you like to share?"

How did he know I was a newcomer? I am on the spot, but I talk. The words flow from deep inside of me. "Hi. My name is Jesse, and I think I may be an alcoholic."

"Hi Jesse," everyone shouts.

"Two nights ago, I ended up in jail. I called a friend in the middle of the night and asked him to throw my bail. I hope that I have hit my bottom. The only way that I can be sure that it's my bottom is to stop digging.

"Drinking for me was like Halloween. I could wear a different mask every day. I could be anyone that I wanted to be. If I was pumped up, booze would calm me down. If I was down, booze would pump me up. If I was alone, booze made me fit in. If I was trapped, booze helped me escape.

"At some point, booze stopped working. I keep trying to find the old feelings, but they are gone. Now, when I drink, I make bad decisions. When I drink, I keep digging my hole.

"I am tired and sick. I am full of fear. I am scared. I am alone. You guys in AA tell me to do this one day at time. I haven't had a drink for the last thirty hours. I'm glad that I am here, and I am glad that you are all here, too." I manage to smile at them.

I don't know one person in the whole room, but after the meeting strangers come forward and offer hope. We all stand in the church basement and talk. Even though I drink two more cups of coffee, I can barely keep my eyes open.

I drag myself to the car and drive back to the motel. On the way, there is a detour and I am brought back to reality by flashing lights. Three police cars are involved in some kind of disaster.

An overweight cop is leaning against a black king cab pickup that is parked diagonally across the road. He waives me on. He is very businesslike but will not share the details.

I follow the detour signs and stop at a mini mart on the way. The young cashier is more than obliging. She is getting good at telling the story. "A drunk driver nailed two high school kids and they were both killed. They just arrested the driver," she says with a gleam in her eye.

When I get to the motel, I decide to take a ten-minute nap, but sleep for three hours. It is now too late to go back to Saint Anselm College.

I call Fig. "I'm sorry that you had to rescue me from jail," I say.

I tell him I have given up booze, but there is no comment. He's heard it all before. Then I relate everything I have found out about Tommy Button and his obsessive, blonde girlfriend. I tell him that she was different in some way. Fig is still mad and doesn't say much before ending the call.

The next morning, I go back to the alumni office. Margaret has been expecting me.

"I don't remember who the blonde was," she says, right off the bat. "But yesterday, I told you that after she stopped seeing Tommy, she started dating someone else."

"I remember you saying that," I reply.

"After you left the building, I looked at the yearbook. One of the pictures is of a student who also dated the blonde. It was Blake Vanderbeek. I remember him so well. Everyone remembers Blake! He came into our community like a roller coaster. He was bigger than life! He was tall, handsome, rich, sure of himself, full of mischief, and very, very popular. Every girl wanted to date him. I bet that he slept with twenty girls in the short time that he was here. Hearts were broken, all over campus.

I also remembered something else," Margaret says. I slowly turn so that I am facing her, head on.

"I remember what was different about the blonde. The thing is that she couldn't hear. I guess that she could lip read from a mile away, but she couldn't hear a sound. The blonde girl was deaf!"

# 61

It was late at night, but the lights of Yankee Electric Supply were still on. The radio was on, too. Rusty's wife had gone to bed hours ago, but he couldn't sleep. Instead, he got up and went to his office. For the past hour, he had been re-reading old messages from Kiki.

Rusty stood and stretched. He walked to the office window. The quarter moon was partially blocked by quickly moving clouds. The melody from the wind chimes was increasing in tempo, and it felt like a storm was moving in. Rusty's thoughts were restless, too. He couldn't stop thinking about his old lover. Even though he had only seen her for a minute, she had been on his mind constantly. He felt like a horny schoolboy.

He wanted to send Kiki a note, and he'd rewritten the message a dozen times. He wanted it to sound upbeat and caring. He wanted it to sound cool. Then, he wondered why he needed to send a note at all. Rusty was having an emotional fur ball. He was trying to cough up some reason to steer clear of her, but it wasn't working.

He sat down and wrote the message one more time.

Date: Sept 16
From: Rusty@Yankeeelectricservice.com

To: Kiki222@hotmail.com
Subject: Great to see you!

Hi Kiki,

God, it was so great to see you again after all of these years. You look fabulous. How come I am getting older and you keep getting younger? It must be that New Jersey weather!

I am so sorry that I couldn't spend time with you. The woman in the restaurant was my mother-in-law. You suggested we meet in a place where I wouldn't be recognized, but I really screwed that up, didn't I? What a shock. Anyway, I hope that your trip to New Hampshire was successful. My business is going well, and life is good. Will you be coming up this way again? If we get together again, I promise we will not run into any of my friends, employees, or in-laws.

Kiki, I would love to see you one more time before I die!

Love,
Rusty

# 62

KIKI READ RUSTY'S EMAIL AND BROKE out laughing. Rusty said he wanted to see her one more time before he died. He must be a mind reader.

After scrubbing her face and taking the polish off her nails, she fell into the most wonderful sleep that she had had in years.

When Kiki awoke, she gazed out of her patio window and compared last night's deep rest to her endless nights of turmoil. She had not slept so soundly in years. This morning, she felt like a new person. She slowly slid her legs out from under the covers and sat on the edge of bed. After dangling her feet, she sauntered to the bathroom. She used the facilities and thoroughly flossed her teeth. She took her hairbrush and walked to the window while she brushed one hundred strokes, just like her mother had told her to do, so many years ago. She stepped out of her PJs and pulled on a red tank top and a loose pair of running shorts.

Kiki stood in front of her full-length mirrors and marveled at her new glow.

She decided to take up yoga again. She hadn't done this in years. Yoga would help maintain her level of peace. She went right into Sun Salutations. Stretch to the ceiling, fold, lift your head halfway up, fold like a rag doll, pushup pose, king cobra, downward dog. She went through twelve repetitions, six on each side. Then she lay on her back and stretched her legs. Finally, she did a few gentle kidney rolls. She was totally rejuvenated.

After her shower, she realized that things had been slowly changing for the better. Her outlook was brighter, her mood was more upbeat, and her smile was returning. A few people at work had mentioned how good she looked. "Healthy" was the word one girl had used to describe her new glow. Someone had asked what she was doing to make herself so positive. She wished she could tell them. After each horrible man had been eliminated from her life, Kiki had tried to describe her feelings in her journal. There was a brief release from pain. There was a short period of time when she could totally relax.

She made a fresh pot of coffee and filled her cup to the brim. She took her journal out of the desk drawer and went out to the patio. She wrote:

## Date: September 16

*During the last twenty years, I have been saddled with feelings of guilt, humiliation, and revenge. I have been living under a mushroom cloud of hate and embarrassment.*

*Today, I feel a hundred pounds lighter. Now the fog is starting to lift, and the sun is shining in. I no longer need to obsess about Blake, Woody, or Tommy. What a blessing.*

*When I saw Rusty for that brief moment in Manchester, I was all aflutter. My heart was pounding so rapidly I thought it might set off the pistol in my bra. I really wanted to talk with Rusty. I wanted to suggest that we get back together. And if he didn't see things my way, I would end the humiliation and shame once and for all. I was prepared to take action. I couldn't accept the situation, and I couldn't leave the situation. So I had to change the situation with Rusty, just like I did with the others. Rusty was different, though. He had mellowed. He was a little wider in the hips and a little balder on top, but he was definitely the same Rusty I fell in love with twenty years ago. He looked confident, and he walked with a spring in his step.*

*I must admit I was very disappointed when his mother-in-law spoiled the whole meeting. If it hadn't been for that old bat, my mission would finally be over. One way or another.*

*I got an email from him today, and I was thrilled. He was trying to play it cool. He was trying to act as if it didn't matter if we got together or not, but I knew that he wanted to see me. Maybe he wants to have me back in his life. We would make such a wonderful couple. Of course, he would have visitation rights to see his kids, but I would be a perfect stepmother to the children, and we would all have fun together. I would be a good friend to his kids.*

Kiki became excited about the possibilities. What a perfect ending for her life. To be with the man she loved and his beautiful children. They could call her Mom, if they wanted, but they would probably just call her Kiki. It would be a dream come true.

She looked at Rusty's email and laughed again. She continued her writing:

*I would like to spend the rest of my life with Rusty, but if he doesn't take me back, I will complete my mission. I will finally live a normal life. I will get rid of the bad memories and feelings, and I will get rid of the gun. I will get rid of the shoe box. I think I will wait a few weeks before I reply to him. He deserves to sweat.*

# 63

RUSTY SPENT A LOT OF TIME checking his email. He had two thoughts: he was anxious to hear from her, and he hoped he never heard from her again.

Date: Oct 9
From: Kiki222@hotmail.com
To: Rusty@Yankeeelectricservice.com
Subject: Hi again.

Hey Rusty,

Thanks for your message a while ago. I was sorry we couldn't spend some time together, but I understand. Things happen.

As it turns out, I do have to come back to Manchester on business.

Probably in a few weeks. Would you like to try to get together again?

Love,
Kiki.

Rusty was on cloud nine. He let his mind wander. He thought

about how good she had looked. He could see her tiny waist and her dazzling, pearly white teeth, and he let himself think about how good she was in the sack. As the bulge in his pants started to grow, he decided right then and there to see her. Where could they meet without being caught?

He didn't want to be bold, but he decided to suggest a hotel right at the Manchester airport. He would get a room at the Highlander, and they would be alone. They would order a meal from room service, and no one would ever see them together.

He spent an hour on an email. It had to sound upbeat and funny. He wanted to make sure she would see him. He laid out his plan and asked her to tell him when she would be coming back. After rereading the message six times, he hit the send button.

# 64

I HAVE A FEW DAYS OF sobriety under my belt, but I am going nuts. Little things are hitting me broadside. When I reserved this motel room I only considered one factor: price. Now that I am here, I know why it was inexpensive. It's drafty, dirty, dingy, and dumpy. Tonight, after unlocking the door, I walk into a mess. My room looks worse than it did this morning. The bed is unmade, there are towels on the floor, and the waste can is overflowing with leftover take-out food. I pick up the phone and punch "0".

"Front desk."

"Hi. This is Jesse Collins in 134. My room wasn't cleaned today."

"Oh, I'm sorry, Mr. Collins. The maid must have forgotten. I'll talk with her tomorrow."

"My room is a mess. Could you send someone down to clean it?"

"I am the only one here. I can't possibly leave the front desk. I'll take two dollars off your bill."

"I'm out of towels!"

"Come down here, and I'll give you some clean towels. I have another call coming in." Click.

My thoughts start to fester. Could this filthy room be jeopardizing my sobriety? If I go back to drinking again, it won't be over something big; it will be over something as stupid as wet towels.

Not only is my room a dump, but the service sucks, too. I've been in this motel for a week, and it seems like a month. The mattress is lumpy, the carpet is filthy, and the twenty-five-watt bulbs make reading impossible. The room smells like stale cigar smoke and Lysol.

After I get clean towels, I turn on the TV and rotate among the same eight channels for an hour. There are two stations showing old sitcoms, three programs for kids, two religious channels, and one home shopping network that sells exercise equipment. I grab the TV remote and jam my fist against the power button. The room is silent.

I take yesterday's newspaper out of the trash and try to read it again. There's nothing left. I stare at the cheap picture hanging over the bed. The abstract collage of black lines on a blue background in a cheap, maple frame looks tackier every time I see it. A first grader could do better. I am getting jittery and start to think about drinking.

I had planned to go out for a nice dinner tonight, but I don't feel strong enough to sit in a restaurant that serves booze. I pace back and forth in my little room. I am a prisoner in my own world. As I walk, I start talking to myself out loud.

"I can afford a steak," I say. "Why don't I just leave the room?" As usual, there are too many temptations and not enough willpower to go around.

It's now 7pm, and I still haven't eaten. My blood sugar is shot. It's no wonder I am going nuts. To fight off the dizziness, I get my box of Fruit Loops out of the bottom drawer. I take the filthy bowl out of the bathroom sink, rinse it out, and pour in the cereal. The ice cubes that were in the Styrofoam cooler have melted, and the milk has gone sour. I pour it on the cereal, anyway. I start to gag and dump the whole mess down the toilet.

"What is the problem?" I say out loud.

"I can go to a restaurant and order dinner like a normal person. I don't have to have a drink! And if I do have a drink, who the fuck cares? I'm a grown man! I can do this! I just need to practice control, like other people. I can have one damn drink! I can even have a few drinks, if I want." I say it out loud again, just to see how it sounds.

I think this through. I could certainly go to a bar and order just one Jack Daniels. Just one. That's it. There is no need to drink the whole damn bottle. I have as much self-control as the next guy. I can drink in moderation. I've done it before, but I don't remember when.

"Moderation!" I say out loud. "Moderation is the key!"

I flop on the unmade bed. My resolve to stay sober fades. Was my drinking as bad as people would have me believe?

"Sure, I've been thrown out of a few bars, but that's not a problem. I just chalk that up to having too much to drink on that particular night. I spent a night in jail, but that happens to thousands of people each year. So what's the big deal?"

I feel like there is a devil on one shoulder and an angel on the other shoulder. They are yelling at each other, and my head is in the middle. I think my brain might explode.

"Go get a God-damned drink, you pussy," yells the devil.

"Don't do it," yells the angel. "You'll be sorry."

I get up and walk to the bathroom. My head is spinning. I change my mind eight times while I brush my teeth. I am uncomfortable and uncertain. I am having trouble deciding what is real and what is bogus.

I have to get out of this room. I have to get out of myself. I remember seeing a neighborhood tavern four blocks away and decide to go for a walk.

"That's it," I say to no one. "I'll just get out into the fresh, night air, take a walk, and have a coke."

I promise myself that I won't drink. I will sit at the bar, but I will only have a soda. It's a great plan. I leave my room and start walking like a man with a purpose.

# 65

On the way to the tavern, I see a small neon sign flickering down a side street. It reads All Night Diner and I realize how very hungry I am. I decide that food may temper my mood swings and calm my insanity. At least this diner won't be serving martinis.

As I near the entrance, I look in the kitchen window. The cook is stirring a large aluminum stockpot with a wooden stick. The contents are boiling over the edge and running down the side into the flames of the gas-fired cook stove. Smoke is everywhere. The cook is oblivious to the fumes. The ashes from his cigarette bounce off his huge stomach and fall into the stew.

An exhaust fan had been installed to remove the fumes, but it is undersized and can't do the job. The small blades can't move all of the grease, and some of it congeals as it hits the cool night air. As the lard runs down the side of the old, brick building, it thickens and creates a black, lumpy goop. The grease forms a slimy slab that's eight inches wide and three inches thick. It's never been scraped from the wall and I wonder if this is what my insides look like after a lifetime of fries? Some of the grease has actually dripped to the ground and formed a pile that is rising back up to meet the fan. I briefly wonder if this is called a stalactite or a stalagmite.

Police have a saying about restaurants. The blacker the grease, the better the burger. I walk in the front door. The light bulb hanging from the ceiling by a bare cord is too bright. It shines on a cork-board with business cards, notices, and hand-written signs. Some are brown and dog-eared. Most have been there for years.

I climb on to a counter stool and order a double burger, extra fries, and two pieces of cardboard coconut cream pie.

"Bring it all at once," I tell the grandmother behind the counter.

I look in the mirror behind the counter and stare at the man sitting next to me. He is wearing a faded blue work shirt with a name embroidered on the pocket, but in the mirror his name is backwards. I say the letters backwards to myself: yrneH

Henry is about thirty, with short, uneven hair, a day-old growth of stubble, and big, dirty, callused hands. He is staring into a half cup of black coffee. Paper sugar packets are lying next to his cup, and the napkin has many coffee rings. He has been here for a long time, and his head is shaking from left to right. I hear him quietly weeping.

"Are you OK?" I ask.

He chokes, and all of a sudden I am sorry I asked.

"No, no, no, I'm not OK, and I don't know what to do, 'cause she said don't come home no more, and locked the door, and she is mad, but I only stopped for one beer, and why is she so mad?" His head shakes again.

He is almost whispering, but unfortunately I can hear every word.

"I want to see my babies but can't go home, 'cause she kicked me out and said don't never come here no more, but I ain't got no idea why she is mad, and why the babies were crying, and why she was yelling so loud at me to get out, and she says she don't want nothing to do with me, ever, and don't never call her, ever again, and she was screaming, and the neighbors woke up."

I try to back out of this conversation. I sit quietly, hoping that it is over.

"She said that I am a pig, and not a good husband to her, but I ain't no pig, just 'cause I threw up. She yelled at me when the dog started to eat the throw-up off the floor. It's not my fault, 'cause I'm sick, and she said she hates my guts and pushes me out into the dooryard, and my dog was barking and growling at me. My dog!"

We are looking at each other's reflections in the mirror, and then he spins on his stool and stares straight at me. There is a gash from a fresh wound on his cheek. His eyes are bloodshot, and tears are slowly running down his face. This big, burly man is sitting in a public restaurant crying. He just stares at me as if I have the answer. The silence is deafening, but I have heard too much already.

I look around for my burger, but Henry keeps talking.

"She said I drink too much, just like her father, but I ain't as bad as her father, and I don't beat her, and I only had one beer, or two, but she thinks that I'm an animal when I drink, and she yells at me to stop the yelling, but I ain't yelling; she is yelling."

I waive to the waitress. "Miss, can you hurry my burger along?"

"She says I do this all the time, but I don't do this all the time, just last night, 'cause I was tired from working, and she said don't come back no more."

He comes up for air, and I hope he is finished.

"I want to see my babies." He looks at me, and his head slowly drops down. He starts crying again.

I said three words to this man and he has replied with the world's longest sentence. He is spilling his guts. We are now sharing a one-sided conversation. He starts mumbling again, and I cringe.

"She says it's midnight, but how can it be midnight if I only stopped for two beers. Or maybe three beers. I don't know. When I got home, all the lights were on, so it couldn't be too late, and, when I got out of my truck, I slipped, and she thought I was drunk, but I'm not drunk, and she threw the ash tray, and it hurt my face, and she yelled at me to stop bleeding on the floor. Then I threw up, 'cause she hit me. She pushed me out of the house, and the babies were crying, because their mother was yelling, and she slammed the door, and then she opened the door again and kicked my dog out. My dog! He was barking at me, and I tried to sleep in the truck but couldn't sleep, 'cause the dog was barking, and the neighbors were yelling. Why were the neighbors yelling?"

He gasps for air and takes a gigantic breath.

I feel sorry for this man; he needs to tell his story.

I feel sorry for me; I need to listen to his story.

My burger is delivered, and I gobble.

In between bites I ask, "How often does this happen?"

"Few times, not too much, sometimes, but I go to work every day, and not like her father who lost his job."

"Would you like to go to an AA meeting with me tonight?"

"AA? You mean a meeting for al-co-hol-ics? Like her father who beats his wife? I ain't like him. I ain't no pig. I ain't no jerk who comes home drunk. All the time. I ain't no al-co-hol-ic."

I pay my check and rush out of the diner.

# 66

Instead of going to a bar, I make a beeline to my motel. I call the AA hotline and ask directions to a meeting. I race out the door and find the church basement just as everyone is settling in.

The meeting is in a black recovery center, and I am the only white man within miles. Someone shouts from the front of the room and says, "Hey, Whitey. There's a seat down here."

The meeting is good, and it gets me out of myself. I find peace and the strength to stay away from a drink for the next twenty-four hours.

After the meeting, I take a long drive back to my motel. I am calm. I had been thinking about drinking, but another man's story changed my plan. I couldn't help him, but I helped myself. When I get to my room, I go straight to bed and sleep soundly.

I wake up at 6am feeling rested and look out my motel window. I have been in New Hampshire for several days, and this is the first time that I notice the foliage. It's early for the leaves to start turning, and the colors are beautiful. Bright maples are turning red. Oaks are turning yellow. I think about New Hampshire weather. The air is crisp and clear. Today the temperature is perfect.

Later in the day, I talk with Fig.

"I have some information about this Kiki girl."

"Shoot."

"There is a reason that there were no phone messages on answering machines, and no calls from her on telephone reports. She was not using the phone to communicate, and now we know the reason why."

"What's that?'

"Kiki is deaf."

# 67

KIKI TOOK CASH OUT OF HER backpack and laid it on the bed with her clothes. She spent time putting her outfit together. A short, tan skirt, a black tank top and a black sports jacket. Black, spike high heels to match. She added the yellow scarf to complete the picture. She looked in the mirror and approved. What a great outfit. *Rusty will love it,* she thought. After she put her outfit together, she spent an hour on her hair. Every curl was perfect.

When she got to Newark airport, she checked her car into long-term parking and jumped on the shuttle for the terminal. She boarded the 737 for the 4pm takeoff to Manchester. An hour later, the plane was still at the gate. She flagged down the flight attendant and asked why there was a delay.

"There is a problem with the navigation system," she was told. "We might have to go back to the gate for repair, but right now we will sit here while maintenance tries to fix the problem."

To pass time, she angrily thumbed through a travel magazine that had been left in the seat-back compartment. As she absentmindedly flipped from page to page, her eyes stopped at a full-page ad showing a happy couple on a beautiful, white, sandy beach.

The ad suggested that she visit Aruba, the place for lovers. The man and woman in the picture were running along the edge of the beach. Water was splashing under their feet. They were healthy, trim, and tan. In these types of ads, the man was always in his forties with salt and pepper hair. He looked like a successful executive. The woman was always twenty years younger, gorgeous, and in a bikini. No fat, no gray hair, and no wrinkles.

Kiki wondered what happened to the executive's wife. Is she stuck at home with the kids while the husband is playing on the beach with his secretary?

*Men are such bastards!*

At 7pm, Kiki was still sitting on the plane. People near her were talking, but she couldn't hear the announcement. She asked the elderly lady in the next seat what was happening.

"We have to sit on the plane for a little while longer," the gray haired lady said. Kiki realized that even if the flight did go to Manchester, she would be hours late for her date with Rusty. And the FedEx office would be closed.

# 68

I FINALLY FINISH MY INTERVIEWS AT Saint Anselm College. My original theory was that someone had a grudge against old acquaintances, and my hunch was right. The blonde was settling her differences by eliminating old boyfriends, one by one. I spent days interviewing people who worked in the school and people who lived in the town at that time. I have been looking for a deaf girl who may have lived there. I have been looking for a needle in a haystack. But a lot of things change in twenty years. The girl and the needle are both gone. My work in New Hampshire is done.

I call the Chief to report on my progress. "Not only did the three dead guys go to this school, but they also dated the blonde. It appears that the girl in question was a townie. She didn't attend that school, so there were no records on her, but I have interviewed people in town to try to find her."

"I'm getting nervous," he says. "It's been a while since the last killing, and I wonder if the Ball Buster is getting ready to pull the trigger again. I wonder if she has you in her sights. Maybe we should take you off this case."

"You can't do that, Chief. I've been working on this case for too long. I finally feel like I know the girl. I want to have Fig call all of the victim's relatives again and talk about girls they dated in college."

"I want you to finish up and get out of that town," the Chief says.

After I reserve a Saturday morning flight back to California, I check out of my sleazy, in-town motel and try to find a hotel that is closer to the airport. I look in the phone book and call The Highlander. The bubbly girl at the front desk tells me they just had a cancellation. I take the room.

I turn on to Route 93, southbound, and stomp the gas. I ramp up to eighty miles an hour and race to my new hotel room.

The Highlander is only a mile away from the Manchester airport, which means I should have no trouble catching my early morning flight. This hotel is in a different league than the Motel Six that I stayed in all week. The lobby fireplace is lit, and music is playing in the background. On the way through the lobby, I stop at the front desk and request a 5am wake-up call. I am confident that I will not drink tonight.

I take the elevator up to the room and crash. Even though I slept like a baby last night, I am still tried. I am more aware of my feelings, and I want to take care of myself. My friends in AA have told me that there are four situations that I should avoid: "Never get Hungry, Angry, Lonely, or Tired," they say. I am all four.

I sleep for hours and wake up at dinnertime. In the lobby, I look into the restaurant. I can sense that it's way out of my price range, but I don't want cold cereal. Tonight, I will have the biggest steak on the menu.

I walk into the restaurant and ask for a table.

"There will be a thirty-minute wait. I'll come and get you in the bar when your table is ready."

The lounge at the Highlander Hotel is noisy, smoky, and packed, but I find an empty stool. I don't plan to drink, but the booze smells wonderful. The guy next to me seems to be wired, wasted, or loaded.

He is working on a pack of matches and slowly splitting each match in half, one at a time. It also looks like he has been folding napkins into little squares. His ashtray is full. When the bartender comes by, I order O'Doul's.

"Well, are you ready for winter?" It's the wired guy asking.

"I sure am, I'm heading back to California," I say.

"What brings you out this way?"

"I'm a detective, working on a case."

"A California detective working a case in New Hampshire?"

"Yep. What brings you here?"

"I have a date with an old girlfriend. I haven't seen her in twenty years. Well, actually, I did see her a month ago, but my mother-in-law caught us, and I had to walk away. It was pretty nerve-racking. We are supposed to meet here tonight, but she is late. Really late. I wonder if she got held up, or if she changed her mind."

He is rambling so fast that I can't tell if he is drunk or nervous. I think that he is going to tell me his life story, whether I want to hear it or not.

"Late, huh? Wouldn't she call you?"

"Oh no. She couldn't call."

"So, you're meeting an old girlfriend from twenty years ago, huh?" I am trying to make conversation. "It must have taken a lot of balls to call her after all that time."

"Actually, she got in touch with me."

"Lucky guy! When you saw her after twenty years, how did she look?"

"Oh man. She looked great! Tiny little waist, white pearly teeth, short curly hair, and she's still a blonde. Well she's a blonde upstairs, but I have no idea what color her hair is downstairs." He laughs at his own joke and takes another swig of his drink.

Man, did she ever turn me on! I guess I'm a sick puppy, huh?"

"Well, if you are sick, then most of the male population is sick, too! Where did you meet her?"

"Right here in Manchester. I was working for my dad then. He's an electrician, and we wired the office where she worked." The man ordered a double CC and told the bartender to give me a drink, too. He stuck out his hand and introduced himself.

"I'm Rusty. "

"Hi Rusty. I'm Jesse. Thanks for the offer of the drink, but I just gave up the sauce, and I can't drink O'Doul's as fast as I used to drink Black Jack. I'll pass."

"Oh, I'm sorry about that! I heard that when you give up drinking, your pecker shrivels up. Is that true?"

"It couldn't get much smaller." We both laugh.

"Yeah, so anyway, when I met this chick, she had just broken up with a guy from the local college. Actually she asked me out the first time."

"What was she like, way back then? Did she like to party?"

"No, not that much."

"Did she like to dance?"

"No, not much."

"Well, for God's sake. What did she like? Oral sex?"

"Bingo."

"I'm beginning to see why you are so excited!"

A small hand rests on my shoulder.

"Your table is ready, sir."

The hostess stands very close to me as I get off my barstool. She is cute. I am glad to get away from the bar, but before I head to my table, I say goodbye to my new friend Rusty.

"Good luck finding out what color hair your girlfriend has downstairs."

"If there is any," Rusty laughs, as he downs his drink. The hostess looks at Rusty and then at me.

"Men!" she says.

She shakes her head and starts walking to the dining room. I follow her.

# 69

AT 8PM, KIKI'S PLANE HAD NOT moved. When the passengers started to deplane, the little old lady looked at Kiki and spoke slowly. "A repair part is being flown in, and it would take at least an hour for the work to be completed. The captain said that we could get off the plane and grab a snack."

Kiki's date with Rusty was a dead issue. Rusty was still alive, but the date was dead. She was undecided whether to wait another hour or to just go home. She sat down to look at her ticket. She was so lost in her thoughts that she didn't notice the tall, thin man approaching. He knelt down in front of her so that he was at eye level. He almost scared her half to death. He smiled and spoke very, very slowly.

"Excuse me," he said. "I hope you don't mind, but I was watching you while you were talking to the ticket agent. Were you lip reading?"

A little smile came to her face.

"Yes," she told him. "I am deaf. I have been lip reading since I was three years old."

"I am deaf, too," he said very slowly. "My name is Huff. Were you going to Manchester on a business trip?"

"Actually, I was going to see a friend," she said, "But now that the

242

trip is so late, I was thinking of just going home. I live in Asbury Park, and it's a long ride."

"What a coincidence," Huff said. "I live down the shore, too. I live in Point Pleasant, not too far from you. I was going up to Manchester to visit my sister for the weekend, but now I am going to have Deaf Contact let her know that I am stranded. I guess I'll just go up next weekend."

As the conversation continued, Kiki realized that she was talking with a very attractive gentleman who was about her age. Even though he was kneeling, she could tell that he was tall and thin. He was clean-shaven, and his dark hair was cut close. His blue eyes sparkled, and he smiled a lot. He had no wedding ring, so she assumed he was single. He asked her if he could sit down, and, when he did, their knees touched. It was like an electric spark. They talked about work, the weather, and their families. He said he lived alone and had never been married. Kiki told him that, after her mother had passed away, she bought a condo with the insurance money, and that she lived alone, too.

They seemed to have a lot in common, so they just continued talking. Neither of them wanted to end the conversation.

On a whim, Kiki asked Huff about his plans for the rest of the evening. He said that, now that his trip had been cancelled, he had no plans.

"There's a new restaurant in Sea Girt, right on the water," she said. "It's called the Lazy Lobster, and my friend from work said that it was great. Would you be interested in going there for a snack?" she asked. "It's right on the way home for both of us."

"I would love to go to the restaurant with you!" he said. He seemed genuinely happy to accept the offer.

They went to the payphone together. Huff used his portable TTY and made a call to Deaf Contact. As they walked to the parking lot, he offered to carry her suitcase. *What a nice man,* she thought.

"I'll follow you to the Lazy Lobster," Huff said, heading for his car. As they took off from the parking lot, her head was spinning. She was thinking about the evening ahead. She was also fantasizing about the possibility of a lasting relationship. Her date with Rusty was the furthest thing from her mind. The next morning, Kiki couldn't wait to write in her journal.

### *Date: October 11*

*I am exhausted, but I have never been so energized in my life! Last night, I met a wonderful gentleman at the airport. His name is Huff, and he is also deaf. I think we had a date, because we went to the Lazy Lobster together. The restaurant was packed, and I was secretly thrilled that we would have a long wait. We sat in the lounge and talked continuously. Even though we had to wait for over an hour, the time went by in a flash. After a few drinks, the hostess escorted us to the most romantic table in the restaurant. We settled into a window booth with a fabulous view of the harbor. Instead of sitting across from me, Huff asked if he could sit next to me. I could tell that the hostess was jealous.*

*There was a row of sailboats with spotlights shining up from the dock, and the masts were gently rocking back and forth. As we had dinner, we never stopped talking! When I realized that we were the last customers in the restaurant, I had to laugh. Huff laughed, too. Our waitress was young and looked very tired from a long night at a busy, new restaurant. She sat at a nearby table, waiting for us to leave.*

*Although we both knew we had to go, neither of us wanted to* be first to make the move. When the kitchen crew came out and started stacking chairs up on the tables all around us, Huff asked for the bill. The waitress looked so relieved. I wanted to split the tab, but he insisted on paying.

At 3am, we sat in Huff's car and talked for another hour. We had the dome light on so that we could read each other's lips. I wondered what other people thought we were doing. I couldn't believe how much we had to talk about. We talked about private school and training. We talked about the problems with our disability. We talked about our goals and fears. We talked about what we do for fun.

At 4am, a sliver of light started to peek over the horizon, and the night started to turn into early morning. Huff suggested coffee. We left my car at the restaurant, and he drove to the amusement pier in Seaside Heights. We parked at the south end of the boardwalk near the log flume and slowly walked north. As we started our journey up the boardwalk, he took my hand. My heart almost stopped.

I have lived on the Jersey shore for many years, and I love the salty mist from the ocean waves. I love the smell of creosote from the boardwalk. I love the colors of the concession stands, and I love the feeling of being in a relaxed atmosphere where most people are on vacation.

This morning, while holding Huff's hand, it all looked new. It was like the first time I had ever been at the beach.

I was surprised to see how many people were up at this hour. Two joggers passed us, and an older couple peddled by on rusty, old, beach cruisers. Their long, gray hair was blowing in the breeze. A few people were walking on the beach, and a man was scanning the sand with a metal detector.

A young girl was sitting alone on a bench. She was crying. I bet she had been up all night, and I wondered if a boyfriend had just dumped her. I could relate.

It was amazing how quickly the evening went by. Here it was, morning, and I was having one of the absolute best times in my life. We had been together for ten hours, and we never stopped talking. After a short, five-minute walk in the early morning light, we came to an all-night snack shop, and we ordered coffee to go. As we continued our journey, we both realized it was going to be a beautiful day. Every few blocks, we stopped to talk about something. A few times we laughed. We walked to the Heights pier and started back. It was now near 6am, and the first sun worshipers were starting to stake their claim for a spot on the beach. The beach badge booths were opening up along the boardwalk and a city employee was cleaning up the beach with a huge, gasoline-powered vacuum.

We found a bench facing the ocean and just sat holding hands. We had finally run out of conversation.

Huff broke the silence.

"Why don't you follow me back to my place?" he asked. I had been thinking about the same thing. I had my answer rehearsed.

"I would love to," I said, "but I have a lot to do today. Could I please have a rain check?" He looked disappointed but said OK. To let him know I cared, I reached over and kissed him. It started out as a friendship kiss, but slowly our mouths opened and *we allowed our tongues to explore. The kiss lasted a long time. Huff put his hand near my breast, and I was hoping he would touch me, but he didn't. My hand was on his lap, and I could tell he was excited.*

*As I drove home, the sun was streaming through my windshield. I thought about Huff's offer. I'd really wanted to go to his apartment, but I knew we would end up in his bed. The thought of sleeping with Huff made me tingle, but I had a huge reason for saying no. I really liked this man, and I didn't want him to think I was a slut.*

# 70

MY STEAK DINNER LAST NIGHT WAS satisfying, and I slept well. On my final morning in New Hampshire, I wake up without a hangover. After a quick shower, I take the shuttle from the Highlander Hotel to the Manchester airport and get to my gate with plenty of time to spare.

Once we take off, I order black coffee, settle in, and let my mind wander. I think about Maggie. I think about work, and I think about the case.

I also think about Rusty; the guy I met last night in the bar. I'm wondering what color hair his girlfriend had downstairs. I am wondering if he got laid. What a riot. I sit quietly as I replay the conversation with Rusty. The facts start to slowly whirl in my mind. Something is wrong. My mind starts racing. My head starts pounding. *She got in touch with him.* His old girlfriend got in touch with him. *Oh my God!*

*What the hell was I thinking?* I bolt upright so quickly that I knock the coffee out of my neighbor's hand. *Oh my God.* Rusty said she couldn't call. She worked in an office in Manchester twenty years ago. She had dated a guy from a local college. She's a blonde with short curly hair. *Oh my God.*

I pick up the GTE Airphone and place a call.

"Highlander Hotel, how may I help you?"

"There might be a man staying there whose name is Rusty, and he is in serious danger."

The operator just listens.

"I have to find out what room he is in. It may be a matter of life and death."

"Sir, there is no way that I could find someone by their first name. And if I could, that information would be confidential. I cannot tell you what room he would be in.

"I'm a detective, and this is urgent."

"Sir, to see my records, you will need a search warrant."

I say "Fuck," and hang up. Every single person near me is staring. I call Fig and explain the situation on his voice mail. It's still only 6am in California. I ask Fig to call the police department in Manchester, New Hampshire, and have them get to the hotel, pronto.

My years of drinking have dulled my mind. I am devastated. The clues were right in front of me, and I didn't see them. I am definitely not fit for this job. I should resign.

When the flight attendant comes down the aisle, I order two nips of vodka. "Just to calm me down," I say to myself. I get a glass of ice and a twist of lemon. I open the nips and pour them into the glass. I stare. My mind is twitching as if two thousand volts of electricity were passing through me. I watch the ice melt. It takes forever. The temptation to drink is overpowering. I wonder why I torture myself. When the ice is completely melted, I carry the glass with the booze and the empty bottles to the men's room. I put the empty nips in the trash, and pour the vodka down the drain. I get on my knees in the tiny men's room and look all the way up.

"Thank you" is all I can say.

Five hours later, Fig meets me at the airport. I am feeble and in shock. I am pissed at myself for letting this opportunity pass through my fingers. Fig has already talked with the police in New Hampshire. They went to the Highlander Hotel, and there was no one named Rusty registered.

We head straight to the station.

I wonder if Rusty is dead.

# 71

As the weeks went by, Rusty continuously checked his inbox. There was nothing at all from Kiki.

He wondered where Kiki was.

# 72

KIKI WAS IN HEAVEN. SHE WAS in love. Huff was working late, and Kiki went to her own apartment. She thought about her new relationship and how much it had changed her outlook. She had never been happier in her life.

After pouring herself a glass of wine, she lit a candle on her desk and decided to journal. It would be nice to write about positive events for a change. She relaxed and started to put her thoughts on paper.

### Date: October 25

*Am I truly in love? Is this the feeling I have read about in every woman's magazine since I was twelve? Is this the feeling that I have been seeking for an eternity? If this is a dream, I hope I never wake up.*

*I cannot see enough of Huff! The last four weeks have been wonderful. It has been the most exciting time of my life. We live an hour away from each other, but we email each other ten times a day. We have been together four or five times a week. He is so attentive and gentle. He is so handsome. He is thoughtful. Most of all, I believe he really cares for me. I am so fortunate to have him in my life. I feel differently about him than any man I have ever known. Huff and I have a wonderful relationship. We have so much in common. I would do anything for him, and I think he would do anything for me.*

*For most of my life, I have had trouble with relationships. People just didn't understand me. Most of my female acquaintances were fair-weather friends who would only include me when it was convenient. Others just stopped returning my calls. And what about MEN!? They have used me, abused me, and then they would dump me. A guy once told me about the "Four F Club." Find 'em, feel 'em, fuck 'em, and forget 'em. That was how I have always been treated.*

*I have tried to be a good friend, but my therapists have described me as needy, insecure, resentful, and unhappy. They have said that I take everything personally and I assume way too much.*

*One therapist sent me home with an assignment. He asked me to write an emotional description of myself. I will never forget the look on his face when I came back and read my self-evaluation.*

*"I am full of jealously, pride, selfishness, lust, doubt, insecurity, fear, and rage. I am oversensitive, immature, self-centered, and delusional. I am an egomaniac with a low self-image. Sometimes I wonder what meaningless, self-inflicted trauma I will put myself through, today."*

*I was hoping he would disagree with me, but he just smiled and told me I did a good job.*

*The harder I have tried to attract people, the more I have pushed people away.*

*But Huff is different. Huff understands me. He is supportive and caring. For most of my adult life, I have heard people say they were looking for a 50-50 relationship, but I never knew what they meant. Now I know. Huff and I are both working at this relationship. I am truly in love with Huff!*

*I have been with many, many men, but with Huff things are different. With Huff, there is a chance for long-term happiness. With Huff, there is love.*

# 73

IT HAD BEEN A FAIRYTALE EVENING. Huff and Kiki went back to their favorite restaurant, the Lazy Lobster. They had the best table and the best service. The food was worth writing home about. The champagne was sparkling, the candle was flickering, and then there was the real magic. There was Huff. Every other girl in the restaurant would have traded places with Kiki in a heartbeat. But Huff was hers.

After dessert, Huff turned so that he was facing Kiki. He handed her a small gift. It was about the size of a box of cards, and it was beautifully wrapped.

Her heart was pounding. *Is this a ring?* She became dizzy.

"It's a key to my apartment." He smiled. "Instead of bringing your clothes back and forth every time you sleep over, why don't you leave some of your things up here? I'll clean out the closet in the guest room, and it can be yours. We can play house!" He smiled in a wicked sort of way.

# 74

It's a big day for me. I have been sober for two months. I am learning how to go through a day without responding to triggers. I am at the local AA meeting, and they ask me to say a few words.

"Hi guys, My name is Jesse, and I'm an alcoholic."

"Hi Jesse!" everyone shouts.

"It's great to be here tonight. It's great to be sober.

"When I was in eighth grade, a girl asked me to dance and I froze. I couldn't imagine getting on the dance floor. I felt so awkward. I felt so alone. I didn't belong. A friend took me outside and gave me some blackberry brandy. All of a sudden, I was fine. For the first time in my life, I fit in. I could do what the other kids were doing.

"From that day on, I did everything in my power to get booze. And booze worked for a long time. But one day it stopped working. By then, I was hooked. It was very hard for me to quit. Every day I would promise myself I wasn't going to drink that night, and then I got drunk. I was so sick of breaking promises.

"Something bad doesn't happen every time I drink, but when something bad happens, it's because I have been drinking.

"I got to the point where the amount of pain outweighed the amount of pleasure. I wanted to be sober. I needed to get sober, or

I thought that I would die.

"It's been sixty days since my last drink. In the last two months, my life has gotten better. I feel terrific. I have energy. I can hold my head up. I can smile. Getting sober was the hardest thing I have ever done, but it has been the best gift I could have given myself.

"I am so happy to be sober."

After the meeting, I stop at the dairy bar for a triple vanilla ice cream cone with chocolate jimmies. I take the long way home. I turn the radio up and listen to Johnny Nash singing about his bright sunshiny day, and wonder if he was getting sober, too.

When I get home the phone is ringing.

"Hello?"

"Happy sixty-day anniversary, Jesse."

"Oh, hi Maggie. Thank you very much for your call! How's the weather in Colorado?"

"Well, tonight the moon is brighter than I have ever seen in my life. It seems suspended over the highest peak in the state. It even has a fluorescent halo. How are you doing in sobriety?"

"Well, I'm still the same asshole I used to be; I just have fewer dents in the car. I miss you, Maggie."

"I miss you, too, Jesse.

"I love you, Maggie."

"Jesse, all I have ever wanted was to be married to you, to be a good wife, and to be able to say that you were my best friend. Being away from you has been tough."

"It's been tough for me, too. I'd like to come and see you."

"I'd like that. Let's plan to get together in a month and celebrate your 90 days of sobriety. I will treat you to an unbelievable steak. And ice cream."

# 75

KIKI WAS SO EXCITED ABOUT MOVING her clothes into Huff's apartment that she had trouble staying in her own lane. The ride to his condo took forever.

More than anything, she wanted to use the new key to Huff's apartment.

What a thrill when it fit, and the door opened.

"Honey, I'm home!" Kiki stood at the door of his condo with a cardboard box full of shorts, tank tops, and a bathing suit. She also had some underwear, a few sweaters for chilly nights, and an extra pair of jeans. In the bottom of the box, she had hidden her new baby-doll PJs. It was to be her surprise.

This was a special occasion, and Huff made a big deal of showing her the closet he had just cleaned out. He had moved most of the contents to his storage area in the basement, but there were a few things left. As she started to unpack, Huff took a jacket off of a hanger and lifted the last box down from the top shelf. He placed the box on the bed and absent-mindedly opened it. As quickly as he opened the box, he shut it again. Kiki saw the look on his face, and she also saw a framed picture. She tried to grab it. He turned his back and pushed past her.

"It's nothing," he said. "I'll just put it in the storage area."

She quickly moved in front of him.

"Let me see your picture," she said, with a fixed smile on her face.

"It's nothing," he said again. "I'll just put the box down in the basement with the other stuff."

"If you have pictures of your life, I'd like to see them," she pressured, but he refused. She asked again. He began to feel threatened.

"No," he said forcefully.

Kiki reached for the box again and said that it would be fun to look at his pictures, but she was not smiling. She could feel herself slipping back to her old, obsessive self. She had a terrifying look on her face. Huff was pushed into a corner, both physically and emotionally.

"What could the pictures be of?" she snapped. "Pictures of your childhood, or your family? Pictures of your school days? Did you have a bad haircut that you don't want me to see? What are you hiding?"

She knew that she should have just given up, but that was not her nature.

Huff clutched the box as if it were a basketball and his opponent was blocking his shot. But Kiki would not let up. He couldn't believe the instant change in her personality.

Kiki reached out and tried to pry Huff's arms away from the box.

"God damn it," he screamed. "Go ahead and look!" He opened his arms as wide as he could, and let the box fall. As it crashed to the floor, the cardboard sides split open, and broken glass flew in every direction. Huff stormed out of the room and sat down at the kitchen table with his back to her.

How could things have gone so bad, so quickly? This was supposed to be a special night, but instead it had turned into a nightmare. She knew that she should have backed off, but she couldn't control herself. The damage was done. She bent over and picked up a picture. She wrinkled her brow and made a frown. She was puzzled. In her hand, she held a picture of Huff and another girl. They were in shorts and standing at a baggage claim area. They looked so happy. She looked over the top of the picture and saw Huff sitting stiffly at the kitchen table with his arms folded. She looked back at the picture. Huff and the girl were both tan, and the girl had a straw hat in her hand.

She picked up another picture. It was of Huff and the same girl standing in front of a theater with a ticket window in the background. The next picture was of the two of them in an ice cream shop sitting at a small table sharing a giant sundae.

Kiki was confused, scared, and threatened. Did he have a secret life? She took out another picture. This picture was also of Huff and the girl in a big embrace. Her eyes started to mist. Just to be sure of what she was seeing, Kiki looked at one more picture. This one was of Huff and the girl in a hot tub. Although the water was bubbling, it was easy to see that she was naked. They were both laughing. She started to take out another picture, but she just stopped. What was the use? She walked to the kitchen table and sat opposite Huff. She didn't know what to say. Tears were flowing down her cheeks.

They sat at the kitchen table for a long time without saying a word. Finally, after regaining his composure, Huff slowly started to talk.

"A week before we met, I broke up with my girlfriend. Her name is Tara. We were in high school together, and we dated for ten years. When we broke up, I took down all of her pictures, but I forgot to get rid of them."

Huff got up and walked to Kiki. He took out his handkerchief and wiped her eyes. She stood up and they hugged for a long time.

Kiki looked at him and laughed the whole thing off. Secretly, she was crushed. "I am sorry for acting like a spoiled child," she said.

Huff said that it was OK. He started to clean up the broken glass and put the pieces back in the box.

When he came back to the table, Kiki had one burning question. It couldn't wait.

"Did you love her?" she asked.

His smile slowly disappeared from his face. He started to look very sad. Tears came to his eyes. Then they were both crying.

"She was my best friend, and I loved her very, very much," was all he said.

After a few more minutes, he got up from the kitchen table and walked into the bedroom.

He looked back at her and said that he was going to bed.

Kiki got her things and left without saying goodbye.

# 76

AFTER THE LONG RIDE HOME, KIKI got out her notebook. She wiped her eyes, and as she started to write, big wet tears fell on the page. The salty dots blurred the ink, but she would never have trouble reading this entry.

### *Date: October 25.*

*Pictures, pictures, and more pictures. They were all of Huff and some bitch. She had long, red hair and she was gorgeous. She had a fabulous figure and a beautiful smile. And she smiled at my Huff in every picture.*

*How could Huff do this to me? He knows how I feel about him, and yet he gives himself to someone else. What about me? What about my feelings? What about the time I have given to him? What am I supposed to do now? He is inconsiderate, childish, insensitive, and immature. He is only thinking of his prick. He is just one more selfish man in a world of self-centered men.*

# 77

"I'M HAVING SUCH A HARD TIME getting through to Tippy" I say to Erica. "All I want are a few pictures of her dead husband, but she never returns the calls." I dial Tippy's phone again.

"This is the Vanderbeek residence. Please leave a message."

"Eh, Hi Mrs. Vanderbeek, eh, Tippy. This is Jesse from the San Diego Police Department. I've left a few messages, and, eh, I'd like to talk with you about a few things. Could you please give me a call? Thank you."

"Five calls in one week, and she never calls back. I wonder if she's left town. Maybe she just isn't answering her phone."

"Do you want to talk with her or just see what she's wearing today?" Erica asks.

"Both! I'm trying to get pictures of some of her dead husband's friends. And I'd like to get some pictures of Tippy, too."

Erica picks up a half-eaten bagel and throws it across the room.

"Ouch. That hurt. Just for that, I'm going down to console the poor widow right now.

"Don't forget your Polaroid," says Erica.

The gate to Vanderbeek's house is open, When I get to the door, I can see through the house and out to the pool. There is a woman lying at the pool, and it looks like she is naked. I stare for a full minute before ringing the bell. The person at the pool gets up and looks toward the door. It's Tippy. She takes a shirt off of the back of the chaise and drags it behind her as she walks toward the entrance.

She walks very slowly, like a model in a fashion show, with one foot in front of the other. She is not naked, but is either wearing flesh-colored Victoria Secrets or Haynes for Her. Jesse becomes faint. Tippy is halfway to the door before she starts to put her shirt back on.

I stutter as I introduce myself again.

"How about a drink?" She walks to the bar.

"No thanks; I'm on duty."

She fills two tall stem glasses with chilled white wine.

"Chardonnay OK?" She hands me a glass.

"Cheers," she says, as she downs half her drink.

I am trying to look into her eyes, but it's impossible.

"Mrs. Vanderbeek, I'd like a list of your husband's business relationships."

"Please, call me Tippy."

"OK, Tippy. Also I'd like some pictures of his friends. Do you have any old photos of him? We are trying to find out if the victims had any acquaintances in common."

She suddenly wrinkles her nose and reaches up under the back of her shirt. She starts scratching. With her shirt pulled up to her rib cage, she walks toward me and turns her back to me. She pulls her shirt up even higher.

"Can you see if I have a bug bite?" she asks. "Something is itching like crazy."

I awkwardly scratch Tippy's back as she moves up and down to get my fingers at the right place.

"Oh, that's it. Ooh, a little to the right. Oh, that feels so good. I'll give you two hours to stop. She reaches back with her other hand and pulls her panties down. "A little lower, please." She squeaks a tiny laugh as she turns around and looks me straight in the eyes. Suddenly, she becomes serious.

"Let's go to the bedroom." She takes me by the hand and leads me down a long hallway. She stops at the last room and puts her hand on the doorknob.

Tippy turns and looks at me. "This is the bedroom. My husband is dead. Take anything you want." My heart almost stops.

She pushes the door open and I see a room full of boxes.

"Here's all of his stuff." She giggles. "I'll be at the pool."

As she walks away, she takes her shirt off and lets it drop to the floor.

I look at the room full of boxes.

"I'm such a sucker. I always fall for that trick!"

After an hour of digging and rummaging, I carry two boxes of files to my car. I go back in to thank Tippy. She is lying on her stomach. It is, after all, a great day to work on a tan. I stick my head out and ask for some pictures of Blake.

"On the mantle over the fireplace."

"Thanks"

"I think I have another bug bite."

I force myself to leave.

# 78

IT'D BEEN WEEKS SINCE KIKI FOUND the pictures of Huff and his old girlfriend.

To try to make amends, Huff invited Kiki to a festive family reunion at the beach. She would finally be able to meet his relatives. And she had been thrilled at the spectacle of it all. She silently vowed that she would never bring up Huff's relationship with the redhead again.

But the family reunion was not a good idea. It wound up being the worst day of Kiki's life. It was a disaster.

When she got home from the reunion, she sat and cried for hours. She knew what she needed. She needed to write. She wiped the tears out of her eyes, got out her journal, and tried cathartic healing. She squeezed the pencil so hard that it broke.

### Date: October 31

> When Huff asked me to join him at the family reunion, I felt so hopeful, but I was also scared. My old feelings of insecurity kicked in. What if they didn't like me?
>
> The party was on a secluded beach, south of Point Pleasant. It

*was a beautiful, warm, sunny day. As we walked toward the group, Huff was very attentive and held my hand. It was exciting. We could see the colorful umbrellas. We could smell the charcoal burning. Coolers were everywhere.*

*We passed four little boys who were building a sandcastle. Their backs and noses were covered with white sun block, and they were oblivious to the rest of the crowd.*

*A group of little girls was playing with Barbie dolls under an umbrella. They were exchanging outfits, and they too were in their own world.*

*Several boys were tossing a Frisbee back and forth and trying to keep it away from a smaller boy.*

*The teenage girls had their own agenda: they were working on their late summer tan. Two of the girls were lying on their stomachs, and their tops were undone. One girl was on her back, and I was amazed at how tiny the bottom piece of her bikini was. Maybe it was last year's bathing suit, and she had grown. Or maybe this was the new trend.*

*A heavy-set man was filling plastic cups and handing out drinks. People were talking and laughing. A mother was changing a baby. This was a typical family, as I imagined it should be. I have never had a typical family, and I was jealous.*

*The older folks were in little groups, talking. At one picnic table, a thin man in his fifties with a very short, gray, crew cut was telling a joke or a story. Everyone at the table was watching him as his arms spread out to measure the size of something. As we walked toward that group, I could read his lips. He said, "This* is big, and this is rare!" Everyone howled at the punch line. He had a drink on a picnic table near him, and he downed it after he finished his story. Everyone had a plastic cup handy.

As we walked up to the crowd, Huff said he wanted to introduce me to his crazy in-laws. The first group was still smiling from the joke, but, as we approached, they all jumped up. They made a big fuss over Huff, and they were happy he was there. It was clear they liked him, and he was the center of attention. People were tapping him on the shoulder to get his attention. They were talking slowly so he could read their lips. They told stories and asked him about the trip. One uncle asked if he had trouble finding the beach. He got hugs and handshakes. One aunt gave him a big, sloppy, wet kiss on the lips. Everyone laughed as he tried to get away.

"This is my favorite girl cousin, Mattie" Huff said to me with a big smile. They looked to be the same age and had a special bond. She put her arms around him and they hugged for a long time.

After the initial hellos, other people started to look at me and then back at Huff. Their heads went back and forth. I have never felt so self-conscious.

Huff introduced me to the group, and most of them smiled politely. One lady came up and took my hand. She said, "Hi." Everyone else just stared. I felt as if I was invading their space.

As we made the rounds to folks at other picnic tables, we got the same reaction. I was intruding.

One of the little boys who had been working on the sand castle ran up and asked the question I was afraid of. He spoke very clearly for Huff's benefit, and I could read his lips. "Where is Tara?" he asked.

The little boy was the first to ask the question, but the others wanted to know about his ex, too.

Huff went to the grill to get some food, and the uncle who had been telling the jokes came up and sat next to me. I could tell that he was tipsy.

"Too bad that Tara couldn't come," he said. "Did you know her?" I shook my head and tried to hide the tears.

As Huff was waiting in the food line, Mattie cornered him. She looked at me and turned her back so I couldn't read her lips. Her hands were moving, and she kept looking at me over her shoulder. He just kept shaking his head.

I felt self-conscious, awkward, and out of place. I felt like an ostrich, but I couldn't bury my head.

We left the party early, and I drove home. On the way, Huff was quiet. He put his head between his knees. We were doing sixty on the Garden State Parkway, and I couldn't stop. When we got back to his place, his eyes were bloodshot. I knew that he had been crying. I asked him what was wrong. Communication was difficult. Finally, he looked at me and answered my question.

"My cousin thinks I was crazy to break up with Tara."

He looked so sad. After a long silence, he added, "Maybe she was right." He turned away from me and walked to the bedroom.

*I got my things and left.*

*Once again, I was being dumped.*

*Should I drive my car over a cliff? Should I slash my wrists in a thousand places? Should I fire my pistol in one ear and out the other?*

*I have to find something to do, or I will go crazy! I need a project. I need to keep busy. Maybe I should do something positive to get my mind off my negatives. I should go visit an old friend.*

Kiki sat and thought.

*Maybe I should go back into the past and rekindle an old flame. That will take my mind off of my problems.*

Kiki found the determination to take the next step. She got into her car and drove towards the city. She would search for a new Internet café and send an email to Rusty. It was time to return to New Hampshire.

# 79

It has been ninety days since my last drink. I wake up a different person than I was before.

It's not easy to stay sober. I still think about drinking every day, but today I pray for the grace to find the space between the thought and the action. Today, I don't act on the impulse.

It's another beautiful, San Diego day, and I notice the little things. I pay attention to a light breeze blowing across the garden. I take time to smell the roses. I am aware of my emotions, and I take care of myself. I am eating and sleeping on a regular basis. What a concept.

I have a new group of friends, and we acknowledge a common enemy. Our enemy is the drink. We celebrate our successful, sober days, and understand relapse when it overtakes someone that we care about. We all pray to stay sober. If one of us has a slip, we are accepted back into the group with a simple "Welcome back." No applause or lectures. When a member goes a year without drinking we say "Congratulations," but we also say "Happy daily reprieve." We don't dwell on someone's occupation, and it's not important what kind of car we drive. It's not unusual for a successful executive to reach out to an unemployed laborer. For us, success is not the destination. It's the daily journey.

I walk into an AA meeting and I sit next to Chuck, who has been sober for nineteen years. Chuck has a gray goatee, a pleasant smile, and tons of serenity. He enjoys eating, and it shows. Chuck makes fun of our disease, and he helps me relax.

"Hey Chuckie," I say, "Wanna hear something strange? I haven't thrown up in about three months."

"How long have you been sober?"

"About three months."

"Any correlation?"

"Gee, I never put the two together." We both laugh.

At 8pm, the meeting starts, and the leader of the meeting makes an announcement.

"We have a special occasion tonight. Erica would like to give a token to Jesse for ninety days of sobriety."

Everyone smiles as the two of us amble up to the front of the room. People shake my hand or touch my arm as I walk by.

Erica starts. "Hi, everyone. My name is Erica, and I am an alcoholic."

"Hi, Erica!" everyone yells enthusiastically.

"This is my friend Jesse." She looks up at me with a genuine smile. "Jesse and I have been friends for a long time," she says. "We worked together, laughed together, and cried together. We have been drunks together, and now we are trying to stay sober together. Jesse has grown so much in the last three months. I am very proud of the work that he is doing."

People are as happy for Erica's recovery as they are for mine. She has been around longer than I have this time. She has tons of support and a lot of friends. Erica has changed so much since she got sober. She glows with enthusiasm and energy. She is no longer a girl with tears in her eyes, fear in her voice, or vomit on her blouse.

"Happy ninety days of sobriety, Jesse." Erica hands me a bronze token with the inscription, "To thine own self be true." She gives me the biggest hug I have ever had.

It's my turn to say a few words.

"Hi, guys. My name is Jesse, and I am an alcoholic."

"Hey, Jesse!"

I smile to my friends who are sitting in the room and wave to a few who are standing in the back.

"People say that there's a fine line between use, abuse, and addiction. I crossed each line and never even noticed the change. Other people noticed it, but I thought I was normal.

"From the minute I took my first drink, I abused alcohol. I loved booze and everything that it did for me. Alcohol made me feel taller, thinner, and blond. It helped me feel good about myself. Alcohol made me feel like I belonged. And I wanted to belong, so much. When I was a kid, alcohol helped me overcome my shyness. I could talk to the girls, I could tell jokes, and I became the life of the party. I was the kind of guy who would light a glass of Yukon Jack and drink it while it was still burning. I couldn't get enough booze.

"When I was lonely, alcohol was my friend. When I was scared, alcohol gave me courage. When I was down, alcohol bumped me up. Towards the end, I couldn't do anything without drinking. I couldn't drive without a drink. I couldn't go to the beach without a drink. I couldn't work without a drink. I couldn't get laid without a drink.

"But at some point, booze stopped working. I would go to a bar to hear a band and get thrown out before the band started. I would take a girl on a date and black out before the night was over. The next morning, I would cringe while I listened to the answering machine. There's a hole inside of me. For most of my life, I have tried to fill the hole with booze, drugs, sex, work, and money. I spent too much time trying to compare my insides with your outside. At the end, I spent too much time alone. I was a dead man walking. Alcohol built me up but it let me right down again.

"Today, I realize that I have a disease. The disease is called alcoholism. I am not ashamed of my alcoholism; it's just a disease. Today I believe that my strength will be measured by how I confront my weakness. My weakness is booze. I need to stay away from booze for twenty-four hours. I can do that by going to a lot of AA meetings, by talking with my friends in this program, and by helping other people who have the same demon.

"I've broken many things because of my drinking. I have broken a lot of ten-dollar bills that I couldn't account for the next morning. I have broken the heart of someone who loved me. But most of all, I have broken promises to myself.

"I'm happy to be sober today, and I have gotten a lot of my old life back. But I know how fragile my sobriety really is. There are still days that I am not comfortable in my own skin. Sometimes, the obsession is so strong that I would give up everything I have for five minutes of blackness.

# 80

"This is a great burger," I say to Fig.

It's another beautiful day and we are sitting on his deck.

"Can't take the credit," he says. "All I did was fire up the grill."

The conversation goes back to our favorite subject.

"I wonder what ever happened to the Ball Buster?"

"Well, it's been a few months, and Kiki hasn't had target practice on any guys lately. Maybe she ran out of bullets."

"Maybe she ran out of boyfriends."

"Maybe she is dead," Fig says.

"I really would like to spend some more time on this case, but the bad guys keep popping up. We never seem to run out of new challenges. I wonder if that guy from New Hampshire, Rusty, ever got to see her?"

"How's the AA thing going?

"Well, I haven't had an alcoholic beverage for three months."

"Man, that's a long time between drinks! Congratulations, Jesse."

"Thanks for being my friend, Fig."

# 81

RUSTY THOUGHT ABOUT THE LAST FEW months. Since the day he tried to hook up with Kiki, his life had been hell. His wife would not forget the fact that he came home at 5am. She was convinced that he'd had an affair.

"I did not have an affair," he shouted back. He wasn't lying.

At least business was good. A big school job was finishing up, and two more bids had just been awarded in Rusty's favor. After placing orders for material, Rusty logged on to check his email.

"Finally, a message!" He says out loud. At once, he was relieved and challenged. Her message was positive and upbeat. There was no mention of the night she had stood him up, and no mention of the fact that she hadn't been returning his messages for the last three months. Instead, she just told him about her job. She talked about the weather in New Jersey. And then she said that she was coming to New Hampshire soon.

"Can we get together?" she wrote.

Rusty leaned back and mumbled to himself. "That girl has caused me so much grief. She is nothing but trouble. I don't care how good she looked or how much I was attracted to her. I'd rather die than see Kiki again!"

# 82

THE CHIEF SLOWLY WALKS IN MY direction and stops in front of my desk.

"What's up, Chief?"

"The Ball Buster just struck again!"

"What? Where?"

"New Hampshire."

"Oh no! No! No! God damn it! No, no, no!" I shout as I pound the desk with my fist.

The Chief stares at me.

"Was his name Rusty?" I say.

# 83

THE NEXT MORNING, I BOARD A plane to Manchester, NH. It's been two days since Rusty was found in a parked car with multiple gunshots to his groin. Ballistics confirmed that the fatal bullets came from the same Kel Tec pistol that was used in the other murders. Hair samples are identical. Saliva matched the samples that were found on two other dead men's lips.

When I get off the plane in Manchester, NH, photographers are everywhere. Bulbs are popping. Questions are being hurled. I'm used to this.

The airport newsstand is trying to sell papers. They are displayed so that the most creative headlines are visible.

**Parking Lot Killer Hits New Hampshire.**

**Ball Buster Takes Another Shot.**

**The PLK Strikes Again.**

**Away Team Scores in New Hampshire.**

The reporters don't know the facts. They don't know the killer is deaf. They don't know she has curly blond hair. The biggest secret is her method of communication. They have no idea how she has been getting in touch with her victims.

# 84

"I'm sorry about your loss, Mrs. Harding. I know that this is a bad time, but I would like to talk with you about your husband, Rusty."

I know that I can't expect much cooperation from her now, and I feel like a slime ball for asking, but I need to get a few answers.

She is overwhelmed. Her husband has been dead for three days and the police have already interviewed her twice. Newsmen have parked their mobile vans on her front lawn. She clearly does not want to talk to another cop.

She looks at my business card.

"Why is a California detective interested in a New Hampshire crime? Was my husband in some kind of trouble?"

I explain that there has been a string of crimes with the same MO, and I am trying to put the pieces together. I ask Rusty's wife the usual questions about motives and activities leading up to the time of the murder. I ask her about any leads she may have, but my heart isn't in it. I know who killed her husband. I go through the motions, anyway.

"Do you have a few recent pictures of Rusty I can take with me?"

She nods her head and goes off to get a pile of Kodak envelopes. As she sifts through the pictures, she hands me a picture of Rusty. This is the same man that sat next to me on a bar stool three months ago, but I don't need to share this information with the widow.

Rusty is the first victim who did not go to Saint Anselm's college, but I know how Rusty met his killer. His father did electrical work in Kiki's office twenty years ago. Rusty was on the job.

"Please tell me about Rusty," I ask. "I would like to know about his life when he was about 20 years old. Did you know him then?"

"You want to know about something that happened twenty years ago? How would that help now?" She seems agitated.

"I'm trying to piece together patterns" is all I say. "Did you know him then?"

"I have always known Rusty. We went to grammar school together. We dated through high school, but then we drifted apart. He worked for his father and went to night school to get his journeyman's license."

"Do you know who he might have dated way back then?"

"He was dating some bim-, er, girl named Kiki. I heard that she was attractive, but she was handicapped. Deaf. I was seeing someone else, and we didn't get back together until we were twenty-five. We got married when he was twenty-six and had just taken over his father's electrical business."

"What can you tell me about Rusty that would help me in my investigation? Has anything unusual happened lately? Has he been acting strange?"

Mrs. Harding looks at me, and her eyes start to mist. She looks towards the floor and tells me about a night three months ago when he came home at 5am. She says that things had been tense since then. She admits they had a big fight two weeks ago. He slept in his office, and one day he never came home from work.

Mrs. Harding shows me to the office, and I borrow Rusty's computer.

I am forcing myself to go through the motions. I want to be like a dog that pisses on every rock.

# 85

IT WAS A PUNKY DAY ON the Jersey shore. It had been raining off and on for hours. Kiki had been driving endlessly for most of the morning. At noon, she stopped at a sandwich shop and got a turkey sub to go. As she ate, mayonnaise dripped on her blouse, but she didn't even notice. She didn't even care.

She was having trouble seeing the road. The windshield wipers were clearing the window, but they couldn't remove her tears. The fog in her mind was thicker than the fog that was coming in off the ocean. She was almost paralyzed with grief.

Instead of moving forward with her life, she had regressed. She was listless, depressed, and disappointed. Nothing was fun. Getting rid of Rusty hadn't made her happy. The project that she had been working on for years had left her empty and disillusioned. She had completed her mission, but she had never felt worse.

Without a plan, Kiki ended up in the Lazy Lobster parking lot. This is where she and Huff had their first date together. She pulled into the same spot where they had sat and talked for hours while waiting for the sun to come up. This was their spot. This was their restaurant. This was supposed to be their life, but now she was alone again. Dumped again! Fucked over again! She rested her head on the steering wheel.

She thought about Huff and played out different endings in her mind. It didn't have to be over. *There must be some way I can get his attention,* she thought. There must be a way that she could repair the damage. There must be a way that she could get back with the man she loved. She had to see Huff one more time.

It had been weeks since they'd seen each other. Surely he was lonely, too. He was a very proud man, and would not lower himself to get in touch with her. She had to take the step if they were going to get back together.

As she sat in the parking lot, an idea started to form. It was an interesting plan. She still had a key to Huff's apartment, and it would be fun to surprise him. She could bring a bottle of his favorite wine.

As she thought about seeing Huff again, her mood changed for the better. She started the car and headed towards the store where she bought some wine, cheese, crackers, and a bouquet of flowers.

"Huff will be thrilled to see me," she said to herself as she drove toward her condo. She took a shower, changed into a new outfit, and started to pack an overnight bag.

"This is the best idea that I have ever had," she said out loud.

When she finished packing, she grabbed her pistol, just for luck. She had been holding it a lot lately, just for its calming effect. She planned to get rid of it soon, but for now it gave her comfort. She wanted to be in control of every situation. It was all about control.

The Garden State Parkway was not crowded, and the drive to Huff's apartment was peaceful. Kiki was planning what she would say when they met. She would give him the wine and start off by apologizing for being such a big baby. He would like that. Her mind was racing with anticipation.

"After we finish the wine," she thought out loud, "I will pop into the bathroom and change into the sexiest little baby doll that I own. I will even wear my new high heels. Huff will be shocked and embarrassed. He is such a prude. We will make love for hours, and it will be a wonderful evening."

It was getting dark when Kiki finally got to Huff's apartment. She took out the key and squeezed it tightly as she walked to his door. The lights weren't on in his apartment, but that was not unusual. Sometimes, he watched TV in the dark.

Should she just go in, or should she activate the light alarm first? She decided to be adventurous and just go for it! After all, this was going to be a wonderful treat for Huff. He was going to be so excited! She couldn't wait to see the happiness on his face. She let herself in and tiptoed into the living room. The room was dark, but there was a crack of light coming from under his bedroom door. She expected that Huff would be lying on his bed, just thinking about her. He would be so thrilled. She slowly opened the door. She was ready to shout, "SURPRISE!" at the top of her lungs.

What a surprise.

Huff was lying on his back and Tara was sitting on top of him. Her naked body was slowly moving up and down, glistening with sweat. Her figure was perfect. Her head was tilted back, and her long red hair was hanging everywhere. Huff's eyes were closed. They were too involved with each other to notice the intruder. In her shock, Kiki dropped the bottle of wine. Tara's head jerked towards the noise, and then, sensing that something was wrong, Huff snapped his head in her direction, too.

In a split second, Kiki sought the comfort of her Kel-Tec. She grabbed her pistol, just as an angry dog would grab a bone. She needed to have her finger on the trigger. Without warning, the gun went off. One shot hit Tara in the back and she reared up from the thrust of the explosion. She twisted towards the far wall and landed on the floor. The second shot hit Huff in the stomach. He shuddered, and his body twitched as he looked toward her. He was moving his mouth, but she knew that no words were coming out. Within seconds, his head fell back. There was no more twitching or kicking. There was no flexing or thrusting.

Kiki was blind with rage.

She walked to the foot of the bed and pulled Huff's legs apart. Without a second thought, she left her autograph. The final five shots from her revolver were spent at close range. Kiki headed blindly for the door as tears started to roll.

# 86

It's midnight when Fig and I deplane in Point Pleasant, New Jersey. We get to our hotel and crash. At 7am, we meet Dino Santaro for breakfast. He is a career detective in this seaside town.

Dino is tall and lean, and his curly, black hair is cut close. He is dressed in clean, starched khakis and a very neat, blue, button-down dress shirt. His conservative, plaid sport jacket fits perfectly, and it is either new or it just came from the cleaners. He looks more like a male model than a cop.

Like many people in the law enforcement community, Dino has been following our case in the news. There are lots of crimes in the world, but there is not too much creativity in the killing business. Few serial crimes are so unique that they attract everyone's attention. People all over the country are discussing this case, and Dino is no exception. He is one of thousands of cops who would love to crack a high profile event like our Ball Buster mystery.

We introduce ourselves and make small talk. Our waitress finally comes by with a pot of coffee and menus. Her restaurant uniform is a white, nylon dress with a striped apron. It was obviously picked out by someone who was thin. On our waitress, the apron causes an optical illusion. To say that she looked pudgy would be a compliment.

I can't tell if the stripes are going the wrong way, or her body is going the wrong way. She is definitely a throwback from the fifties. Her eye liner is way too black, her lipstick was put on with a putty knife and her hair teased with two cans of spray. We order cheese omelets all the way around, and I hope that our waitress doesn't comb her hair within twenty feet of our food.

Dino starts his story. Two days ago, he was called in to a crime scene. Two people had been killed in bed, obviously during the act of lovemaking. That was not unusual. The twist was that the man in question had been shot six times. Five of the shots were from very close range.

Dino immediately called the San Diego Police and ended up talking with Erica. He needed to share a few details about this murder in his town. Although there was no parked car, there was one resemblance to all of the cases that we have been working on. The shots that were fired from close range were into a very private area. Also, curly, bleached-blonde hair was found in the apartment.

A broken bottle of wine had fingerprints that matched the killer.

After breakfast, we decide to touch base with the chief of detectives. We might need his help, and it's better to have him with us than against us. The chief's name is Dave Cosgrove, and he is out for the morning. We leave a card and head out to the deceased's apartment.

As we get to Huff's apartment, our level of excitement is rising. Is it the coffee, or is it the fact that this might be the case-breaking trip? There are people everywhere, and we have to fight through the crowd to get to the entrance of the high-rise. The crowd looks like locals, but we have one of the uniforms take pictures of the onlookers. While I go in to talk with the apartment owner, Fig walks through the crowd to look for blondes with short, curly hair.

The manager of the building is a dark, burly man with a full beard.

He is Greek and says his name Alexander Tsjonis, very slowly. We can call him Zander.

He brings us a small cup of strong, dark, black coffee, and we sit down. We have no firm idea of what Kiki looks like, but we have a few clues. The only living person we know who has ever seen Kiki was Margaret from the college, and that was 20 years ago. We know about her height. We can guess her weight. But the most important identifying fact that we can talk about is that she is deaf. Someone who lip-reads should stand out. We ask the manager if he remembers a deaf girl with curly, blonde hair. Before we can go too far, he says that the deceased was also deaf. We didn't know that, but it makes sense. He said that Huff had one girlfriend for years, but there was a different guest who visited him recently. Since we are there early in the morning, he invites us to come back later to interview his staff.

Back at the police station, we finally meet the local police chief. He makes up for his lack of height with an abundance of gruffness, a long crew cut, and boots with extra-thick soles. He is all business. He looks as sharp as a tack and tough as nails. He obviously works out, and he is as wide as he is tall. His handshake is bone-crushing. He reminds me of a Brillo Pad.

He is a cop on the move, and his office is decorated with black-and-white photos of politicians. There are some cheap frames holding certificates. His small, black desk is neat, but his side table is a mess.

He has been following our serial case and thinks we are wasting our time in his town.

"We don't have those kinds of people here," he says. I wanted to tell him to dream on, but that wouldn't help my cause. We tell Chief Cosgrove about the Ball Buster's signature shot, and how we now have matching hair samples to boot. He wishes us well, but he doesn't like the publicity that will come with our search.

"Keep your investigation quiet and make it quick," he says. I give him a card. Without looking, he tosses the card on the pile of junk on his side table. It's so nice to be welcomed.

When we return to the scene, there are a few people who remember seeing a girl who seemed to be lip reading. Since Huff was deaf too, they took special notice when two of them were talking. We make an appointment for sketch artists to come in and work with the staff.

Fig and I go into Huff's apartment and look for some clues. We find an address book and decide to track down contacts. Since this is a small, loose-leaf notebook, I take the book and the first half of the pages. I remove the second half of the pages and give them to Fig.

He heads north, and I head south. I meet with a cousin, who is devastated. She loved Huff! I go and visit an uncle. I start to find a pattern. They each had met Huff's new girlfriend a month earlier, at a cookout on the beach. The uncle has a group picture and points to a blonde with short curly hair.

"That's her, the bitch," he says. "Her name was Kiki, and she killed my nephew!"

Bingo.

"Where did she live?"

"Damned if I know, but if I find her before you do, she is dead meat!"

I sit in the car and go through Huff's phone book again. There is no Kiki listed anywhere in the book. I look at a hodgepodge of names on the inside front cover. Some entries are in ink and some are in pencil. Some have mailing addresses and some have email addresses.

At the bottom of the haphazard list, the last entry is a capital letter K, scribbled very lightly in pencil. No name, no phone number, but there is an address.

I call Fig on his cell, but I get voice mail. I leave a message with the address of "K."

I know that I should get in touch with Fig. The first rule of engagement is to wait for backup. I know how dangerous it is to confront a killer, alone. How many times have we talked about this at the bureau? How many times have we had meetings about this? I know the potential risks.

But something else is going through my crowded mind. This is a very selfish thought. I am totally off base, out of line, irrational. I am reckless, irritable, and discontent.

I want to redeem myself in the eyes of my boss. I want my partner's respect. I need to win my wife's affection. If I find Kiki by myself, some of these things may happen. I was a great agent at one time, and I haven't lost my touch. I can do this by myself.

I rush off to the address of "K."

# 87

Kiki had been crying for two long days. She hadn't slept. She hadn't eaten. She hadn't showered or changed her clothes. Her nose wouldn't stop dripping. There were crumpled tissues all over the apartment. She sat at her desk and tried to write, but today there were no words. She glanced at her reflection in the full-length mirror. She was traumatized by what she saw. She seemed to have aged ten years in the past two days. Her face was a deathly gray, and dark circles accentuated her hollow eyes. She fell to the floor.

They had all hurt her, and now they were gone. All of them. Even Huff. The men who had controlled her life were dead. Her mission was complete. She should be happy. Sobs turned into convulsions.

Kiki crawled to her umbrella stand. She took her pistol out of the backpack. She sat at her desk and loaded the chamber. She caressed the handle. She put the barrel into her mouth as far as it would go and almost gagged. As she put pressure on the trigger, she wondered what it would be like to squeeze a little harder. If this pistol had put so many other people out of their misery, wouldn't it help her, too? What would it feel like? How long would the pain last? Would there be pain? Would there be peace? She thought about the flash of light that would come just before the darkness. Her own hot flashes made her perspire, but she was shivering involuntarily. She was dizzy and felt like she was losing her balance. If she fainted and fell, would the pistol go off in her mouth? Would she hear the sound? Would she see the explosion, or would she die first? She pointed the pistol toward the side of her head, and inserted the barrel into her ear. She slid the pistol between her legs.

She started to write a suicide note, but what would she say? Who would read it? Who would care? For the first time in her life, there should be tranquility, but instead, there was a huge hole. Every nerve ending in her body had frizzled. She had become numb. Something was buzzing inside of her head as if a thousand honeybees were tending to a dying queen. A hot, bright, white light started to appear in front of her eyes.

Kiki regained focus and thought about hanging herself, but the process was overwhelming. And what if she changed her mind at the last second? Imagine clawing at the rope while her breath was slowly being cut off.

Sleeping pills would be an easy exit. Just take a handful and never wake up. But she didn't have any sleeping pills.

Kiki picked up her faithful Kel-Tec pistol and gripped the handle one more time. She always felt better with her pistol in her hand. This was how her story should end. A simple gunshot! It would be a perfect ending to a less-than-perfect life. Suicide was preferable to living. The pistol went back in her mouth and she licked the barrel with her tongue. She slowly increased pressure. "Just pull the trigger," she said to herself. "Just pull the fucking trigger."

# 88

I RACE TOWARD ASBURY PARK AND quickly drive through the intersections of the look-alike streets. I am searching for an address. My cop instincts tell me that "K" is Kiki. The address that was written in pencil may actually be Kiki's residence.

My adrenalin is pumping, and my heart is pounding. I feel like I am paused at the top of a roller coaster for a brief second. I lose my breath and plunge downward. I couldn't stop the momentum even if I wanted to.

I know I should go to the local police department and check in, but I don't want to take the time. I should call for backup, but that would slow me down. I should try to get in touch with Fig one more time, but I don't. Rational thinking is now out the window. There is only the quest. If this is truly Kiki's apartment, I am about to capture a cold-blooded murderer who has killed at least five men. The urge to put an end to this case right now is impossible to resist.

The address is a small condo complex. I park in the street and run toward the entrance. The buzzer by the front gate has white name tags that have been inserted into small plastic holders. Most have full names. I stare at each name carefully. There is only one resident without a last name. It only shows an initial. That initial is "K." It's on the second floor.

I run up the brick stairs two at a time. I get to the door and stop to catch my breath. I know she owns a handgun, and that she is dangerous. I take out my pistol. I am ready to break some rules.

With all of my weight, I crash through the cheap, wooden door. The lock splinters into pieces as I dive toward the floor. I land on carpeting and roll into a prone position. Out of the corner of my eye I see another person rolling, too. My reflection in the full-length mirror scares the hell out of me. When I come to a stop, I instantly see a different motion. A girl sitting at a desk is waving something in her hand. It's shiny. It's a weapon!

She and I stare for two full seconds. Our weapons are pointed at each other.

We fire at the same time.

# 89

KIKI WAS SHOT AT, BUT SHE was not hit. It seemed so bizarre. She felt like she was in a game, but watching from the sideline. She could smell the gun powder, she could feel the fresh air coming in through the busted door, and she could see a body lying motionless on her living-room floor. She was involved physically, but not emotionally. For the first time in her life, she did not take the attack personally.

Kiki looked through the shattered door. Since it was daytime, her neighbors were at work, and no one had heard the commotion. It was time to plan the next phase of her life. She understood that she would have to move. She could see herself flying off to a new location, setting up a house, and living happily ever after.

She quickly cleaned herself up and laid out some clothes. She put on a tan blouse, a maroon skirt, a wide, black belt, black tights, and low, black heels. She went to the umbrella stand and took out her backpack, which still held over $100,000 in cash. She threw in some toiletries and underwear. She picked up her pistol off the floor and grabbed a box of ammunition out of her bottom drawer. She put that in her bag, too. She took a black, cardigan sweater out of the closet and looked at herself in the mirror. She looked terrific!

She closed the shattered door as best she could and walked down the stairs of her complex.

She thought about the man who had just busted in.. It was certainly Detective Jesse Collins. She had seen his picture so many times. She wondered how he had found her.

Her mind churned slowly as she walked across the parking lot. For the first time in her life, she started to think more like a rat in a cage than a free bird.

It was unusual for a detective to travel all the way across the country by himself. Cops were like dogs. They traveled in a pack.

If there were other cops involved, they would probably be here shortly. She wondered about her chances of escape. She stopped in the middle of her parking lot.

Kiki did a U-turn and retraced her steps. She walked back to her apartment. As she walked up the stairs, she realized that she was no longer the hunter, but now she was the hunted. Her mission now was survival.

She stepped over the body and walked towards the bathroom. She took a pair of scissors from her makeup drawer and, without a second thought, chopped her hair. Within a minute, she had a new hairdo. Her sloppy, choppy crew cut made her look younger. Kiki had to laugh. She flushed her cut hair down the toilet. It only took another minute to wash off all traces of makeup.

She kicked off her high heels, rolled down her panty hose, and got out of her skirt and blouse. She stuffed her clothes into the laundry basket.

She reached in her bottom drawer and pulled out some old work clothes. The last time she had worn these rags was when she painted the bedroom. She slipped into a tight t-shirt that flattened her figure and added an old, red-and-black-checkered hunting shirt. She pulled on a pair of painter pants that were covered with brown and green splotches and an old pair of black sneakers. Finally, she topped her outfit off with a John Deere baseball cap. She replaced the cardigan sweater with a black sweatshirt. Within seconds she had switched from class to trash. She had changed from a stylish city lady to a rebellious country girl.

She grabbed the backpack again and walked back to her car. After leaving the parking lot, she drove to a small, corner drug store and picked up a bottle of dark brown Clairol. On the way to Newark airport, she stopped one more time. She dyed her hair in the bathroom of a Texaco. Two rolls of paper towels dried her hair enough to stop the dripping. She was now a brunette. When she finally got to the airport, she left her car in long-term parking, as she had done many times before. Kiki boarded a shuttle to the terminal and sat stiffly in a window seat. She avoided eye contact, and looked toward the curbside baggage area.

Cops were everywhere. They seemed to be checking every female passenger's identification. One policewoman was holding a license up next to a girl's face. They were looking for Kiki, but she wondered how they knew what she looked like.

Kiki's mind started racing, but she kept calm. She slung her backpack over her shoulder and, as she stepped off the shuttle, she made a sharp, left turn around the front of the van. Kiki crossed two lanes of traffic and walked calmly away from the terminal. She walked to the taxi stand and asked the cabbie to take her to Amtrak. They quietly rolled out of the airport, but as they approached the train station, she could see more police. Cops were checking IDs right in front of the main building.

Kiki told the cab driver she had changed her mind and asked him to take her to Route 80. She could see him shaking his head, but it didn't matter. She was in control.

The cabbie put his taxi in gear and took off toward the thruway.

When they reached the on-ramp, she paid him cash and added a generous tip. She jumped out and stood there waiting for him to get out of sight. As soon as he disappeared, she walked up the ramp.

# 90

THE FIRST VEHICLE THAT ENTERED THE on-ramp was a giant eighteen-wheeler. The sign on the truck door said long-distance moving. She stuck out her thumb, and the driver started down-shifting. Kiki ran alongside the truck until it stopped. She grabbed the chrome handrail next to the passenger door and took the three steps up to the enormous cab. She opened the door, climbed in, and smiled. "Thank you for stopping," she said.

"My name is Crash," he said. Crash was fat and fifty. His white beard and red baseball hat made him look like Santa.

"My name is Kiki," she said.

She explained that she was deaf but could lip-read if he talked slowly.

"I just found my boyfriend in bed with some slut, and I want to get as far away from New Jersey as possible," she said.

"I love riding way up here in the cab of this great big rig. Is this what they call an eighteen-wheeler?"

He smiled.

"I like the view."

Kiki was amazed that she could see right into every car that they passed, and she could see what people were doing. In one car, two girls had stem glasses in their hands and a large bottle of wine between them. They were giggling. In another car, a girl was lying across the front seat on her stomach and had her head in the driver's lap.

Her knees were bent and her feet were up against the passenger window.

She was probably being very nice to her boyfriend.

"See all kinds of sights from up here," said Crash. He smiled and talked very slowly.

"Last summer as I was going through a long stretch of highway, I passed two girls in a convertible. Their tops were off. I guess they were working on their tan. I beeped at them and they waved to me."

Kiki liked Crash. They talked continuously. After a while, he started to open up, and he told her about his life. His wife had left him for another guy.

"A salesman. A fucking salesman," he said.

"She even took my two little boys. She disappeared, and I may never see my sons again. Don't even know where they moved to," he said. "But you've been through a lot, too. I understand how you must have felt to find your boyfriend in bed with another girl."

They had an instant bond. Crash seemed comfortable with Kiki. He talked very slowly and made sure that he was looking in her direction so that she could read his lips. If he didn't understand something, he would ask her to repeat it again. She liked that.

Crash was on the way to pick up a load of household furniture in Colorado and then deliver it to Texas. The company he worked for would have day workers at each site to help with the load. Kiki asked if he stopped for the night, and he said that he had a few favorite truck stops where the food was good and the restrooms were clean.

"My first stop is just outside of Cleveland," Crash said, "And we should get there about midnight. I expect you will be sound asleep long before then." Just talking about sleep made Kiki realize how tired she was. In fact, she was exhausted! She kept yawning. Crash suggested that she climb into one of the beds in the back of the cab and take a nap. For some reason, she trusted him. She liked her new friend, and felt very comfortable. She took his advice and climbed between the bucket seats and into the back of the cab. It was such a neat space. It was clean and organized. There were two bunks, and each had blankets and pillows. She thanked him and climbed up into the top bunk. When her head hit the pillow, she was out. She was asleep in two seconds and emotionally escaped the trauma of her two long days. Finding Huff with another woman, her door being busted open, the total change of identity, and the escape, had all left her wasted. The gentle rocking of the moving van was like a giant massaging machine, and lulled her into a long, dreamless sleep.

Kiki felt like she had slept forever when the motion of the rig slowly changed and she came back to life. The big truck was pulling into a long parking space in a truck stop along the expressway. Vans and tractor-trailers were lined up on either side of them, and in the distance she could see a restaurant. Crash was climbing into the sleeping compartment underneath her.

She quickly sat up and looked at him with wide-open eyes.

"Relax, Kiki," he smiled. "I just need to take a nap." With that, he crawled into the bottom bunk and all was quiet. She lay awake for a minute and fell asleep again.

After another long sleep, Crash was gently shaking her.

"Time to get moving again," he said. Would you like to use the ladies room before we head out?"

"You bet," she said. "I really have to pee."

He walked her to the main building and waited outside the ladies-room door while she used the facilities. When she got into the bright light of the bathroom, she broke out laughing. The sight of her short, choppy, brown hair and her ratty clothes in the mirror made her smile. She patted her backpack. She had her money and her pistol. Everything would be OK. Before they walked back to the truck, Crash steered Kiki to the self-serve line in the restaurant. They armed themselves with burgers, chips, coffee, and candy bars. He insisted in paying. As they got back to the cab and she climbed into her passenger seat, she smiled at Crash.

"I could get used to this." Kiki said.

They continued their conversation, and Kiki told Crash about her childhood. She told him about her failed love affairs but didn't tell the last chapter in each broken relationship. He understood her pain.

For a while, Kiki wondered if she could just ride into the sunset with someone like Crash. He was the father figure that she had never had.

As they approached Denver, Crash reached out with a genuine offer.

"Would you continue on with me to Texas?"

"Where do you go after that?" she asked.

"I deadhead back to Newark for a few days and then to Daytona." She thought about going off with him, but that would only be a temporary solution.

"I can't go back to New Jersey," she said. He seemed to understand.

Crash asked Kiki where she would like to get out.

"Can you drop me near an inexpensive motel?"

"Do you need some money?

"No, I have money. Thanks for asking."

At the edge of town, Crash slowed to a stop in front of the Mountain View Motel.

"This place is clean," he said.

Kiki smiled.

"I really enjoyed your company," she said. She reached over the controls and gave him a long, wet, sloppy, open-mouthed kiss. She let her tongue find his. Her hand dropped to his lap as if it were a mistake and let it lay there as they continued to kiss. Even though he was fat and fifty, she felt him start to grow. Before it ended, she squeezed him playfully.

As she climbed out of the big rig, she smiled at Crash. His grin stretched from ear to ear.

# 91

WITH A BACKPACK FULL OF MONEY, Kiki walked toward the office of the motel. The neon sign said "Open 24 Hours." She asked for a non-smoking room and paid cash. The room was clean and faced away from the road. Her courtyard location was inconspicuous.

The Mountain View Motel mattress was lumpy, and the pillow was hard, but Kiki didn't notice. When she hit the bed, she slept like a log. The next morning, after the longest shower in history, she went down to the lobby and paid for another night. The proprietors only cared about the money in advance. Kiki cared only about being invisible.

There was a menu in her room from Dominick's Denver Diner. She could see that name on a neon sign about a block away. She was hungry, and it looked inviting. Dominick's Diner was a mess, but the food smelled great. She sat in a corner table and ordered the house special of scrambled eggs, sausage, home fries, and toast. She ate every single bit. It was breakfast time, but she ordered a piece of carrot cake, too. Her waitress didn't judge.

She ordered coffee and read the Rocky Mountain News while she ate. A small article on page three told about a female killer who had disappeared. There was a very small black-and-white photo of a girl with curly, blonde hair and lots of make-up. Kiki took the paper to the restroom and compared the picture to the person in the mirror. There was absolutely no resemblance.

Back in her room, she slept again.

That afternoon, she went for a walk and found a small grocery store. She bought some additional toiletries, cereal, and a small container of milk. She got cold cuts, some rolls, bottled water, and her own copy of the newspaper. She bought a small, Styrofoam cooler and, when she got back to the room, filled it with ice from the machine in the lobby.

The television in her room was a 12-inch black-and-white, but it served the purpose. She checked the news several times a day and was happy to find that, as each day passed, the amount of coverage she received was less and less. The only photo the cable company aired was her group picture at the beach party. Since she had taken a new identity, she looked totally unlike the girl in the news. The fact that she was wearing baggy paint pants and a tee shirt made her look 10 years younger. When she looked in the mirror, she thought that a lot had changed. She had become a new person. She had become anonymous. She paid for another day in cash.

When Kiki had left New Jersey, she didn't bring her car or any extra clothes. She didn't have a plan. Her trucker friend, Crash, had brought her here and she thought that this was a sign. She loved the crisp, mountain air, and she decided to stay in Colorado for awhile.

She had always wanted to live a simple, clean, uncluttered life, but there were so many issues. There were always people, places, and things in the way of happiness. Being away from the people who had crossed her, the places that caused her stress, and the things that she couldn't control, was a new experience for Kiki. She was happy to be away from the traffic, the chaos, and the congestion. She was happy to be away from New Jersey.

There might be hope for her, after all. She had never achieved a feeling of inner peace. Here in Colorado, she felt for the first time that there might be an opportunity to finally become her true self.

As the next few days went by, Kiki spent more time sleeping than ever before in her life. Each morning, she went to the office and paid for another day in advance.

On her fourth day, Kiki ventured out for a bit of shopping. She thought about buying some new clothes. The lady in the office directed her to a bus that would take her to "LoDo." The Lower Downtown Mall at NW Sixteenth was a long shopping district. Although no cars were allowed, there were plenty of buses and lots of free, public transportation.

When the bus stopped at the edge of LoDo, she stepped into her new environment and her new life. As she walked around the downtown area, she realized that she liked the casual community. This was so different from New Jersey. It was now late summer, and people were transitioning their outfits. She saw many folks wearing sweatshirts with their shorts.

She planned to make a few changes, too. In keeping with her new identity, she put together a whole new look. She paid attention to what other people in Denver were wearing. She wanted to blend in.

Kiki bought casual, comfortable, tasteful clothes. No more starched blouses and no more high heels. She bought a mid-length tan skirt and a new pair of jeans. In another store she bought casual, chino slacks and a two-piece, navy sweater set. She bought a hooded warm-up suit with the Denver Bronco's logo, and she bought a pair of comfortable penny loafers. In the dressing room, she got out of her painter pants and t-shirt. She changed into the chinos and hoodie. The old clothes and hat were discarded in a trash bin.

As she walked past stores, Kiki looked into a mirror and saw an opportunity for instant improvement. She found a hair stylist that welcomed walk-ins. The girl who met Kiki at the door gasped in horror.

"Oh my God! What happened to your hair?" she asked.

Kiki was prepared.

"My girlfriend and I had too much to drink one night," she smiled, "and I let her style my hair. Pretty bad, huh?"

"I guess she tried to color your hair, too. We better get to work," replied the stylist. Two hours later, Kiki's hair was neatly trimmed, very, very short, and the color was jet black. But this time it was a professional job. She looked in the mirror and was happy with her new look. She tipped the girl well and continued her walk.

With her new hairdo, new outfit, and the elimination of most makeup, she was a brand-new person.

Her next stop was a small, Italian restaurant right on the corner. She was ready for a real meal. She ordered a salad with the house dressing, lasagna with garlic bread, and a dish of chocolate ice cream.

When she got back to the Mountain View Inn, she went right to bed and slept for another ten hours. She thought of this time as a metamorphosis. It was like a coming-out party for herself. It was a rebirth. She felt born again. Her naps and long nights of sleep were medicinal, and she started to put her past behind her. She stopped watching over her shoulder, and the sight of a police car slowly creeping down the street didn't send her into panic.

On the following morning, she laid her new clothes out on the bed. This was how her mother always got dressed. She picked out her new, tan, chino slacks, and a plain, black sweater. She gave her new penny loafers a quick shine with the face cloth from the bathroom and added a new ankle bracelet. When everything looked like it matched, she got dressed. She liked her new hairdo, and she liked her new character. She walked outside and took a deep breath of the crisp, clean, mountain air. The fog had lifted, and for the first time she found out why the motel was called Mountain View. She saw the skyline for the first time.

Kiki went back to Lo Do and did more shopping. She bought a small suitcase on wheels. She picked out a travel kit, a gray pantsuit, a pair of sneakers, sensible underwear, socks, and a tweed sport jacket. She bought a few turtlenecks to wear under her sport jacket.

Kiki was beginning to feel comfortable in her new surroundings and in her new personality. She thought she might be happy in Denver. She decided to look for an apartment or even a small house to rent, and she looked at the real estate section of the paper. The ads showed that rents here were much less expensive than they had been in New Jersey.

She was in no hurry to settle down, and living at the motel was safe. She had totally disappeared. For the next several days, she took the bus back to the LoDo area and met with several real estate agents. The first two salesmen went through the motions, and the third was very pushy. All were unhelpful. She was a deaf girl, and none of the agents had any experience with her disability. They couldn't grasp the concept that, in order to communicate, they had to look straight at her so she could read lips. She knew that one agent was shouting by the way others looked at them. This didn't help at all, but this was not unusual for new acquaintances. Within seconds of meeting someone, she knew if they would be able to communicate. If she didn't like them, she would move on. Most of the agents were looking to just do the deal, to get the commission. They weren't interested in her, and Kiki wasn't interested in a settle-for address.

# 92

ON THE FOLLOWING SATURDAY MORNING, KIKI put on her new, tan skirt, a lightweight, black blouse, and a tweed sport jacket. She might have been a visiting schoolgirl. She took the bus to the mall again but, instead of shopping, ended up taking a walking tour of the neighborhood. She had no agenda, but it was such a beautiful day. She wandered aimlessly for hours. She enjoyed the weather, the sights, and her freedom.

Kiki had no idea how far she walked, but by noon she realized she was in a different community. She was probably only a few miles from LoDo, but this town had an entirely different feeling. She stopped in front of a beautiful Victorian house on the edge of a small, town commons. An independent real estate company occupied half the building, and there were neatly framed pictures of apartments and houses on display in the big, picture window. After looking at every single home, Kiki walked in.

The gal on duty was about her age, and she had a small sign on her desk that introduced her as Darlene Hutchens. Compared to the other real estate sales agents Kiki had met, Darlene was refreshing and wholesome. She smiled a lot and didn't seem to be in a hurry. Kiki liked her. Darlene was dressed in tan slacks and a light-blue blouse. She wore a blue blazer with brass buttons. Darlene talked slowly, and they immediately bonded. Darlene stood and pointed across the street.

"Have you had lunch?" Without waiting for an answer, Darlene said, "Why don't we walk across the street and grab a sandwich?"

The girls walked to a luncheonette called Sunshine's.

"This is my favorite table," Darlene said with a smile.

They sat in a booth by a huge picture window. Their view was of the town commons, a neatly cut lawn, and a freshly painted gazebo. There was a statue of a little boy and a few picnic tables. They could see Darlene's office.

Darlene started the conversation right off the bat, and, instead of acting like a sales agent, she acted like a friend who had a lot to say. She talked about the weather, and then mentioned that she liked Kiki's tweed jacket. When the waitress approached the table, Darlene ordered without even looking at the menu.

"I'll have a tuna sandwich on wheat toast, a small salad with ranch dressing on the side, and a root beer."

"I'll make it easy," Kiki said. "I'll have the same." She felt herself smiling for the first time in ages.

During the first half hour, Darlene talked non-stop about nothing in particular. She talked so much that Kiki couldn't get a word in edgewise, and it was nice. It was refreshing for her to just enjoy the attention. She liked her new rental agent.

After a while, Darlene became serious and took a deep breath. "My husband just passed away."

"Oh, I'm so sorry," Kiki said. She reached out and took Darlene's hand. "What happened?"

"He lost his battle with ALS. Do you know about Lou Gehrig's disease?"

"I have read about it. Oh, I am so, so sorry."

Darlene looked as if she were far away and continued talking. "When he was diagnosed, I realized I would be providing for myself. My friend was in real estate, and she encouraged me to take a course. A month before my husband passed away, I took the test and passed. Today is my first day on the job."

Suddenly, Darlene sat up straight. Her eyes opened wide. She realized that this was not a social luncheon, but a sales interview.

"Oh, I'm so sorry," Darlene said, with a big, toothy grin. "I'm doing all of the talking. The fact is you are my first client. Tell me what you are looking for. Maybe I can help." She smiled again.

Kiki was touched by the attention. She slowly started to talk.

"I just ended a relationship that I would rather not discus. I'll be living alone for a while," she said.

"What kind of place are you looking for?" asked Darlene.

"I'm sure that this will sound silly," Kiki continued, "But I've always dreamed of living in a quaint, little cottage. I'd like to be in the country, where I could go for walks. I would love to have room for a small garden. I'd like to have a pet. Maybe a pussycat. But," she said, coming back to reality, "I'm sure I'll end up in another walk-up apartment overlooking a dumpster."

"Do you like gardening?" Darlene asks.

"I would love to have a garden"

"That's great, because if you move to this town, I will ask you to join the garden club."

"I would be honored."

"Tell me more about your dream house," Darlene prompted.

Kiki beamed, and talked about her fantasy home. "If I could design a house, it would be set back from the road, and there would be a long, gravel driveway. It would have a white picket fence. There would be a screen porch. There would be a huge tree for shelter from the summer sun. But," she sighed again. "This place only exists in my mind. I have to stop dreaming."

Darlene's eyes started to widen. She frowned, cocked her head, and looked quizzically at the ceiling. She was a million miles away. She looked straight at Kiki again.

She slowly got up, and without saying a word, she left the table. Kiki didn't know if Darlene went to the ladies room or went back to work. Maybe she had gotten bored with the conversation. Kiki stared at the empty seat and the uneaten sandwich.

The old feeling of rejection took over. She was being dumped, one more time. She looked around uneasily for the waitress. Tears were starting to form in the corners of her eyes.

In a flash, Darlene was back at the table. In her arms, she hugged a gigantic, leather notebook. She had a twinkle in her eye, and she cleared the plates off of the table. She opened the book and quickly started flipping through pages. After passing pictures of five different houses, she smiled and turned the book around to Kiki.

She smiled and slowly said, "Is this your little dream house?"

"Oh my God!" Kiki cried. She couldn't believe it! She looked at a picture of the cottage that she had only seen in her mind. There was a picket fence, a screen porch, and a big maple tree in the front yard. The cottage was small and looked so cozy. When the photograph had been taken, bright red roses were in full bloom. In the distance was a gorgeous view of the mountains.

Kiki started to cry. "Is this available?" She looked up at Darlene and, before she got an answer, looked down again at the picture.

Darlene watched Kiki for a full minute before she reached out and touched her hand. "Let's get our sandwiches to-go and eat them in the car. We'll take a trip to Boulder and look at the cottage."

The girls got into Darlene's car and drove toward the mountains. Kiki sat quietly. Her mind started racing. She wanted to have a calm, peaceful, uncomplicated life, and she would like to have a friend like Darlene, but old fears started to slip in. She didn't feel worthy of this relationship.

As they drove, Kiki found another reason why this was not a good idea. What if she had to fill out a lengthy credit application? What if they matched her name to a crime scene in New Jersey? What if they asked for her bank account? What if they asked for job references? What if, what if?

Her negative thinking came to an abrupt halt as Darlene turned off the country road onto a long, gravel driveway. On the left they passed an antique farmhouse with an attached barn. It was neat and well-cared for. Further back on the property was the cute little house that Kiki had seen in the photograph. It was fabulous!

As she stared at the little cottage, her mind churned up a new fear. The small house was only a short distance from the main farmhouse. The owner of the farmhouse would surely be the landlord. What if the landlord didn't like her? Once again, her mind raced to the worst-case scenario.

As Darlene stopped her car, the two girls got out and slowly walked around the cottage. It was perfect. Kiki wanted to live in this little house more than anything else in the world.

Before they even got to the front door, Kiki stopped her new real-estate agent and asked one important question.

"Who lives in the big farm house?"

"I do."

# 93

IT'S BEEN A YEAR SINCE I was shot. It's been a year since Maggie and I have been back together.

When I ended up in the emergency room, Fig stopped crying long enough to call my wife.

"I have very bad news," he sobbed.

Maggie took an all-night flight and showed up by my bedside the following morning. She kept vigil over me day and night. After being in a coma for weeks, she was the first person I recognized.

The doctors told Maggie that chances for my recovery were slim, so she volunteered to become my caretaker. When it was safe for me to travel, she moved me to her little house in the mountains. Maggie could be near her mother and take care of me, too. She planned for our retirement. My disability pension would provide for Maggie, and Maggie would provide for me.

"We will forget about the past and start a new life together," she said, "but there are two conditions. One: you will never pick up another drink; and two: you will never get into a cop uniform. Not even on Halloween!"

When we moved to Boulder, I had physical therapy three times a week. I was told that I may not walk for a long time.

"I have three legs," I joked, "but none of them work."

The physical pain was one thing, but the emotional pain kept me down. My therapist gave me the news.

You will experience denial, anger, bargaining, and depression before you gain acceptance." She was right. Now, as acceptance kicks in, I am trying to focus on the positives.

During the long, winter months, Maggie and I found new interests.

I took up photography. I tried to see this long, winter season through the camera's eye. As I sat at my window, I looked at the forest as Ansel Adams might have. Instead of dead trees, a colorless backdrop, and endless mounds of snow, I saw something different. For the first time in my life, I could see that pine trees were a shade of gray. The sky was the color of slate. The horizon was a dark shade of maroon just before the sunset, and the snowdrifts were white on white. Shadows let me know where the drifts began and where they ended. The only color in the picture was a single, light-brown leaf that held on to our maple tree long after all the other leaves gave up and dropped to the ground.

The white of winter takes my breath away; it brings me back to reality. This is my day, and it is my life. I can slow my life down by enjoying the changes, or I can slip into oblivion and let the days fly by unnoticed. Today, I choose to enjoy my life.

Maggie fights off cabin fever by working with animals at our local animal shelter. Every day there is a different animal to rescue, and she wants to save them all.

We agreed that, since I am such a needy animal, it's senseless to have another needy animal in the house. One day, Maggie fell in love with an ancient, chocolate lab named Freebee. After months without a placement, Freebee faced euthanasia. Maggie begged for more time, but the policy was firm. Maggie brought Freebee home to spend her last weekend with us. The dog never left.

Freebee and I bonded instantly. She has the most incredibly sad eyes I have ever seen. Because of arthritis, she is in constant pain. It is hard for her to sit, hard for her to stand, and very hard to climb the stairs. I can relate. We make a great pair. At night, when I start my long trip up to the bedroom, Freebee starts her trip, too. It takes each of us a long time, stopping on the landing to catch our breath. We each grimace as we make it up one step at a time.

Each morning, after Maggie gets up, Freebee waits by my bed until I get the courage to face the stairs. For me, the reward is a steaming mug of hot coffee. For Freebee, the reward is the promise of breakfast and a chance to relieve herself outside. Together, we walk down the long flight of stairs one step at a time.

Maggie, Freebee, and I have settled into a peaceful existence. We help each other stay focused. We help each other enjoy the little things. We make each other smile.

I look at my wife with tears in my eyes.

"What a great life!"

"It sure is!" she replies.

# 94

AFTER MAGGIE GOES TO BED, I think about my past year. The place that I am in now is great, but it would not have been my first choice. For the thousandth time, I relive my impulsive night in New Jersey. What was going through my mind? Regardless of how many times I ask this question, I never allow myself to answer. Tonight, in the solitude of my peaceful settle-for existence, I ask the question. Why did I go in to Kiki's apartment alone? I answer the question: I was trying to overcompensate for my addiction. There: I said it! I had fucked up so many times, and I wanted to show everyone that I was still a good cop. I wanted to let everyone know that I was still sharp, capable, and quick-thinking.

I guess I showed them. Here I am: A cripple.

# 95

"LIBBY! FIG! OVER HERE!" MAGGIE YELLS at the top of her lungs. The Denver International Airport's baggage-claim area is packed.

With tears in their eyes, the three friends hug. They back up and look at each other and hug again. Then they all start talking at once. They are so busy catching up that they don't even notice that all of the bags have been claimed from the carousel except theirs.

As they walk towards the car, they see me leaning on my crutches.

"Oh, my God," says Fig. It's the first time he's seen me in over a year. Since then, I have lost weight, and my mustache has turned completely white.

As we approach the car, no one speaks. I try to breaks the ice by saying, "I don't always look this bad. Sometimes I look worse."

Fig's laugh is nervous.

"You look great, Jesse." He's a terrible liar.

Maggie helps me into the back seat as Fig puts the crutches into the trunk. He climbs in next to me.

"Hey guys. Before we even get started, I want to apologize: I'm sorry I'm not going to be as much fun as I was when I was drinking,"

"Who the hell ever said you were fun?"

"How do you feel, Jesse?" Libby asks.

"I feel like an M&M. I'm hard on the outside, but mush on the inside."

The drive from the airport is pleasant, but only the girls are talking. Fig steals a glance at me. I feel like I am a hundred years older. He winces.

"How's the police business, Fig?"

"Every time we catch one bad guy, three more hit the streets. There's a lot of job security in this line of work."

"Well, that sounds great to me. Retirement ain't all it's cracked up to be. I'd rather be directing traffic in Tijuana than directing Maggie around the house. I'm pretty tired of sitting on my ass all day."

"But you have such a nice ass." We are chuckling together as we pull into the driveway.

"What a wonderful house," says Libby. "I love the view of the mountains."

"We like our view, too. It's better than TV."

When they walk in, Freebee shows new signs of life. He jumps and barks for the first time in weeks. After some sniffing, he goes back to his spot by the wood stove and curls up.

"Jesse, do you mind if we all have a glass of wine to celebrate?" Maggie asks.

"You can celebrate the fact that I am not having a glass of wine!"

"That's for damn sure." They all laugh.

"What's the best think about being sober?" Libby asks.

"Most people have lots of emotions to deal with. Since I stopped drinking, I only have two."

"Oh, that's wonderful. What are they?"

"Suicidal and homicidal."

We talk nonstop about the weather, the Padres, and the differences between California and Colorado. We talk about the little things in our lives.

Maggie and Trudy set the table for dinner. We all enjoy broiled salmon, twice-baked potatoes, and asparagus. The homemade, chocolate-mint pie with fresh whipped cream is devoured. After dinner, we sit around the fireplace and gab for hours.

On the following day, we all take a driving tour of the Colorado countryside. The scenery is beautiful, and the day is pleasant. We stop for lunch at LoDo, and I insist that they walk around the shops and boutiques. I find a bench and watch the tourists.

"Tonight, I'm going to cook the best damn rib-eye steaks that you have ever had," I tell them.

"He's been looking forward to cooking for you guys for two weeks," says Maggie. "I tried to talk him out of it, but you just can't separate a man from his grill."

As dinnertime approaches, Fig and I walk out to the deck to start the grill. Even though I am balancing on my crutches, I light the charcoal without a hitch. I haven't lost my touch.

"Have a beer, Fig." I suggest.

"Why don't you have one too, and just drink in moderation."

"Drinking in moderation is like having half of a blowjob."

We laugh.

While we wait for the coals to glow, our conversation once again goes back to the girl from New Jersey.

"I just can't imagine what happened to her," I say. "I got to meet her, and then she totally disappeared!"

"Just like most of the girls you meet."

"Yeah, but this one changed my life."

"She sure left her mark on you."

"I was just looking for a quickie, not a lasting relationship. I still look at the newspaper clippings once in a while."

"Do you like the pictures that they published of you?"

"I should have used more mascara."

"I think about that day a lot," Fig says. "I should have been with you when you broke into her apartment."

"Don't blame yourself. I should have called you, but I didn't want to wait. The thing that keeps going round and round were the two seconds before shots were fired. I can't imagine why she was holding her pistol, unless she knew I was coming."

"Maybe she was cleaning it."

"Maybe she was going to commit suicide. I wish I had gotten there a few seconds later. I should have stopped for a beer on the way."

"I told you not to quit drinking!"

"I don't remember that part. Anyway, I'll never forget the flash and the shot! I got a round off, too, but I guess she was a better shot. She hit my chest, dead center."

"You were a good shot. You hit her wall, dead center," Fig smiled. "And then she completely disappeared. Her apartment was abandoned. She just walked away. They had a stakeout on her apartment for months, but she never came back to get her stuff. She never claimed her car at long-term parking, either."

"What do you think happened?" I ask.

"My take is that she is on an island someplace, terrorizing tourists."

"Do you think that there are other boyfriends on her list?"

"There may be other boyfriends, but she has changed her operating procedure. Or else the other boyfriends are wait-listed. She may just be in a holding pattern. According to her New Jersey bank, she had lots of cash at one time. She could live on that for a while."

"But how did she get out of Dodge? They checked every single person that took a plane, a train, or a bus for weeks. They checked every single car rental agency."

"I think she's been arrested in another state. She's probably in jail now, but we just never heard about it."

"I don't think she is in jail. I think she was too smart to be caught.

I think she's somewhere else in the country, with a new identity and a new life. I think she will show up again."

"Fig." I say to my best friend, changing the subject. "I fucked up so badly. If I had followed protocol and waited for you, the end might have been so different. The two of us could have easily taken her down. I blew our opportunity."

"Jesse." He says, looking serious for the first time in two days. "I've never asked you this, but I can't put it to bed. Why did you go in by yourself? Why didn't you wait for me on that day in New Jersey?"

"I think about this all the time, too, Fig. The best answer I can come up with is that I wanted to redeem myself. My drinking was out of control. I was out of control. The chief had put me on notice. My wife had left me. I was missing clues. I didn't have hunches. The booze had me captive. I consciously thought that if I caught the girl, everyone would get off my back. When I was with the bureau, I could do this stuff. I was a star. I was good at my job. Then I got hooked on booze. The old me was gone. I wanted it back. I felt that if I got the girl by myself, I would be a hero again. That's what I was thinking."

"When do we eat?" Maggie yells from the kitchen.

"Right now, if you like it raw!"

During dinner, our conversation becomes more somber.

"What's the biggest problem you deal with these days?" Libby asks.

"Well, I got the squirrel thing going on. I can't stop the wheels from turning."

"What else?"

"I've seen my mortality. Life is pretty fragile, and I'm thankful for every day. I'm thankful for Maggie and I'm thankful for friends like you guys."

"Do you have some words of wisdom?"

"I know that I can't add years to my life, but I want to add life to my years."

"How's that working out?"

"Not too good!"

As the girls clear the table, Maggie gives everyone a rundown of the next day's activities.

"The local Garden Club is having a plant sale and cookout tomorrow."

Both men groan at the same time.

"No way," Fig says. "Jesse and I will stay here and watch the game."

"Yeah. Count us out," I say.

"We will count you guys in!" Maggie says, emphatically. "We have to eat lunch anyway, and it's for a good cause. They are raising money to renovate the gazebo in the commons. It'll be fun!"

As Maggie and I get ready for bed, I look at my wife. Out of the blue, I admit that I love her: "Maggie, I would be glad to spend the rest of my life with you."

"That's so nice." She smiles.

"But I don't want to go to a plant sale tomorrow."

"We'll see."

"That's what my mother always said."

"Have a good night, Jesse," she says, toying with him.

"We'll see."

# 96

THE NEXT DAY FEELS LIKE SPRING. The weather is warm, and the sun is shining. After a big breakfast, we take our friends on another sightseeing tour of the Colorado countryside.

"I can't believe how beautiful the mountains are," says Libby. "We have nothing like this in San Diego."

"The problem is all of these trees," says Fig. "What are you going to do with all the trees? The developers in San Diego have the right idea. Just take all the trees down and build lots of houses."

"Take all the trees, and put 'em in a tree museum," sings Maggie.

"Charge all the people a dollar and a half, just to see 'em," sings Libby.

At lunchtime, without any fanfare, Maggie steers the car toward the town commons. The sign says "Garden Club Cookout today!"

"Oh no!" I complain. "I thought you forgot about this cookout. I bet the Garden Club ladies have thirty kinds of three-been salad!"

"Will you please pipe down and get with the program?"

"My mother used to say that, too. Right now I feel like a little boy who is being controlled by his mother," I grumble.

"Yes, and if you don't behave," Maggie says, "I'll pull your pants down and give you a spanking. I bet she used to do that, too."

"Yeah, right up until I turned eighteen."

"Hey, I've been a bad boy, too." Fig pipes in. "Can you pull my pants down?"

When we get to the town commons, I climb out of the back seat and lean against the car.

"Where does it hurt?"

"Some days, it's in my back," I say. "But today it's just a pain in the ass."

Fig laughs and gets the crutches out of the trunk. Maggie parks the car.

Fig and I slowly navigate the walkway toward an empty picnic table in the park. The sun feels good.

Some people are sitting on blankets. Others are standing near the gazebo, listening to a small band playing oldies. Little kids are dancing to the music.

The plant sale is in full swing, and some of the visitors are making trips to their cars with new purchases. A few people have started to line up at the long, serving table.

Men and women are cooking burgers, and smoke gently fills the air. There are bags of charcoal piled up in the bed of a pickup truck, and coolers of all shapes and sizes are stacked up behind the line. The cooks are all wearing tall, colorful, chef's hats. Every few minutes, a hat falls completely off, but that's all part of the fun. All the men have red-and-white-checkered aprons, and most of them have a beer.

The ladies on the serving line are all wearing white blouses and bright red aprons. They each have a colorful bandana tied around their neck. It's quite a sight. There seems to be a lot of camaraderie, and the chatter is endless.

"Whoever put this party together did a great job," Maggie says.

"The burgers will be too small, too expensive, and too burned.

We should have just sent the money and stayed home."

"Will you stop being such a jerk?"

The girls head off to get in line.

"This could be worse," Fig says.

"Let's eat quickly, buy a plant, and get home to watch the game."

"I'm having a great time, Jesse. Let's just enjoy it."

I smile as I realize what a drag I have been. *It's time to change my attitude,* I think. My life is good, I am sober, and back with Maggie. Fig and Libby are visiting, and I plan to walk again someday.

In a short while, paper plates are delivered. They are heaping with beans and potato salad.

"Where's the burger?" I ask.

"It's on the bottom. You have to eat the salads first."

"I'm not a salad kind of guy," I say, as I push the beans aside. "How much did this burger cost me?"

"More than you can afford. Now eat."

We all stop talking and start eating.

"Can you get me another burger?" I ask.

"Just eat your beans. Have some salad," Maggie replies.

"I hate two of the three beans in three-bean salad."

"Well, eat the one that you like."

"I want another burger."

"There are people who haven't had their first burger, yet," she says.

"If you don't want to get another burger for me, I'll get it myself," I say. "No one would refuse a cripple." They all laugh, nervously.

As Libby, Maggie, and Fig start to chat, I become quiet. Something is wrong. I still have incredible mood swings and fight to keep from riding the roller coaster of emotions. Sometimes my whole personality can change in an instant.

"Dr Jeckel and Mr. Hyde" is what Maggie calls me.

Something is gnawing away at my serenity. I feel my mood

changing but don't know why. Nothing is really wrong. Am I becoming anxious because other people are drinking? There are beer cans, wine bottles, and little, paper cups everywhere. The young group at the next table is getting tipsy. Am I romanticizing a drink? I've been fine all weekend. Are my friends bringing back memories of the past? Are all of these healthy people having too much fun? I feel like I am in a vacuum. I have no idea what Maggie, Libby, and Fig are talking about. Something is definitely wrong. I feel light-headed and fuzzy.

To pass time, I turn toward the serving area again, and slowly scan the crowd. After a moment, everything becomes a blur, and I slip into a haze. I shake my head and refocus on people in the line again. I close my eyes and try to try to label each person that I have seen. I try to compare them to an actor or movie star. Maybe one of them looks like a sports figure. It makes remembering them a little easier, later on. How would I describe each person to a sketch artist? It's a cop thing.

Some vaguely familiar image is nudging me. Was it conscious or subconscious? I stare at the folks who are working near the food, and a strange, uneasy feeling overcomes me.

"What's wrong, Jesse?' Maggie brings me back to reality.

"Yeah, Jesse," Fig says. "You haven't said a word in an hour!"

I smile and pat Maggie's knee. This is the same pat that I give her after physical therapy, when my body hurts. This is the same pat I give her when I am depressed and my mind hurts. And this is the same pat that I give her when I can't make love and my ego hurts. Everyone at the table smiles and sits still for a while.

When they resume their conversation, I return to my feeling of confusion.

Sometimes, when I am upset, I sort through my emotions until I come up with the reason. It is usually something small and insignificant. Sometimes, the only thing that bothers me is the way that someone looks at me. Or maybe it is the pain of physical recovery. When I get to the root of my unrest, I feel better.

I scan the serving area again, one person at a time. I start to feel ill. My mouth gets dry. I wonder if the color has disappeared from my face. I shiver as a chill runs down my spine. I try to speak, but nothing comes out.

I sit and stare. Are my eyes playing tricks? People around me are talking, but I can't hear a word. I feel my heart racing like a fire truck, and my blood begins to percolate like an old-fashioned coffee pot.

Should I ask Fig about my suspicion? Do I have a hunch, a sixth sense, or a silly intuition? I was with the bureau. I know how to investigate. I can figure this out. I grunt slowly as I pick up my crutches, and wince as I try to stand.

"Jesse, where are you going?" Maggie asks.

I don't answer. Instead I put one crutch in front of the other and start to hobble across the uneven field toward the service line.

"I'll get you another burger, Jesse! Can't you just wait a few minutes?"

I ignore her and keep walking.

In my peripheral vision, I see Maggie shake her head and start to get up but then sit back down.

"Sometimes, he is in his own damn world," I hear her say to Libby and Fig.

Fig hesitates, but then follows Maggie's lead and also stays put at the table.

They watch me slowly maneuver my crutches toward the line and then go back to their conversation.

When I get to the serving table, I cut in front of an overweight man in a bright, Hawaiian shirt. He looks at the crutches and moves back to give me space. Without saying a word, I walk up to the edge of the table and position myself in front of a small woman on the other side of the line. She is vaguely familiar. I feel that I have met her once before.

The small woman slowly looks up. She frowns and there is confusion in her eyes. There is disorientation. Then, there is denial as she shakes her head.

"Hi Kiki," I say.

She closes her eyes as if to wish me away.

In a single instant, I lunge over the table and try to tackle the woman. As the weight of my body crushes the flimsy folding table, its aluminum legs collapse, and it smashes to the ground. I crash to the ground, too, and scream out in pain as I grab hold of her. I have her for a second, but lose my grip as three other servers are knocked to the ground. A big urn of coffee spills, and scalds everyone within ten feet. People are screaming.

One of the cooks is shoved into a red-hot barbeque grill. He accidentally grabs the edge of the grille to steady himself, and, as he goes down, white-hot briquettes sear his flesh. He shrieks at the top of his lungs. His apron starts to burn. His hair singes, and the smell of burning flesh fills the air.

In the middle of this commotion, I start to lose consciousness. My old wound feels like it has opened up. I try to grab the woman again, but slip in a mound of coleslaw. My last vision is of her wiggling away.

Suddenly an ear-piercing explosion penetrates the town common. It sounds like a gun shot.

Some people are shouting.

People are praying. "Oh my God" is coming from many directions.

Parents instinctively grab their kids. Some folks drop to the ground and hide their heads under their arms. Others are crawling to a tree for cover. The noise of the gunshot is quick, and it is deafening, but it is impossible to tell where it came from.

After a few seconds, folks start running toward the parking lot. Others are walking quickly. Babies are crying, and young kids are yelling to their parents. Every single person is in motion.

In the middle of the commotion, the small woman squirms out from under the pile of servers, and pushes herself up to a kneeling position. She quickly crawls for a long distance, then rises up to a standing position. She drops her bandana, removes her apron, and walks calmly toward the parking lot. She blends in with fifty other people who are trying to get away from the upheaval. To add to the confusion, cars are being started and tires squeal as frightened townspeople make a hasty exit. The small woman makes an exit, too.

Within seconds, it is over. The people who are lying on the ground are being helped up. As Fig arrives at the scene, people are crawling and squirming on the ground. The man who was burned is in shock and is involuntarily shaking and moaning. Someone is administering mouth to mouth. Fig also sees blood.

# 97

A FEW MILES FROM THE PARK, Kiki got out of her car. She was shaken but in control. It was all about control. She walked into her little cottage and quickly changed her outfit. Tan shorts and a floral, summer top with spaghetti straps looked good. She pulled down her top and removed her bra. The outfit looked even better. She grabbed a black cardigan with tiny buttons and put it over her shoulders.

Within minutes, she grabbed her backpack full of cash, added some toiletries and a few extra 32-caliber clips. She calmly climbed back into her car.

As she started driving out of town, she passed police cars and an ambulance racing toward the public park in the center of town.

Without even thinking, Kiki drove toward the Denver airport. She pulled into long-term parking. She locked the car and slid her backpack onto her shoulder. Instinctively, she found a cab and directed the driver toward the entrance of Route 80. After the cabbie left, she walked up the ramp.

As a white convertible approached, she put out her thumb. The driver jammed on his brakes. As he backed up, Kiki noticed the name on the car: Mercedes. The driver had a blond crew cut and the whitest smile she had ever seen. He was wearing yellow shorts and a navy tank top. His baseball cap was keeping the sun out of his eyes, but his nose looked burned. He had a flat stomach. She approved.

She bent over the door of the small sports car and wondered if her top was leaving her exposed. The look on his face confirmed it.

"Hi there," he said. "Where are you headed?"

"To the coast."

"I'm headed to Seattle; is that far enough?"

"Seattle? Oh, my God! That's exactly where I want to go."

He moved the bottle of suntan lotion off the passenger seat as she climbed in. She smiled when she saw that his shoes were off.

He grinned. "My name is Jeb," he said, as he reached out his hand.

"Hi Jeb."

"What's your name?"

"Kiki," she said.

Jeb started to pull away from the side of the road. He drove slowly, looking more at Kiki than at the road.

"What's in Seattle?" she asked.

"I'm opening a new branch of my company. I've rented a hotel room for a few months. Normally, I would just fly, but I want to have the wheels. Why are you leaving town?"

"A guy from my past is stalking me. No matter where I go, he shows up."

"Stalking you? What do you mean?"

"We ended our relationship years ago, and he has never gotten over it. One time, after a year with no communication, he walked right into my apartment. He just busted in. Another time, out of the blue, he showed up at a picnic. He made a scene in front of a hundred people."

"He sounds dangerous."

"He scares the hell out of me."

"How does he find you?"

"He doesn't have a life. I think he spends all of his time on the Internet."

"So what's your plan?"

"I want to change my address. I want to change my hairstyle. I want to change my name."

"Do you have a place to stay?"

"Not yet."

"Well, maybe I can help."

Look for the rest of this story in the sequel,
*Five Minutes at a Time,* by Doug Smith

CPSIA information can be obtained
at www.ICGtesting.com
Printed in the USA
BVHW030852291219
568055BV00002B/239/P